PRAISE FOR THE ZODIAC MYSTERIES

THE MADNESS OF MERCURY

"Danger figures in the stars for Julia, along with mixed astrological energies, some wolves in sheep's clothing and an amiable stranger with a down-under accent."

—*BookPage*

"With *The Madness of Mercury*, Connie di Marco begins a fascinating new series set in the intriguing world of astrology in San Francisco. I really loved this book! The writing is clever and compelling and the protagonist is smart and gutsy. The villains are seriously sinister and the darkly intricate plot will keep you turning pages late into the night. I'm looking forward to many more in this series. Connie di Marco knows her stuff!"

—Kate Carlisle, *New York Times* bestselling author

"Connie di Marco blends real-life tragedy, heart-rending betrayal, loyal friends, and the kindness of strangers in this fast-paced, entertaining read."

—Leslie Budewitz, two-time Agatha Award-winning author of the Seattle Spice Shop Mysteries

"The stars may not align for the unlucky characters in *The Madness of Mercury*, but they certainly do for readers who discover this book. An astrologer with her eyes on her charts and her feet planted firmly on the ground, Julia Bonatti is an original sleuth, juggling astrological readings with a mysterious death and a Jim Jones-like cult leader. Dark wit and darker motivations unite to create a satisfying read."

—Kim Fay, Edgar Award finalist for *The Map of Lost Memories*

"A great read is in the stars! With the Zodiac Mysteries, Connie di Marco gives us a bright and interesting heroine and a mystery with plenty of twists and turns. Lots of action and well-written suspense equal good fortune for readers."

—Casey Daniels, author of *Graveyard Shift*

"An enjoyable read."

—*Reviewing the Evidence*

All Signs
Point to Murder

All Signs Point to Murder

✵ A Zodiac Mystery ✵

Connie di Marco

MIDNIGHT INK
WOODBURY, MINNESOTA

FIRST EDITION
First Printing, 2017

Book format by Cassie Kanzenbach
Cover design by Ellen Lawson
Cover illustration by Mary Ann Lasher-Dodge

Midnight Ink, an imprint of Llewellyn Worldwide Ltd.

Library of Congress Cataloging-in-Publication Data
Names: Di Marco, Connie, author.
Title: All signs point to murder / Connie di Marco.
Description: First edition. | Woodbury, Minnesota : Midnight Ink, [2017] |
    Series: A zodiac mystery ; #2
Identifiers: LCCN 2017011364 (print) | LCCN 2017017658 (ebook) | ISBN
    9780738751788 | ISBN 9780738751078 (softcover : acid-free paper)
Subjects: LCSH: Astrologers—Fiction. | GSAFD: Mystery fiction.
Classification: LCC PS3604.I116 (ebook) | LCC PS3604.I116 A79 2017 (print) |
    DDC 813/.6—dc23
LC record available at https://lccn.loc.gov/2017011364

Midnight Ink
Llewellyn Worldwide Ltd.
2143 Wooddale Drive
Woodbury, MN 55125-2989
www.midnightinkbooks.com

Printed in the United States of America

For Basil

ACKNOWLEDGMENTS

Many thanks to Paige Wheeler of Creative Media Agency, Inc. for her hard work, good advice, and expertise, and to Terri Bischoff, Sandy Sullivan, Katie Mickschl, and the entire team at Midnight Ink for welcoming the Zodiac Mysteries to their home.

Special thanks as well to my writers' group and first readers—Kim Fay, Laurie Stevens, Cheryl Brughelli, Don Fedosiuk, Paula Freedman, and R.B. Lodge—for their critiques and encouragement.

I would be remiss if I didn't say thank you to Llewellyn Publications for all the wonderful astrology books they've published over the years. Without that esoteric knowledge, this series could never have come into being.

Last, but certainly not least, thanks to my family and my wonderful husband for their tolerance in living with a woman who is constantly thinking about murder.

If by chance any reader shares a birth date with an unsavory character in *All Signs Point to Murder*, please know that a certain amount
of astrological license has been necessary. I am confident that anyone born on such a date would never contemplate murder and
mayhem—at least I certainly hope not.

—*Connie di Marco*

♈ ♉ ♊ ♋ ♌ ♍ ♎ ♏ ♐ ♑ ♒ ♓

THERE ARE NO OTHER people.

That's one theory at least. The souls we meet on our path are those whom we can perceive, who reflect us, who vibrate at our level. Heraclitus, an ancient Greek, said that character is destiny. If so, we must look to ourselves alone when things go wrong. We must look inward to discover our fatal flaw, the one that led to ruin, the evil we perceive only when it is too late. We ask ourselves, why was I so blind? What is my Achilles heel, that I was unconscious to such danger?

My name is Julia Bonatti—Julia Elizabeth Bonatti—and I'm an astrologer. In my practice, I struggle to keep an open mind, to not judge, or at least not too harshly. To remind myself of my own failings and forgive those in others. So it was that I did not see.

I once believed that no one is born evil—that evil is a learned talent. That there is no such thing as a dark sun. But I was wrong. There are those whose actions defy logic and the heart. In those cases, judgment is warranted. Judgment and retribution.

ONE

♈ ♉ ♊ ♋ ♌ ♍ ♎ ♏ ♐ ♑ ♒ ♓

THE DOOR TO THE dressing room flew open with such force the mirror rattled against the wall. "Where the *hell* did she get to? We're almost ready to start." Brooke's voice hovered on the edge of hysteria.

I paused with a mascara wand halfway to my lashes. "Have you checked the ladies' room?" Brooke's nervousness was contagious.

"Yes. I checked," she groaned. "Julia," she whispered, "I think Moira's been drinking..." She turned back to the corridor, her mauve train catching on the threshold. "Damn." She twisted, tugged on her skirt, and stormed off.

Geneva Leary, my best friend from college, my friend who had seen me through the darkest time of my life, was getting married in just a few moments in the courtyard of the Inn of the Seven Horses in Sonoma County, north of San Francisco. Her sisters, Brooke and Moira, and I were serving as bridesmaids.

The door flew open a second time. Sally Stark, our wedding coordinator, charged in with the same question. "Where is Moira Leary?" she hissed.

I glanced up at Sally's reflection in the mirror. "Brooke is looking for her now." I sighed and replaced the cover on my mascara. Why does everyone get so tense at weddings? It's hardly a Broadway opening.

"I can't have this. I just can't have this. I've never had a bridesmaid who behaved in such an irresponsible manner." Sally, wearing a severe black suit, was painfully thin, her jaw permanently clenched. The tendons in her neck bulged like ropes as she spoke.

Brooke halted at the door to the dressing room. Sally turned to face her. "Mrs. Ramer, this is absolutely unacceptable. I have never seen such cavalier behavior. I assure you, the Inn will never allow you to plan an event here again. That's if I have anything to say about it."

Brooke's face was flushed. I was waiting for her to explode, but instead she took a deep breath and closed her eyes for a moment to regain her poise. "I understand how you must feel."

"No," Sally bit back, "I don't think you do. This reflects badly on *me*. In all the years I've been coordinating weddings, I have never had *anyone*—bride, groom, or bridesmaid—simply disappear moments before the ceremony is to begin!"

Brooke and I had spent the afternoon supervising the preparations. We'd run up and down the stairway to the courtyard wiring yards of white tulle to each banister, with bunches of baby roses, to outline the bridal path. The flowers had arrived, the DJ was early, and one hundred white helium balloons with trailing ribbons had been released under the canopy covering the dance floor. Everything had, up until now, gone smoothly. Unfortunately, Geneva's sister Moira had shown little interest in the festivities. Now, with the ceremony about to start, and more than a hundred guests waiting in the heat, she was nowhere to be found.

"We can't delay any longer." Brooke surrendered to Sally's anger. Sally sniffed dismissively. "Fine. I'll signal the harpist." She left the dressing room, slamming the door behind her.

Brooke stared at me and silently mouthed the word *bitch*. "Let's go, Julia."

I stood and followed Brooke out of the dressing room. Clutching my small bouquet of lavender roses and purple iris, chosen to coordinate with my mauve gown, I took my place at the top of the stairway behind her. Geneva, sheltered in her private dressing room, had been able to ignore the hubbub and remain calm. I reached behind me to squeeze Geneva's hand. She smiled in response and we started our slow descent to the courtyard, accompanied by the liquid strains of a harp.

We were a wedding party of eight—seven, now, with Moira's disappearance. Their brother Dan, his friend Andy, who was dating Moira, and the best man, Matt, waited at the altar next to Geneva's husband-to-be, David. As Brooke led us slowly to the courtyard, Andy looked at us questioningly, confused that Moira was not in the procession. I raised my eyebrows and shrugged my shoulders imperceptibly to indicate I had no idea where she was. After a few moments of shuffling, he chose to remain standing with the wedding party.

The courtyard was bathed in a shifting dappled light, the last sunlight of the day. Rising levels of brick planters surrounded us, forming an amphitheater of cultivated and wild blooms. The scent of jasmine, poppies, roses, and larkspur filled the air with an intoxicating scent. Brooke's seven-year old daughter, Ashley, was taking her job as flower girl very seriously, scattering rose petals around the patio. Mary Leary, the bride's mother, sat in the front row, tears glistening in her eyes.

Weddings always bring out the best and the worst in me. On one hand, I become embarrassingly teary-eyed and sentimental, sometimes given to outright bawling. On the other hand, a cynical part of me separates and steps back, like an astral body, watching and wondering about all those "till death do us part" vows. Do the participants realize what they're promising? If all marriages end in death or divorce, why the rush to the altar?

I often reflect on the karmic connections between two unique individuals, those connections that propel us to "own" each other in a marital sense. As an astrologer, this stuff interests me. I know long-term relationships must have a Saturn connection—otherwise they tend to be fun and short, or short and not so fun, as the case may be—but Saturn connections can be difficult, restraining, and sometimes even, let's admit it, oppressive.

Geneva wore a simple, ivory floor-length sheath. She carried a bouquet of white roses and delicate stephanotis. She appeared doll-like standing next to her groom. David is tall and fair, and today he'd put aside the wire-rim glasses that normally give him a scholarly look. A hush descended as the ceremony began, broken only by the sound of water splashing against the rocks in the creek below the courtyard.

This was the tough part for me. The intimate moments. Two and a half years earlier, my fiancé Michael had been killed in a hit-and-run accident outside his apartment on a quiet residential street in the Sunset District. Since his death, I'd done my best to avoid weddings, baby showers, and holiday events. But where Geneva was concerned, it was different. She'd been a true friend during that time. I couldn't say no to being supportive on her wedding day. Most of all, I couldn't let her know how difficult this was for me.

Brooke pulled a small tissue from an unseen hiding place to mop her brow. A trickle of perspiration rolled down my back and I prayed the June heat wave would abate after sunset. It was no surprise the weather was brutal; no one had bothered to ask my astrological advice when the date was chosen. Then again, no one ever calls an astrologer when things are going well. I wasn't at all happy about the Moon-Mars-Pluto connection in the heavens on the chosen day, either. But I never for a second thought that death was hovering with beating wings.

TWO

♈ ♉ ♊ ♋ ♌ ♍ ♎ ♏ ♐ ♑ ♒ ♓

I HEARD THE WORDS *"You may kiss the bride."* David, beaming, leaned down to kiss Geneva. The entire crowd broke out in cheers and applause, more I suspected from relief that the formalities were over and the evening would bring cool weather, food, wine, and celebration. The bride and groom, laughing, turned and waved to their guests. Geneva's mother, a plump, dainty woman dressed in a blue silk suit, rushed up and hugged both the bride and groom.

Brooke leaned closer and muttered, "It's so damn hot." The oldest of the three Leary sisters, Brooke is tall, blonde, and striking. I'm fond of her, but I've always found her somewhat intimidating. The superachiever in the Leary family, she's now the editor of a well-known fashion magazine in the city. She has unerring fashion sense and had even hired a designer to create our gowns.

I spotted Sally Stark pushing through the crowd surrounding the newlyweds. She looked upset as she approached Dan Leary and whispered something in his ear. The expression on his face shifted. He shot a glance at Brooke and headed in our direction. He spoke very quietly to Brooke and then turned to walk into the now-closed dining area of the restaurant. Brooke's complexion paled. She followed Dan.

Something was wrong. I glanced around to make sure I wasn't needed at the moment and followed both of them.

Inside the empty restaurant, Moira, still in her bridesmaid's gown, sat holding a cold cloth to her forehead. One of the waiters stood at the ready with a bowl of ice water. Dan stood there glaring at his youngest sister, arms crossed against his chest.

As I entered the room, Brooke turned to me. "They found her at the bottom of the stairs down by the creek. She'd passed out."

"Damn it, Moira, what were you thinking?" Dan demanded.

Moira's face was red and blotchy. "Why don't you get off my case? I had a couple of glasses of wine. That's all." She dipped the cloth in the ice water and squeezed, then replaced it on her forehead.

Dan shook his head. "You expect us to believe that?"

Brooke's lips were pinched. "Couldn't you keep it together just this once, for Geneva's sake?"

"Something was wrong with my drink."

"Like what?" Brooke asked.

"I don't know," Moira whined. "Maybe 'cause I didn't have anything to eat all day. I don't know. I swear I only had two glasses."

We all turned as the door opened. Rob Ramer, Brooke's husband, entered. Almost as tall as David, Rob is darkly handsome and muscular. But his chiseled features had taken on a hard cast and his jaw was clenched.

"So much for the program," Dan muttered. He stormed out, slamming the door behind him.

Rob grasped Moira's shoulder. "Brooke, you and Julia should head back." Moira tried to pull away, but Rob's grip was too strong. "I'll handle this. I'll stay with her until she feels better." Moira dropped her head and stared at the floor. She made no response.

Brooke let out a sigh. "Rob's right. We should get back." I followed her toward the exit. She leaned toward me and whispered, "Rob's in prosecuting attorney mode now. He can deal with her much better than I when she's like this."

I glanced back once at Moira. She was silent, staring at Rob with an expression I couldn't quite read, perhaps a mixture of fear and anger.

The sun had set and the sky was now a deep, periwinkle blue. The courtyard and surrounding gardens sparkled with thousands of tiny white lights. Large candles flickered at each table as the waiters began serving. On one side of the bride and groom, Brooke was next to Dan. Andy, still awaiting Moira, anchored the far end of the table. Andy is thin, with a saturnine face shadowed by hollow cheeks and heavy dark eyebrows. He wasn't looking happy.

Matt, a large man with wide shoulders and ruddy cheeks, was seated next to me. Geneva had mentioned he had played football in college, and, judging from his conversation, his favorite topic was sports. I smiled and nodded a lot, pretending I had some interest in the topic.

With a promise of good behavior, Moira had managed to escape Rob's supervision and joined us. A fresh cocktail stood next to her plate. An argument started brewing between her and Andy, and Moira became louder and more belligerent. Andy leaned over and whispered in her ear, then grasped her arm. He looked very angry. Moira's jaw was set. She lapsed into a sullen silence.

Brooke struck up a fresh conversation with the bride and groom in an attempt to lighten the tension at the table. The three of them chatted amiably, ignoring the simmering altercation between Moira and Andy. Then Moira stood suddenly, swaying slightly, and with a final glare at her date, stormed away. Andy, his face flushed, turned back to his plate and stabbed at the remaining food. Dan glanced at Andy but said nothing.

I'd seen a few episodes of sullen and volatile behavior on Moira's part over the past few days. There was no doubt in my mind that Brooke and Geneva were devoted to their younger sister, but they'd been forced to cut her a lot of slack in order to keep the peace.

Next to me, Matt continued to wolf down his dinner. "So, Julia, what sort of work do you do? Are you a teacher too, like Geneva?"

My appetite was nonexistent after the heat of the day. I picked at my food, choosing small bites. "Uh, no." I was hesitant to answer. Somehow Matt didn't strike me as the type of guy to be receptive to the occult. "How about you?"

"Well, I'm with Lyle & Smart. I'm a stockbroker. Are you interested in the market at all?"

He caught me with my mouth full. "I don't really…know much about investing."

"You know, most people don't, Julia, but I'd be happy to talk to you about it some more if you're interested."

"To tell you the truth, Matt"—I managed to swallow my food—"I don't really have any money to invest right now. I'm self-employed, and…uh…you know, making ends meet, building my business."

"Oh, I understand, believe me. It's tough. What kind of business do you have?"

"I do personal consultations."

"Really?" Matt queried.

He was not going to let this go. "I'm an astrologer."

"You don't say!" His eyes widened. He was quiet for a moment. "You mean you can tell the future?"

I cringed. "Uh, no, not exactly. Not the way you mean."

"Hey, if you don't mind, maybe I could talk to you about that sometime."

"Sure," I replied, surprised and mentally kicking myself for assuming Matt would be someone who'd ridicule my interests. "I'll give you one of my cards later."

Matt nodded. "I'd appreciate that."

When our dinner finished, Geneva and David rose and circulated among their guests, greeting family and friends. I danced to a few romantic ballads with Matt, Dan, and a white-haired Leary uncle. Brooke and Rob then stepped onto the dance floor, while Dan stood by his mother, her arm hooked through his, watching the festivities. David and Matt sat on the sidelines, enjoying a beer while Matt regaled David with newlywed jokes and laughed heartily at each punch line. David, looking a little tipsy, smiled and nodded dutifully. I spotted Geneva chatting with the DJ. Ashley was still scampering around, dispersing rose petals over the courtyard and picking up used ones and dumping them in the fountain. Andy was nowhere to be seen.

At the far edge of the pavilion, Sally Stark had cornered Moira. Sally's face was thrust forward, and she emphasized her words with a finger pointed at Moira's chest. Moira leaned back against the archway, her expression contemptuous. Sally took a deep breath, reached for her wineglass, and downed it completely before storming away.

I breathed a sigh of relief. The celebration was almost over and in spite of some upset, nothing had gone terribly wrong. It was as good a time as any to get comfortable. I headed for the dressing room, kicked off my shoes, and dug a pair of sandals out of my tote bag. I soaked a facecloth in cool water and held it to the back of my neck. There wasn't much I could do about my hair until I reached a shower and washed the hair spray out. I tucked a few straggling wisps back in place and wandered into the courtyard, empty now that everyone had moved into the dance pavilion.

I had no desire to return to the noisy crowd and instead headed for the stairway that led to the creek below the restaurant. Matt spotted me and hurried away from the dance floor.

"Hey, Julia," he called. He pulled a pen from his jacket and scribbled on the back of his business card. "Here's my birth date and time. Maybe I could call you to set up an appointment?"

"Sure." Well, there you go, I thought. The last person I'd ever expect wants to be my client. I gave him my business number as I glanced at his birth information.

"Where were you born, Matt?"

"Oh. Chicago. You need the birthplace?"

"Yes, for the latitude and longitude."

"Who knew?" He smiled.

"How come you're not out on the dance floor?"

"I plan to be. I've got my eye on that woman who's dancing with Rob right now."

I glanced toward the pavilion and saw a tall, sultry-looking redhead in a dark green clingy dress.

"Do you know who that is?" he asked.

I shook my head. "No. Maybe she's one of the teachers from Geneva's school."

"Well, then, I definitely went to the wrong school." He smiled again and turned away, hoping to position himself near the object of his desire as soon as she was free. Just then, Moira, standing at the edge of the crowd, spotted us. She drifted in our direction and wrapped her arms around Matt's neck.

"Hey," she said, moving even closer to him. "Let's dance." I caught a strong whiff of alcohol on her breath.

"If you insist," he responded, glancing over her shoulder at me and looking slightly embarrassed. As they moved onto the floor, she once again wrapped her arms around his neck and pressed her body close to his. Andy had reappeared and glared at them darkly from the sidelines.

I left Matt to Moira's wiles and headed toward the creek. Darkness closed in as I descended. Light from the Inn's windows offered slight illumination, enough to see outcroppings of rocks lining the creek bed. It was deliciously cool, and quiet except for the gurgling of the creek. I sat and gathered my dress around my knees. Leaning against the banister, I drank in the night air. A full moon had risen over the hills to the east and the sky was filled with stars never visible in the glow and fog of the city.

Voices from above filtered down. I turned and looked up to the top of the wooden stairway. Two figures were outlined against the light of the Inn's kitchen windows. A man and a woman. A woman who wore a gown exactly like mine but was shorter than Brooke. It was Moira. I couldn't identify the man standing against the light. Was it Andy? There was a glimmer of a cigarette as he inhaled. They hadn't seen me and were arguing in sibilant whispers. Suddenly, Moira's voice became louder.

"I don't need you to tell me…" She backed away unsteadily from the man.

"Look, calm down… we'll talk…"

Only snatches of their conversation reached me. Should I somehow make my presence known, or hope they wouldn't see me? I didn't relish being an eavesdropper at a private argument.

Moira raised her arm to strike at the man, but he grabbed her wrist. She pulled her arm away and turned, stumbling slightly. Her head was down and I was almost certain she was crying. She ran around the side of the building, heading back to the dance floor. The man swore softly, threw his cigarette on the ground, and crushed it with the toe of his shoe. He turned and followed her. I still hadn't been able to see his face.

The mood of the moment broken, I gave up my oasis and climbed the stairway, following the path Moira and her unknown man had taken a few moments before. As I turned the corner of the Inn, I crashed into Dan coming from the other direction. I caught my breath and jumped back.

"Oh sorry, Julia. Didn't know anyone was here. Didn't mean to scare you. Just trying to slip away and grab a smoke." Dan has the brilliant blue eyes shared by the rest of the family. One of his front teeth had been chipped in a teenage fight, and when he smiled, it gave a rakish air to his features.

"Moira was here a minute ago," I said. "She was arguing with someone."

Dan grimaced. "That's no surprise."

"Was it you?"

"Me? No. Probably fighting with Andy."

"I didn't mean to eavesdrop."

Dan sighed. "Well, my sister can be pretty outrageous when she wants. Sorry you had to see her like that earlier, too." He pulled a packet of cigarettes and a lighter out of his jacket pocket. "She's had way too much to drink. I'm keeping my fingers crossed she doesn't ruin the rest of Geneva's night. Fortunately, the party's almost over and Geneva and Dave'll be leaving soon." He offered me a cigarette from the pack in his pocket. "Would you like one?"

"No thanks. I totally quit a few years ago."

"Good for you. I'm still trying," he replied ruefully as he flicked his lighter and lit the cigarette. "Hey, I haven't really had a chance to talk to you alone. I was so sorry to hear about ... " He trailed off.

I nodded. "Michael. Yes."

"How are you doing?"

"I'm getting by. Coping, I guess. But I'm doing okay." I changed the subject before he could ask more questions. "How about you? What are you up to these days?"

"Me? Well, I studied computers and got a fancy certificate, but as soon as I was done, the bottom kind of fell out. I decided to stick with electrical work, like Dad. I set up on my own."

"That's great. Is it going well?"

"Yup. More work than I can handle." Dan took another drag from his cigarette. "I should quit too. Hey, do you know when they're leaving on their cruise?"

"Day after tomorrow. They're staying at David's house while they get ready to get out of town."

"That makes sense. Listen, Julia, after this we're all heading over to Brooke's. Mom and Matt and Andy and everyone. I hope you'll come too? Brooke wants everyone to stay overnight—she's planning a big breakfast party in the morning. Besides, we could use an extra pair of hands loading up the cars with the gifts."

"Thanks, I think I will. Geneva invited me too." What I really wanted was to sleep in my own bed, but my car was at my grandmother's house in North Beach. Brooke had been kind enough to drive me to the Inn, and I hesitated to ask anyone for a ride all the way downtown again. "Are you sure one more guest won't be any trouble for them?"

"Not at all. They have a huge house. Plenty of room. I'm heading home tonight, but I'll be there in the morning. I can give you a lift after that."

We heard shouts from the patio above. "Sounds like they're getting ready to cut the cake." Dan smiled and flicked his cigarette to the ground, crushing it under his shoe. "We should get back."

A high-pitched scream cut the air. He froze. "What the hell?"

"Something's wrong." I gathered up my skirts and hurried toward the sound.

THREE

♈ ♉ ♊ ♋ ♌ ♍ ♎ ♏ ♐ ♑ ♒ ♓

SALLY STARK LAY ON the dance floor, one arm thrown to the side. She had lost a shoe in her fall. A young man was kneeling next to her, checking her pulse while everyone crowded around. The music stopped as the DJ realized the emergency.

The man called out, "She's breathing but she needs help. Someone get help." Several people had cell phones to their ears, but judging by their repeated attempts and frustration, they weren't able to get a signal.

Dan turned to me. "There must be a landline inside." He ran toward the door of the restaurant and I moved closer to the crowd surrounding Sally. Geneva was kneeling next to her. Dan returned a moment later. "They're calling over to Santa Rosa from the Inn. An ambulance should be here soon."

As we waited helplessly, the young man continued to hold Sally's hand. No one moved, and if anyone spoke, it was only in whispers. I spotted Moira in the crowd. Her face was pale, her hand over her mouth in shock. Twenty minutes passed before we heard sirens from the road. The paramedics arrived and pushed through the crowd. One of them quickly checked Sally's vital signs. They lifted her onto a gurney and carried their burden up the stairway to the waiting ambulance. The man who had been attending to Sally followed them, describing his efforts. A few moments later, the ambulance pulled away, its lights flashing and siren blaring.

Everyone let out a collective breath of relief that the emergency was now in someone else's hands. The DJ returned to his console and, lowering the volume, played a soft ballad, hoping to recapture the earlier mood. The young man who'd tried to help Sally approached us. He shrugged helplessly. "I did what I could, but I don't think it did any good. I just don't know."

"You seemed to know what you were doing," Dan offered.

"I took a training course, but I'm no expert."

"Well, I'm glad you were here."

The man nodded and turned away. He and his companion gathered their things and approached Geneva to say good night. In spite of the music, several other people were making plans to leave.

Geneva hurried toward us. "Dan, Julia, we'll do the cake cutting right away before everyone leaves, and then we can wind things up. We'll keep it simple." The newlyweds approached the small pavilion where the cake stood. The DJ made an announcement, and once the first slices were cut, everyone applauded halfheartedly.

"Damn." Brooked moved next to me. "What a fizzle. I can't imagine what happened to Sally. Maybe she's diabetic. Moira was standing near her when it happened. She might have noticed something." Brooke turned to me. "You're coming back with us, aren't you, Julia?"

"I twisted her arm," Dan replied.

"Good." Brooke smiled. "Once everyone's gone, we can pack it in. I'm glad you're joining us."

At that point in the evening, I wasn't, but deciding on tact, I smiled. "Thanks, Brooke. It sounds like fun."

FOUR

♈ ♉ ♊ ♋ ♌ ♍ ♎ ♏ ♐ ♑ ♒ ♓

I RODE WITH DAN in the front seat of his car while Moira squeezed into the back with several large wrapped boxes. Dan and I chatted occasionally during our ride but Moira remained ominously silent. As we approached the city, the sky turned from black to a soft charcoal gray of reflected light. The road curved downward as we descended the long hill toward the Golden Gate Bridge. The topmost pillars of the bridge poked up through a dense layer of fog. The downtown area, still clear and brilliantly lit, was outlined against the black waters of the Bay. We drove onto the bridge. The stars were swallowed up and the temperature dropped another ten degrees, misty droplets covering our windshield.

Brooke and Rob's home is at the corner of Clay and Cherry just two blocks south of the Presidio. By the time we arrived, the front door and street-level garage were wide open. Rob had pulled his car into the garage next to David's car, parked there for safekeeping during the honeymoon. Matt had pulled in behind Rob and was supporting a not-very-sober Andy out of the car and up the inner stairway to the house. Given Andy's condition, Brooke had insisted on driving his car back to the city. The garage was full and Dan was forced to find a spot on the street two doors down.

As he cut the engine, Moira leaned forward and grabbed her brother's shoulder. "That was meant for me," she whispered.

Dan turned and glared at her. Moira climbed out of the car and, without another word, walked up the stairs to Brooke's front door.

I shot a glance at Dan, but he ignored my look. "What did she mean?"

"Who knows?" He shrugged. "Everything's a drama with Moira." He climbed out and I followed him around to the trunk. He reached inside and began to load my arms with presents. "Can you manage all this, Julia?"

I nodded. "I'll be fine."

"Great. I'll get the rest."

I climbed the long stairway and entered the foyer. Brooke and her mother had already rearranged a jumble of presents into an organized pile on the hallway table. Dan entered behind me. We dropped our boxes and cards at the end of the table and I did my best to incorporate them into the arrangement.

Dan touched my shoulder. "I'll see you in the morning. Don't forget, I'll give you a ride."

"Thanks, Dan. Hope it's not a bother."

"Not at all. I'll just say good night to everyone."

I followed him down the hall into the kitchen. Dan gave Brooke a kiss on the cheek and bent down to hug his mother. "Night, Mum. I'll see you tomorrow."

Brooke took me by the arm. "Julia, I left some pajamas and a robe and slippers for you. We have a sofa bed in the den that's very comfortable. Matt's already settled into one of the guest rooms and Moira and Andy have another. I hope that's okay with you. Sofia, our housekeeper, isn't here tonight—she's visiting her daughter—but I'll help you make up the bed."

"Oh, I can do it, Brooke. Just point me to the linen closet."

Brooke led me out of the kitchen and through the foyer to the other side of the house. She opened two cabinet doors next to a guest bathroom. Reaching inside, she pulled out a stack of linens. "Here you go. There are extra blankets too in case you need them. Come back to the kitchen after you've settled in and we'll have a nightcap."

The den was directly over the street-level garage, on the same floor as the foyer, living room, library, dining room, and kitchen. The second and third stories were bedrooms and a home office. Geneva had given me the grand tour of Brooke's house the night of the rehearsal dinner, and the space was starting to feel familiar. The main stairway connected all the levels, and a back stairway, originally designed for servants, led from the backyard to the kitchen and then to the upstairs rooms.

I hauled the sofa bed open and pulled sheets over the mattress, adding a blanket and pillow. I dug my jeans and a T-shirt out of my bag. I couldn't wait to extricate myself from the bridesmaid concoction I'd worn all day. I folded the dress and wrapped up the shoes, knowing full well they'd end up as a charity donation. Once I was decent, I washed my face, brushed my teeth, and headed back to the kitchen.

Brooke and her mother were already at the table with glasses of wine. Brooke, elegant as always, wore a white silk robe highlighted with a black embroidered floral design that trailed over one shoulder and across the back.

"Julia, dear, come sit down and join us." Mary twinkled up at me and patted the chair next to her. Brooke placed a delicate crystal wine glass in front of me and filled it with a pale white wine.

"I'm exhausted, Julia, I don't know about you. Mom, another one?"

Mary shook her head. "No, dear, I've had enough. I'm off to bed. I'll see you in the morning, darling." She stood and, touching the top of Brooke's hair, kissed her cheek. "I love you."

"Love you too, Mom." Brooke squeezed her mother's hand.

"Good night, Julia." Mary smiled as she pushed through the swinging door to head to her upstairs room.

Brooke breathed a sigh of relief. "Well, at least we got through it all. I still can't believe Moira pulled that stunt today."

"It's strange she'd lose consciousness like that, don't you think? Just from two glasses of wine?"

Brooke shrugged. "If that's all she had. She's *supposedly* not drinking any more."

"Where is she now?"

"She and Andy went up to her room. She always stays in the same guest room when she's here."

"She stays over a lot?"

"Oh, yes. It's her second home. I mean, she has her own place, her own apartment, but it's small, and she's head over heels in love with Ashley, so she stays over a lot to spend time with her. I'm really upset about today. I just can't have her around Ashley if she's drinking or ... worse. Rob would go ballistic..." Brooke took a sip of her wine and gave me her full attention. "So … what about you, Julia? We haven't had much time to chat. Anyone in your life right now?"

I smiled. Brooke was well aware of Michael's death, and like everyone else, she expected me to have moved on. I was getting tired of explaining why I hadn't.

"No, not yet." I shook my head. "Maybe someday." The subject of Michael reminded me that I hadn't returned a call from Celia, Michael's mother, my former would-have-been mother-in-law. The business of the wedding had given me an excuse to delay. I dreaded returning her call. After Michael's death, Celia had done everything possible to avoid speaking to me. According to her logic, I was responsible for his death. If he hadn't been rushing to meet me, he would never have been struck by a hit-and-run driver. His sister Maggie had done her best to heal the breach, but it had gone on so long, I'd given up hope. The fact that Celia had called was decidedly strange. I had no idea what she wanted, but I could guarantee one thing. The conversation would be psyche-bending.

I'd procrastinate one more day and call back tomorrow, I decided. I finished my wine and felt a sudden fatigue wash over me. I knew if I didn't fall into a bed soon, I'd collapse on the floor. "I better turn in, Brooke. Thanks again for putting me up."

"No bother at all. You go ahead. I just have to let Cassie out."

"You have to walk the dog at this hour?"

"Oh, no. I take her down to the garage. Her doggie door leads to her run in the backyard. Thank goodness the gardeners clean up out there." She laughed and rose from the table. "We let her out to play in the yard as well, but she loves to jump the fence when we're not looking."

Just then, Cassie, a large yellow lab, bounded into the kitchen and nuzzled against my hip.

"She's beautiful. Is she good with kids?" I asked.

"Oh, yes. She's a retired service dog. She's really more Rob's dog than mine. He's trained her. She's very smart." Brooke nuzzled Cassie's face and was rewarded with a big slippery lick. "Aren't you, girl?"

Cassie sniffed my leg and I patted her head. Before I could get out of the way, she lifted her head and lapped at my cheek. I laughed. "I guess I'm used to my cat, who's a lot less demonstrative."

Brooke stood up. "Come on, Cassie. Let's go downstairs." Cassie, nails clicking on the tile floor, bounded after her as she left the kitchen.

I stifled a huge yawn and found my way back through the foyer to the den. I slipped out of my jeans and T-shirt and into the pajamas Brooke had loaned me. Snuggling under the sheets, I pulled the comforter up to my chin. I was forgetting something. Oh yes—Wizard, my cat. He was at my grandmother's house in North Beach, where I'd stayed while helping my friend Gale reorganize her shop, the Mystic Eye. This had been followed by almost three days of wedding preparations. With all the activity, it was easiest just to camp out in North Beach, close to everyone. I live out on 30th Avenue, in the outer Richmond. My place is small, but I love it. I'm just a few blocks from China Beach and the Golden Gate straits, where the fog rolls in every afternoon and the foghorns lull me to sleep at night.

I knew Wizard wouldn't be dealing with my absence well at all, in spite of the fact that my grandmother constantly feeds him treats. He usually climbs onto the bed with me as soon as I'm in it and his purring lulls me to sleep. Poor Wiz. I sent him mental kisses. *We'll both be home soon.*

I heard footsteps and a door closing. The walls of the house were solid, but I was sure I heard Brooke downstairs in the garage calling Cassie back into the house. After that, all was quiet. I picked up the book I'd packed and settled in to read a few chapters. I was working my way through a study of astrological chart comparisons.

The page began to blur before my eyes and I must have drifted off. I slept until the explosions woke me.

FIVE

♈ ♉ ♊ ♋ ♌ ♍ ♎ ♏ ♐ ♑ ♒ ♓

I CAME TO INSTANTLY, my heart banging against my rib cage. Every nerve in my body was alive and singing. There had been two, then a third. They were gunshots and they were close. Very close.

I leaped out of bed, pulling on my robe as I ran down the hallway and pushed through the door to the foyer. A lamp on the table cast a soft glow over the room. Mary Leary was standing on the stairway. She seemed groggy and confused.

"Mary, I heard something. I think it came from the garage. Can you wake Brooke and Rob up?" Mary nodded but continued to stand, transfixed. My tone firmer, I said, "Something's really wrong, Mary. Please go get Rob and Brooke."

Mary finally nodded. Her face was white with fright. She turned away and climbed the stairs. I headed for the hallway door that led to the garage and tried the knob. It was locked. Then I heard footsteps thundering down the stairs and Matt appeared beside me.

"What the hell was that?"

"Gunshots. I'm pretty sure."

"That's what I was afraid of." He'd pulled on a pair of jeans and was rubbing his tousled head.

"I was in the den, right above the garage. I think that's where they came from."

Matt grabbed the doorknob and pulled, but the door didn't budge. "It must be locked from the other side. Let's see if we can get in there from the back yard."

"Wait. I hear something." We backed away in unison, unsure what to do. The door flew open. Rob stood in the darkened doorway, his face ashen. He stared at us for a long moment and finally said, "Call 911. I think I've shot an intruder."

Matt and I stared at him, unable to speak.

"He … he shot at me first. I was in the library. I couldn't sleep. I … I heard the door at the back of the house … the one that leads into the garage. It squeaks. I was afraid someone was trying to break in so I went down. Look, I'll explain later. Can somebody please call 911?"

I glanced around and spotted a phone on the side table. My fingers were shaking but I managed to punch in the numbers. The operator answered immediately. "Please send someone to 793 Clay Street. There's been a shooting." The dispatcher wanted more details. I gave her my name, but kept telling her I didn't have any answers.

I looked at Rob. "We have to go down. We need to see what's happened there."

Brooke had appeared at the top of the stairs. Her face was pale.

"I'll go first," Rob said. "There's no light at all. The switch didn't work for some reason. I'll find the emergency light." Matt and I descended the stairs, following him. The garage was pitch dark. I smelled engine oil and gunshot residue as I clung to the handrail to keep my balance.

29

"Stay put while I find the switch," Rob said.

He moved quietly along the side wall. I heard a click and a large battery-operated emergency light came on. It was bright but didn't illuminate the entire area.

A figure in black pants and a black hooded sweatshirt lay on the floor between Rob's and David's cars. A small pool of blood had formed under the intruder's head. I turned and saw that Brooke had followed us. She looked terrified. I moved toward the figure on the floor very slowly. A lock of fair hair had slipped out of the hood.

"Rob," I called. "You need to come here."

Rob had backed up until he was against the stairway and could go no further. He gathered his courage and slowly approached. He knelt next to me as I pulled the hood back, revealing Moira's face. Brooke screamed.

Rob jumped backward. "Oh, no. Oh, no. Oh my God. No!"

Mary had followed Brooke down and now clung to the railing at the bottom of the stairway. Her face had turned ghastly white. Her eyes rolled back in her head and her body went limp. Matt saw what was happening and rushed to her side, holding her upright.

Brooke screamed. "It's Moira, Rob. You've shot Moira!"

Was I imagining it, or did Moira's lips move? The pool of blood oozed slowly over the concrete floor. I leaned closer and whispered. "The ambulance is on its way, Moira. Hold on."

Rob cried, "I'll get a blanket." He grabbed a rough blanket hanging on a peg and rushed over, covering Moira quickly. Matt ran upstairs and returned carrying several towels. I pressed one to the back of Moira's head, afraid it was already too late. Brooke was making a sound deep in her throat that threatened to become a scream. Rob had sunk to the floor, his back against a car door.

We heard sirens in the distance. Rob leapt up, hurried to the garage control, and pressed in his code. Nothing happened. "Damn! There's no electricity to the door. Wait. There's a release here. I'll get it open."

Matt called out, "I'll check the fuse box." We heard a squeak as he cracked the metal box open. He fiddled with the fuses. "One's loose."

Rob found the release and pushed the garage door open just as the power came on. The entire garage was now brilliantly lit. Outside on the curb, the flashing lights of a patrol car and an ambulance throbbed blood-red against the night. Two patrolmen emerged from their car and walked slowly toward the garage opening. Rob stopped in his tracks as the patrolmen approached.

"Sir, can you tell me what happened?"

"I...I shot her." Tears were streaming down Rob's face. "It was an accident...I mean...I thought someone was trying to break in...I came down to the garage. I heard whispering. There was someone else here."

"Where's the weapon now, sir? Can you tell me where you left it?"

"Yes. Yes. It's..." Rob moved slowly, a naked look of confusion on his face. "It's my Glock. I dropped it on the floor...over here." He walked toward the gun lying on the concrete and reached for it.

"Sir, don't touch that. Leave it right where it is." The officer turned and gave a signal to the two paramedics standing at a safe distance. They rushed in with their equipment.

Brooke turned to Matt. "Take my mother upstairs. Please, Matt. She shouldn't be here."

I stepped back and watched as the two men knelt next to Moira. One of them swore under his breath. There was no need for questions.

31

The position of the body, the blood, and the acrid smell still lingered. They started an IV in one of Moira's arms and, placing her on a board, rushed her to the waiting van.

Brooke followed them, tears streaking her face. "Where are you taking her?"

His eyes never leaving his charge, the paramedic replied, "Mount Sinai. It's close and they're better equipped for gunshot wounds."

"I'm going with you," Brooke announced.

"Right now, lady. It's load and go. There's no time to waste," he replied.

Tying her robe tightly around her waist, Brooke clambered into the back with the second paramedic.

"Brooke!" Rob stepped forward. "I'll meet you there."

She turned back to him. "No. Stay here. Make sure Ashley doesn't wake up."

One of the officers took Rob carefully by the arm and turned him toward the stairway to the house. "You'll have to stay here for the time being, sir. The detectives are on the way now. They'll want to talk to you."

Andy stood by the stairway. I hadn't seen him arrive. His face was drained of color. He stepped back as Rob and his escort climbed the stairway to the foyer. The other officer stood in the opening to the garage, the night still dark behind him. Two shadows moved on the street, perhaps curious neighbors who'd been wakened by the sirens.

"Please follow the others," the second officer said to me and Andy.

"Shouldn't we shut the garage door?" Andy asked.

I thought Andy seemed remarkably calm under the circumstances. Or maybe he was in shock and wasn't able to take everything in.

"No, sir. The detectives will want to see this when they arrive. They'll be here very soon."

Andy nodded and started toward the stairway. He stopped and stared at me. "Julia," he said, looking at my robe and slippers. "I think you better take those off."

I looked down at the robe I'd borrowed from Brooke. Large spots of blood stained the hem where I'd knelt on the floor. My slippers had left dark tracks on the floor.

"Oh God." I started to cry. I felt as if I hadn't taken a breath since I heard the gunshots. I untied the robe and Andy lifted it away from my shoulders. I kicked off the bloodied slippers and left them in a small pile with the robe on the concrete. Could they be cleaned? Would Brooke even want to see them again? My mind was occupied with the trivia of what a good houseguest should do in such a situation. For some reason, my pajamas were clean, and at least I was clothed. I shivered violently and followed Andy upstairs.

Andy slipped out of his jacket. "You're cold. Put this over your shoulders."

"Thanks."

He dropped his jacket around me. "Moira's tough," he said. "She'll pull through. Everything will be okay."

I looked up at him, still unable to speak. I doubted anything would ever again be okay.

SIX

♈ ♉ ♊ ♋ ♌ ♍ ♎ ♏ ♐ ♑ ♒ ♓

THE FRONT DOOR FLEW open as we entered the foyer. Dan Leary stood in the doorway, his face mottled with red blotches. Andy and I came to a halt and watched as Dan marched through the foyer to the living room. Rob was seated in a chair, his head in his hands. Mary looked up at Dan as he entered the room. She was silent, her face drained of color.

"You bastard. You shot her. You shot my sister." Dan lunged toward the chair, but before he could reach Rob, the lone patrolman stepped in his way and, with a deft movement, twisted Dan around and pinned him to the wall.

"That'll be enough of that or I'll cuff you and bring you in."

Dan's body went limp.

"You gonna stay calm now?"

"I'm okay. I'm okay. Get offa me, please."

The officer stepped back and Dan turned, shooting a hateful glare at Rob. It was then that he noticed his mother sitting on the couch next to Matt. "Mom. Are you all right?"

Mary nodded, her body hunched in pain. Dan glanced at the patrolman and hurried to his mother.

She tried to stand. "I need to go upstairs," she said. "I want to make sure Ashley's still sleeping." Ashley's room was on the third floor and we all hoped the gunshots hadn't woken her.

Matt volunteered. "I'll go check on her, Mary. She might not have heard a thing up there."

Dan asked, "Where did they take Moira? Where's Brooke?"

Andy spoke up. "Mount Sinai. Brooke went with her in the ambulance."

Dan knelt next to his mother. "Mom, I'm going over there now to be with them. I'll call you in a little while, okay?" Mary shuddered and nodded in return.

"I should have gone with them." Andy's hands were shaking. "I wasn't thinking straight."

I slipped Andy's jacket off my shoulders and passed it back to him. "How did Dan find out about this?"

"I called him," Andy replied. "I thought he should know right away."

The officer stepped forward. "Both of you. Take a seat. No one's going anywhere right now."

Andy halted but Dan ignored the order and hurried to the front door. "Like hell. Don't even try to stop me." He slammed the door behind him before the officer could reach him.

Rob was still sitting, his head down, running his hands through his hair. He rocked back and forth, murmuring to himself. Cassie trotted into the living room and laid her head on Rob's knee. Her paws left a trail of muddy prints on the carpet. Rob reached out and patted her head absentmindedly.

We waited together in the living room, silent and in shock. Matt returned and joined Mary on the sofa, telling her that Ashley was fine and still asleep. Half an hour later, the doorbell rang. I walked back to the foyer and opened the front door to two men in street clothes. They followed me into the living room. The slender, dark man with a wolf-like face was in charge. He wore an expensively tailored suit and patent leather shoes. He held up his badge as he entered the room.

"I'm Detective Paolo Ianello. I'm very sorry to inform you that we've just spoken with Mount Sinai Emergency. Ms. Leary was pronounced dead on arrival."

Mary cried out. "No, not her. Not my baby."

SEVEN

♈ ♉ ♊ ♋ ♌ ♍ ♎ ♏ ♐ ♑ ♒ ♓

By the time the police left, taking Rob with them, the sun had risen behind a gunmetal gray sky. Rob had been allowed to change into street clothes under the watchful eyes of the police, while the detectives and their team took measurements and photos, bagged Rob's gun, and searched the house and garage.

Brooke and Dan returned to the house just as Rob was being led away. There was an exchange between husband and wife in the foyer that I couldn't hear. Dan stood silently to the side, his eyes downcast as Rob left with the police.

Mary had fallen into an exhausted sleep, leaning against the side of the sofa. Brooke, still in her robe, approached and sat next to her, taking her mother in her arms. "Let's go upstairs, Mom. We're going to lie down and I'll have you take a sleeping pill, okay? You need your rest. There's nothing else we can do."

"No dear. I don't want to sleep."

"I know, but you have to. It's the best thing. I'll be right here in the house with you. I'm not going anywhere. I'm not going to leave you alone." She looked at me. "Can you help me, Julia?"

Together we led Mary up the stairs. I could feel the small bones of her rib cage as I put my arm around her. She'd become so much more frail in the past few hours. We led her to her guest room and I smoothed out the bed while Brooke removed her mother's robe and slippers.

"I'll be right back." Brooke walked down the hall to her bedroom and retrieved a sleeping pill and a glass of water from the bath, carrying it back to the guest room. "Here, Mom. Take a sip and swallow this. You'll sleep for several hours, and I'll come in and nap with you in a bit."

Mary dutifully took the small pill that was offered and drank the glass of water. She looked up at her eldest daughter and whispered, "She was our baby, wasn't she?"

"Yes, Mom. Our baby."

Brooke's eyes were red and tear-stained. "Julia, will you sit with Mom till she's asleep? I need to call her doctor and a lawyer and try to figure out what to do next. Matt's going to stay upstairs with Ashley. I don't want her around all this."

"Yes, of course."

Brooke left the room, shutting the door gently behind her. I climbed onto the bed and propped myself against the headboard with an extra pillow. I stroked Mary's head. She lay quietly, finally closing her eyes, her small frame barely lifting the covers. I must have dozed off myself at some point, but woke to hear voices in the downstairs hallway. I lifted my head and peeked over at Mary. She was breathing deeply and fast asleep.

I sat up and moved very carefully off the bed. I tiptoed barefoot to the doorway and slipped out to the hallway. Leaning over the railing, I heard Geneva's voice, and David's as well. My heart ached for Geneva. Her lovely wedding and now this.

I waited until the voices diminished and hurried down the stairs to the den, where I splashed water on my face and stripped off my pajamas. I dressed in fresh clothes, pulled the sheets off the bed, and bundled up the laundry. I badly wanted to shower, but under the circumstances decided to wait until I was home.

In the kitchen, Sofia, Brooke's housekeeper, was at the stove pouring a ladle of batter onto the grill. She was a tall Russian woman with a round face and pale blue eyes that were swollen from crying. The smell of pancakes and bacon assailed my nostrils. Geneva, David, Dan, and Brooke sat at the table with barely touched breakfast plates in front of them. They all looked up as I entered.

"Oh, Julia." Geneva rose and came toward me. We hugged and she held on to me tightly. "My sister ..."

"I'm so sorry, Geneva."

She fought back tears. "Come sit down with us and have some food. We can't eat anything at all." I sat in the empty chair between Geneva and Dan. "Where's Matt? Where's Andy?"

Dan was clenching his hands, his knuckles white. "They left a little while ago."

A tense silence followed. I'd interrupted a family discussion. Geneva and David appeared to be the peacekeepers in the situation, while Brooke and Dan faced each other across the table.

"What are you going to do?" Dan finally spoke.

Brooke looked at him. "What should I do? What am I supposed to do?"

Sofia placed a dish with pancakes and strips of bacon in front of me. It smelled delicious, but my stomach turned at the thought of food. She set a napkin and silverware next to my place and then silently gathered up all the untouched food.

"It was a horrible accident, Dan. He didn't intend to hurt anyone. Someone took shots at him. What could he do? He didn't realize it was Moira in the dark."

"So he claims."

"What the hell are you saying? That this was deliberate? That Rob knew Moira was in the garage? That he intended to shoot her? Come on, Dan."

"I don't know," Dan grumbled. "I don't know what the hell to think."

Brooke turned to me. "They found bullets in the wall near where Rob was standing. That's evidence that someone did shoot at him."

"Do they think it was Moira? I didn't see another gun." I looked around the table and everyone fell silent. Finally, Brooke spoke.

"I think that's what the search was all about last night. And I don't know what they think. They'll find out she had problems. Drinking was just part of it. She had issues with me, with Rob, with everything. We thought she was doing much better lately, though. We did everything we could to help her out. I helped her with money. We gave her one of our cars. But in a way … I don't know … I think maybe it just made things worse. I think she resented me for it."

I glanced at Dan, but he'd remained silent. David heaved a sigh and shot a concerned look at Geneva.

"How's Mom? Is she still asleep?" Brooke asked me.

"Yes. It looks like she'll sleep a while longer too."

"Good. It's going to be so hard on her." Brooke turned to her sister. "Geneva … do you think Mom should stay here with me?"

"Not if they're going to release Rob. It might be better if she wasn't here for now."

"Can she stay with you and David?"

David said, "She's welcome to. We're certainly not going anywhere now. I don't think she should be alone either, but there's construction going on at our house. It might be too disruptive for her."

Geneva spoke up. "We can stay at Mom's for the time being. There's plenty of room there."

"Good idea." David responded. "I might have to be at the house sometimes for the construction crew, but..." He smiled ruefully. "I'd rather be with you at your mom's than alone in the house right now." He reached for Geneva's hand under the kitchen table and clasped it tightly.

The phone rang and Brooke jumped up to grab it. "Maybe that's Rob now." She answered, then listened carefully.

"Thanks for letting us know." She hung up and turned to Geneva. "That was the manager at the Inn. They heard from the hospital that Sally Stark, your wedding coordinator, is still unconscious."

"What?" Geneva paled.

"They're trying to diagnose her condition."

"Oh my God," Geneva mumbled.

"The police might want to talk to us," Brooke replied.

A chill ran up my spine. I recalled Moira's words: *That was meant for me.* I had a clear recollection of Sally Stark belting down a drink by the dance floor. Had she drunk from Moira's glass? Moira thought her earlier drink had been tampered with. I shot a look at Dan. His eyes widened and he returned my look. He made a barely perceptible gesture, as if asking for my silence for now.

41

"Our lawyer, Marjorie, called a while ago," Brooke said. "She's a former colleague of Rob's. They're meeting downtown. I don't think the police were particularly impressed that Rob's a well-known criminal defense attorney." She sighed. "But he was a prosecutor with the district attorney's office years ago. He still has friends there. Marjorie thought maybe some of them might put in a good word for him. There's a chance he could be released on his own recognizance."

"Brooke, I'll stay here with you for now," Dan said. He turned to me. "Do you mind, Julia?"

"No, not at all. You need to be here. I'll get a taxi."

Geneva and David made plans to take Mary home as soon as she awoke. There was nothing more I could do except clear out and let them grieve in peace. I went to the den, straightened up the room, and when everyone had moved into the living room, I returned to the kitchen. Sofia was working in the laundry room. She turned and took the bundle from my arms.

"Thank you. You're very thoughtful." She spoke with only a slight trace of accent.

"Sofia, last night I was wearing Brooke's robe and slippers and I think they might still be down in the garage."

"Police say I can't clean down there yet. But I throw them away later. I don't think Mrs. Brooke should see those things again." Sofia turned away and muttered something under her breath in Russian.

"What did you say?"

Sofia looked at me and blushed. "Sorry. Something my grandfather used to say…" She hesitated. "Not to clean blood until murder is avenged."

I stared at her and shuddered involuntarily. I headed down the stairs to the garage. My bedclothes of the night before were still in the pile where I'd left them. I looked around at the walls and saw numbered tags where bullets had been removed, a rough outline where Moira had lain, and an area of dried blood staining the concrete. Sofia's words echoed in my head.

I went back upstairs to say goodbye.

"Goodbye, dear, and thank you. Is very sad day, but I know Mr. Ramer never meant this."

"How did Rob and his sister-in-law get along?"

"Oh, not good. Not good at all." Sofia poured detergent into the washer and set the dials for the next cycle.

"How come?"

"Mr. Ramer, he is a very...uh...stiff person? Is that right word?"

"You mean rigid?"

"Rigid. Yes. Not a bad person, very kind, but he never liked his sister's drinking, worried about little Ashley too." She pursed her lips. "I don't blame him for that. He is good father."

"Moira was around a lot?"

"All the time. She stay over a lot too. She love that little girl, and Mrs. Brooke always like to have her sister here, but Mr. Ramer worried, he didn't like her sister around so much."

"I see." It backed up what I'd already heard.

"But this is terrible thing. I don't know... how everyone can get over this." Sofia pushed the lid down on the washer and pulled the knob out. Water gushed as she wiped her hands. She shook her head and returned to the kitchen.

I called a taxi from the phone in the den and somehow managed to get all my things, even the rolled-up bridesmaid gown and shoes, into my tote bag. I found Geneva and David in the living room and said goodbye, telling Geneva I'd call her later.

"Brooke's on the phone in the library, talking to the attorney." Geneva replied.

"Please tell her I had to leave but to call me if there's anything I can do for her."

"I will. It's probably best if we're all out of her house soon."

I trudged down the stairs with my belongings and sat on the low wall in front of the house amid the hydrangea bushes. A few side-long looks were aimed at me by curious neighbors walking by. I slipped on a large pair of sunglasses. A news van turned onto Clay and cruised slowly down the street. I spotted my taxi coming in the opposite direction. As I stepped onto the street to wave, a curtain slipped back into place in an upstairs room in a house across the street.

The taxi stopped and I tossed my tote bag onto the back seat and climbed in. The well-tended façade of 793 Clay gave away nothing of the previous night's horror.

EIGHT

♈ ♉ ♊ ♋ ♌ ♍ ♎ ♏ ♐ ♑ ♒ ♓

IT WAS ALMOST NOON by the time the taxi pulled up to my grandmother's house in Castle Alley. I paid the driver, lugged my bag up the granite stairway, and let myself into her apartment.

My grandmother, Gloria, still lives in the house where I grew up, a three-story clapboard in North Beach divided into two flats. Kuan Lee, her old friend, lives on the first floor while Gloria occupies the second and third floors. A small sign hung on Kuan's doorway to alert anyone who might knock that he was with a client. Kuan is an herbologist and practitioner of Chinese medicine who sees clients in his home. He's in his seventies now, and like my grandmother, remains spry and healthy. He's become quite famous in the city and his services are always in demand.

I had a raging headache and my body ached all over. Whether it was the shock of the previous night or the lack of sleep, I didn't know, but at that moment I would have happily availed myself of his services.

I locked the door behind me and climbed the stairway to the up-stairs flat, calling out to my grandmother. No answer. I was secretly relieved I wouldn't have to face her right away. I wasn't in the mood to relive the events of the night before so soon.

Wizard trotted down the stairs from the third floor, his bell tin-kling as he came to greet me. I picked him up and hugged him. He butted his forehead against mine—his way of returning a hug. Glo-ria had been spoiling him horribly, and his twenty-pound fat black body would weigh twenty-five pounds if I didn't get him home soon. He jumped out of my arms and ran to the kitchen, expecting a treat. I ignored him and climbed the stairs to my former bedroom, now Gloria's sitting room. I dumped my purse and tote bag on a chair and grabbed two aspirin from the medicine cabinet in the bathroom. I downed them with a glass of water and plopped on the bed, clothes and all. I dragged a crocheted quilt up to my chin and fell into a leaden sleep.

———

I woke after a dreamless three-hour nap. Wizard had disappeared and my grandmother still wasn't home. It was Sunday, which meant she'd gone to church in the morning and would probably be busy all day with some sort of endeavor. Her latest hobby was kick-boxing. I worried she'd hurt herself. I stumbled down to the kitchen and heated a cup of leftover coffee in the microwave, chugged it down, and returned upstairs to straighten up. Finally I took a shower, happy to be washing chemicals out of my hair, changed into fresh clothes, and brushed my teeth. I pulled my mop of unruly hair, still damp, back in a clasp and slapped on a little makeup.

Lists of things I needed to do were forming in my head. And at the top of the list was returning Celia's call. I grimaced, took a deep breath, and looked up her number in my address book. I know Michael's mother's number by heart, but a strange mental block always forms whenever I pick up the phone to call her.

Michael had been the warmest, most caring person in the world. I couldn't reconcile what I knew of him with the woman who was his mother. In Celia's mind, no one was good enough for her son. She'd disliked me on sight. I know that now. At first, I'd been terribly wounded by her cold courtesy and barely concealed resentment. After Michael's death, I found that there was no comfort from that quarter, nor did she want any consolation from me. I'd tried, but there didn't seem to be any avenue to improve the situation. Logically, there was no cause for guilt on my part, but emotions are never logical. And Celia was a class A guilt trip.

I dialed her number. The phone rang three times and I prepared to leave her a message. She picked up on the fourth ring.

"Celia. Hello. It's Julia." I hadn't spoken to her for several months. For the first year or so after Michael's death, I'd made a point, for my own sense of propriety, to call her at least once a week. Later, the calls were once a month, to ask if there was anything I could do for her. I always received a chilly "No, thank you" in a tone that implied *I* had asked a favor of *her*. Eventually my calls became less and less frequent and finally stopped. I wasn't proud of my reaction to her, but I told myself that had she been a different person, I would have made it my business to stay in better touch.

"Julia. Yes. I'm sure you know why I'm calling."

"Uh, not exactly." I wracked my brain, wondering if I'd forgotten a conversation.

"It's about Michael's things."

"Michael's things?" What was she talking about?

"At your apartment. I'm sure there are personal items that you haven't returned to me."

"Well…" I mentally reviewed the contents of my closet. There undoubtedly were things that had belonged to Michael, things of his that had accumulated at my old place. We'd planned that when Michael returned from a cave exploration in Guatemala, I would give up my apartment and move into his larger space. After his death, I moved to 30th Avenue in the Richmond instead. I couldn't bear to look at anything of his and just packed everything except his letters away quickly, before I was swamped with grief once again.

"I don't think—" I began.

"I'm quite sure I'm correct. I must ask you to go through your things and check. I'm sure there are clothing, books, notebooks, whatever. Under the circumstances, I feel I've been extremely patient."

I wondered what circumstances she was referring to. "Celia, as you know, I moved not that long ago. I do have some boxes still unopened and I'll be happy to check as soon as I can." I wasn't looking forward to picking at old wounds, but now I'd have to do just that.

"Anything you have of Michael's belongs to his family." Ah, there it was. The unspoken cut. We hadn't married. I was not family. I felt the knife blade slip smoothly between my ribs. That old familiar sense of not belonging… the child with her face pressed against the windowpane, looking in, never being a part of. My parents both died when I was five years old, killed in a collision on the Bay Bridge. Gloria raised me, and although there's no doubt in my mind that my grandmother loves me with all her heart, I've always carried the sense of being an orphan. Celia knew instinctively how best to hurt.

I took a deep breath, not wanting to react with anger. "Of course it does, Celia. I will definitely go through everything in storage and I'll give you a ring in a few days."

"I'll call you again if I don't hear from you." With that parting shot, Celia hung up without a goodbye. I felt an angry flush rise to my cheeks. To an empty phone I replied. "I'm sure you will."

I dreaded the thought of having to search through at least six or seven boxes still packed away. There were a lot of old mementos from childhood or college in there. But there would definitely be some items—perhaps books, and of course photos and letters—that Michael and I had shared. Celia was not getting my photos and letters. Had she always been this cold and difficult, or since Michael's death had she gone further off the rails? I'd heard through a mutual friend that Michael's former bedroom at her house had become a shrine to the son who no longer lived. A sense of sadness swept over me. Who was I to judge? What tortures did Celia suffer daily? I had lost my lover, but Celia had lost a child.

I bundled the bridesmaid dress and matching shoes into a separate bag. My grandmother would know if there was a current clothing drive going on at her church or in the neighborhood. She'd been a seamstress most of her working life and was always in demand for those types of fundraisers. I could come back later in the evening for Wizard and all his paraphernalia.

Gale had left a message for me two days earlier that some astrology books I'd ordered were in. She was holding them down the street at the Mystic Eye. I hadn't had a chance to pick them up yet but I was anxious to get them. Since I was already downtown and it was Sunday afternoon, I knew the shop would be open. If Gale wasn't there, our friend Cheryl, who manages the Mystic Eye, would be, and she'd have my books handy.

The sun had peeked out during the afternoon, but it wasn't going to last long. From the upstairs windows, I could see a fog bank hanging out at sea. I grabbed my purse and a jacket and carried my tote bag down to the car. I dumped it in the trunk of my Geo and left the car in the driveway. I turned down the hill and walked the few blocks to Broadway, where the Mystic Eye occupies a conspicuous spot on the main street, close to foot traffic and coffeehouses.

Gale's shop caters to occult tastes—books, jewelry crafted by local artists, candle-burning supplies, Tarot cards, sage bundles, and religious items from religions even I haven't heard of. The shop was just one of Gale's many business projects that was making a nice profit. Once the Eye was on its feet, Gale had become bored and wanted to move on to other ventures. She's one of those amazing people who makes money at anything they touch. I, on the other hand, just manage to make ends meet with my astrology practice. But I can't complain. I'm doing something I love, and sooner or later my income will increase.

Cheryl manages the Eye by herself for the most part. When she and Gale first met, Cheryl was looking forward to a messy divorce and felt completely lost. Her husband of ten years, Frank the endodontist, had left her for his dental assistant. A homemaker all her life, with no real job skills and no children to care for, Cheryl had been devastated by Frank's exit. She walked into Gale's shop one day for a reading at one of the psychic fairs, saw a *Help Wanted* sign, and applied for a job on the spot. She was, according to Gale, as nervous as a cat. She confessed that she hadn't held a job since college and was renting a room in a residence hotel on Bush Street, having left Frank in possession of their large house in Berkeley. Gale was enraged when she heard the whole story and took Cheryl under her wing, hiring her on the spot. Since then, the three of us have become close friends.

I was in similar shape myself when I first met Gale. I'd earned a masters in anthropology, but after Michael's death I couldn't seem to pick up the threads of my old life. That was when I discovered the Mystic Eye and became a regular and a devotee of astrology. Gale opened new doors for me, as she later did for Cheryl, and I never looked back. I've written some articles, and one book on love triangles, while keeping up with my private clientele.

I peeked through the front windows of the Eye. Customers were milling about in the aisles. I cut down the alley around the side of the building. Gale's parking spot was vacant, but Cheryl's VW was there. I wiggled the knob on the back door. Locked. I tapped on the glass pane and saw Cheryl approaching from the office to unlock the door.

"Hey, I expected you yesterday. You got the message your books arrived?"

"I did. I didn't have a chance to call you back. I had the wedding yesterday."

"Oh, that's right. I forgot." She smiled suddenly. "Did you have a blast?"

"Uh … we should talk about that later."

"Oh. Sure." Cheryl could tell she'd upset me. "I didn't mean to pry."

"That's all right. I just wanted to catch you before you closed up."

"Come on in." She locked the door behind me and I followed her into the storeroom. An energetic, petite blonde, Cheryl is rail thin and full of nervous energy. Like Gale, she doesn't pay a lot of attention to the occult arts, but she recognizes the money-making possibilities for the Eye. The aroma of incense, scented candles, and sage bundles filled the back room.

"Listen, Julia. I'm *so* glad you came by. We're not closing for another two hours. We have a psychic fair going on."

"Oh?" I had a premonition of Cheryl's next statement.

"And the astrologer I lined up just called. His car's broken down. He won't make it for another hour or so, if he makes it at all. I'm desperate. I've been stalling five customers, telling them he'll be late. Can you fill in? *Please?*"

I groaned. "You know I don't like to do fairs. They're a pain, especially for astrologers. Besides, since I bought my computer program, I'm spoiled."

"I'm begging." She clasped her hands together and bowed from the waist. "Please. You've got to help me out. Gale's not here. She left earlier, before all this happened. It's not the money so much, it's just that I hate to turn people away and possibly lose future customers. Gale sets these things up for marketing."

"I don't even have my laptop with me," I said. Cheryl looked desperate and I folded. "Two hours?"

She nodded.

"Who else do you have working today?"

"I've got Eric for past-life readings."

"Oh, he's good. I like him." Eric is a slight man who seems to barely maintain consciousness during readings. He dresses in dark suits two sizes too large for him, always with a white shirt and a tie. While he reads, his eyes roll back and he speaks in slow, lugubrious tones. His readings are based on past-life relationships and, whether you believe in that sort of thing or not, he's unerringly accurate in describing the circumstances of current-life relationships.

"And I've got Zora," Cheryl continued. "And Ankaret. You know her. She uses the Tarot."

"Zora's very talented," I agreed. "She did that séance for us last winter and I've heard she's a wonderful psychic too." A hefty woman, Zora dresses in long skirts and tunics, wraps multiple shawls around herself, and calls her clients "babe" while shouting advice at them in a gravelly voice. "But I don't know the Tarot lady."

"Yes you do." Cheryl leaned closer and whispered, "She's the Joni Mitchell wannabe. Nice, but she spent too many years smoking dope in Big Sur. Somebody needs to tell her the seventies are long over."

I heaved a sigh and hung my jacket on a hook in the back room. The shop had been designed with four tiny rooms along the side, each just large enough for two people to sit at a small table. The private spaces were hidden from public view by a curtain over each entryway.

"I'll need an Ephemeris and a Table of Houses, and do you have one of those little gizmo wheels that guestimate the rising sign? Oh, and a large pad of paper and a pen, and a timer or a clock."

"Oh, thank you, thank you, you're a doll. You're a lifesaver! You know how we sell these readings—a dollar a minute in fifteen, twenty, or thirty minute increments. You just have to talk to each person for fifteen minutes or whatever. That's not hard, is it?"

"No," I agreed. The problem was that I hated to do any kind of reading flying by the seat of my pants, so to speak. Fifteen minutes doesn't allow enough time to do more complicated calculations by hand. If I'd brought my laptop with the computer program, I would have been able to set up birth charts instantly. The best any astrologer can do in a situation like this one is to ask for the birth date and birth place and hope the client knows their birth time. Then make a quick judgment about their personality from the planets in signs and in aspect, and hope that a significant transit was occurring to one of the natal planets, in order to say anything meaningful. Even though I did plenty of fairs at the beginning of my career as a way of building up my business, I've never been crazy about doing readings under these conditions.

Cheryl led me to a tiny side room and rushed back with the requested Ephemeris that would give me planetary positions by date, a Table of Houses reference book that could tell me the sign and degree on house cusps—assuming the client actually knew their birth time—and all the other items I'd requested. Then Cheryl ducked out and walked through the shop calling for someone named Shandra.

A young woman in her early twenties peeked through the curtain and hesitated.

"Hi, Shandra." I smiled. "Please have a seat."

The girl looked terrified and sat with her hands clutched around her purse. She was dressed in overalls and a T-shirt with a scarf wrapped around her curly brown hair. She gave me her birth information and even the time. I sketched out her chart as quickly as possible.

"It looks like your Ascendant is fifteen degrees of Aries." I estimated the movement of her progressed Moon for her current age. "I'm sorry I don't have my laptop with me, but it's likely your progressed Moon is approaching your seventh house cusp." I looked up. "Are you planning to get married? Or perhaps making a big emotional commitment, moving in with your boyfriend?

54

"Yes," she breathed. "That's amazing you could tell that. We're supposed to be getting married in a month. The wedding invitations have been sent out already." Her voice quavered.

"I see. Well, the seventh house is all about relationships. But you're having second thoughts, aren't you?"

She nodded but offered no further information.

I took a deep breath and dove in. "In your natal chart there's a difficult aspect, one that has colored your early years, your childhood. So, undoubtedly, your fears are connected with this placement." Shandra stared but did not acknowledge my statement. I knew I was on the right track.

I turned the pad of paper toward her. "You see, your Sun is near the tenth house cusp, right between Neptune and Saturn. Opposing that stellium is Chiron. The fourth and tenth house cusps are the nadir and the Midheaven. This axis indicates parental influences in your life, and since Saturn conjuncts your Sun, I'd maybe say this pertains more to your father than your mother. You've suffered a great deal in your life because of the lack of a father figure, but you've been very strong. The Saturn conjunction has given you strength and you've been able to compensate."

"Yes. That's true."

"Did he abandon you or your mother? Did he disappear in some fashion? Maybe even close to the time you were born?"

Shandra nodded. "He … he drowned in an accident when my mother was pregnant with me. Just before I was born. It took them a long time to find his body. It was terrible for my mother." Her face crumpled and she started to quietly cry. I passed her the box of tissues. Neptune, I thought, the ruler of watery places. How terrible and how apt.

"I'm sorry. I haven't thought about this for a long time."

"And your mother raised you alone?"

"My mom and I are very close." Shandra blew her nose and wiped her eyes. "I'm really sorry. I didn't mean to come here and blubber."

"It's okay. We all blubber sometimes. Even me … especially me." I smiled.

Shandra laughed nervously.

"Let's get back to the wedding invitations. Do you love him?"

"Yes. Very much."

"And he of course loves you."

"Yes." She smiled shyly.

"Well, let's look at his birth information. Even if you don't have all the information now, you can always call me later with it. We can set up a very quick solar chart for your boyfriend and see if there are any real problems." She gave me his birth date and I quickly sketched out his approximate chart.

"My mom really wants to see us get married. I think she's afraid I'll be alone and won't have anyone to look after me."

I thought of my grandmother. This all sounded very familiar. "I can understand that. So what are you afraid of?"

She stared at me silently. I let the silence lag, and then asked her softly, "You're afraid that if you marry him, he'll die. If you invest in this, you'll be left like your mother?"

"Yeeees." At this, Shandra burst into tears again. I passed her the tissues once more and handed her a glass of water.

"Don't feel bad about crying. Crying's great. It gets all the demons out into the light of day."

"It sounds so stupid when you say it like that, but I guess that's why I'm afraid."

"Okay, now look at this." I pointed to the paper. "Here's the solar chart of your boyfriend. What's his name?"

"Rick."

"Okay. Rick seems like a pretty well-balanced guy. There are many, many good connections between your charts. He balances you out very well. You're complementary to each other in lots of ways. With the information I have, I don't see anything negative here. It's very positive. What does your mother have to say about this wedding?"

"Oh, she's got her heart set on it. That's why I've been so upset. I've been thinking of calling it off. I've been so scared and I didn't want to hurt her or hurt Rick. I've backed out twice before, and this time, he says he can't do it anymore. He loves me, but he says if I don't want to marry him, he just has to go away."

"Well, the decision is yours, of course. No one should force you to do anything you don't want to do." I waited to see her reaction.

"What do you think I should do?"

I always have such a hard time biting my tongue. "I really can't tell you what to do. But I can give you some good advice. I think this is a very positive relationship. You're good for each other and, frankly, with his Saturn return coming up this year and your Moon progressing to your Descendant, this is the right time. The Saturn return is considered 'the astrological coming of age.' It usually happens sometime between the ages of twenty-eight and thirty. That's the time we're most free to make decisions that will affect our path for the next twenty-eight or so years. It's a terribly significant time. And your progressed Moon ... well, you may not be fully aware as yet ... but you've already made the commitment."

Shandra was quiet.

"I also think it would help you to see a therapist for a little while, to sort out your father's death and separate that event from your current life. I can give you a few names of good psychologists, if you'd like."

I thought about my own therapist, Paula. Maybe I should give her a call soon myself, but it wouldn't do to recommend Paula to an astrology client. I'd hate to bump into one of my clients in a waiting room. They'd wonder why astrology hadn't answered all *my* questions and doubts. Astrology can offer a lot of support, but it's still no substitute for dredging through your own very illogical emotions.

"Now that it's on the front burner this would be an excellent time," I continued. "There's no need for you to carry these old wounds and fears into a very promising future."

"Maybe I *should* give that a try. I've been so stuck and so scared to make a move, but I'm really terrified I could lose Rick."

"That's it, my dear. I'm afraid our time is up."

"Oh, thank you. I can't thank you enough," Shandra mumbled. "Can I come back and see you again?"

"I'm not always at the Eye, but let me give you one of my cards if you need to see me, okay?"

Shandra took my card and stared at it. She looked up at me. "You're…"

I didn't respond. I suspected what was coming next and I dreaded it.

"You're the astrologer who rescued that woman from the crazy religious cult, aren't you?

I sighed. I'd hoped all the notoriety from months ago would be forgotten. I took a deep breath and smiled. "That's me, all right."

"You're famous!" Shandra's eyes grew wider.

I shook my head. "No, really, I'm not. It's just that they printed my name in the paper."

"Ohmigod, I had no idea!"

"Well, please don't hold it against me." I laughed.

"Wait till I tell my friends that I had a reading with Julia Bonatti."

I groaned inwardly. The events of last winter still haunted me. I didn't like the idea of being in the glare of any kind of publicity, but when my client's elderly aunt was lured into a religious cult that didn't have good intentions, I really had no choice.

Shandra tucked my card into a pocket of her overalls. "Thank you *so* much!" She stepped through the curtain. Through the gap, I could see her two girlfriends waiting anxiously for her. One reached over and gave her a hug as they exited to the street.

I heaved a sigh. I've come to the conclusion that it's a universal law that we're constantly confronted with the very issues we have trouble dealing with in our own lives. If Shandra could overcome her fears, then maybe there was hope for me too.

I managed to get through five more readings in my cramped little space: one elderly woman worried about her grandson, a businessman concerned about a move, a housewife considering full-time work, a single woman worried about marriage, and a professional gambler asking about amulets to help his luck. Thankfully, no one else recognized me or my name. Finally, I heard the bell on the closing door ring for the last time.

I peeked out. "Is that it?"

"Yes. Thank heavens. I'm beat!" Cheryl turned the lock on the front door and flipped over the sign to read *Closed*. "If I have to smell any more patchouli, I'm gonna throw up all over my shoes.

Want to get some Chinese? I need to inhale something totally different before I scream."

"Sure. I'm starving. Where do you want to go?"

"Let's leave the cars. Did you park in the back?"

"No. My car's at Gloria's. I walked over."

"Let's go to that dim sum place up the block."

"The Twin Dragons? Okay." I slipped on my jacket and grabbed my purse and the new books.

"Would you check in the back and make sure everyone's gone and the door is locked?"

I dropped my purse and books on the counter and stepped into the back room. I couldn't find the light switch but felt my way past stacked boxes to the door. A small amount of light from the alley filtered through the dusty window. I heard breathing and the skin on my arms tingled. I wasn't alone in the back room. Then a shadow moved across the light source coming from the front of the shop. Powerful hands grabbed my shoulders. My breath caught in my throat.

"You!" I heard Zora's raspy voice.

My heart was thudding wildly. I took a deep breath. "I thought everyone was gone."

The psychic's powerful grip on my shoulders tightened. "Babe," she rasped at me in the half-dark, "you don't know this yet, but you're in danger."

I froze. "What?"

Pressing her finger into my chest, she barked, "Don't be a do-gooder. Keep your nose out of other people's business, okay?"

She flung the back door open and stepped out into the alleyway. I watched her bulky form cross the tiny parking lot, her shawls flying in the breeze.

Cheryl appeared in the doorway behind me. "Was that Zora? What did she say?"

"Nothing. Don't worry about it." I took a deep breath. "She scares the hell out of me."

NINE

♈ ♉ ♊ ♋ ♌ ♍ ♎ ♏ ♐ ♑ ♒ ♓

NORTH BEACH IS SAN Francisco's Italian neighborhood, full of shops, restaurants, and coffeehouses catering to locals and tourists. Chinatown begins right across the intersection of Broadway and Columbus. Both neighborhoods are crowded all the time, but truly come to life when the sun goes down. We exited from the back door of the Mystic Eye and walked out onto a bustling sidewalk. Turning into the doorway of the Twin Dragons, we climbed a set of creaking wooden stairs to the second-floor restaurant.

Red-and-gold-painted dragons prance around the walls of the restaurant's one large room. Generous booths dominate one side, with windows overlooking the street. There were few patrons at this hour so we had our pick of seating. Cheryl headed for a booth by the front window. I dumped my purse, books, and jacket on the padded seat next to me and settled in. The lighting was dim, but the neon signs on nearby buildings glowed and reflected off the polished tabletop. A smiling waiter arrived wheeling a four-tiered carriage of trays loaded with small concoctions wrapped in soft dough. He placed two plates in front of us and Cheryl and I picked one from each of the trays to start. Soon a pot of hot tea and bowls of steaming white rice arrived.

"So tell me, what's going on? Why did you look so down when you came to the door?" Cheryl asked.

Our waiter returned with a new carriage loaded with different goodies. We pointed at the ones we wanted. I waited until he'd moved away to tell her about Moira's death early that morning. It was a shock to think that not even a full day had elapsed.

Cheryl listened carefully. "How well do you know these people?"

"Geneva is an old friend, a good friend. We went to school together and she was my roommate in the Sunset District for a few years. I know her mother and her brother Dan. Her older sister Brooke I know slightly, although I've heard of her accomplishments over the years, and I first met Brooke's husband at the wedding rehearsal. That's it."

"So this sister … ?"

"Moira was the youngest of all of them—the ne'er-do-well little sister—always in some kind of trouble, always angry and rebellious. Drinking too much, playing around with drugs. Supposedly she was getting it together and staying straight, although her behavior at the wedding yesterday didn't indicate that."

"Julia, I'm so sorry. What a horrifying experience."

"I know … Geneva … can you imagine? She has a lovely wedding, she's thinking about her honeymoon, and now her sister's dead and her other sister's husband caused it. Can you imagine how crushing this is to that family? They're such nice people, Cheryl. They're just very decent. They grew up in their mother's house, near me out on 35th Avenue. In their wildest nightmares, they could never have anticipated anything like this."

"Why didn't you tell me when you came to the shop? I wouldn't have twisted your arm to stay."

"It's all right. I slept a few hours at Gloria's house, so I do feel better. I only planned to stop in and see you, maybe Gale too, and pick up my books. Working the fair took my mind off this thing for a while, but I know it'll haunt me for a long time to come."

We finished our dim sum and when the waiter brought the bill, Cheryl and I split it, leaving a tip. We strolled back to the Mystic Eye. Cheryl checked the locks on the front door one last time, and we cut down the alleyway to the parking lot behind the shop. I waited while she made sure the back door was secure.

"What's happening with your divorce?" I asked. "Is the trial still on?"

"Yes. I'm so nervous, Julia. It's this Wednesday morning, 8:30 a.m., Courtroom 414, San Francisco Superior Court, 400 McAllister. I have it all memorized and written down."

Cheryl rummaged in her purse and extracted a pink slip of paper covered with careful notes. Gale had found a relentless divorce attorney for her, who'd been busy ensuring that Cheryl didn't get completely taken in the divorce. He'd moved quickly through the discovery process and all seemed to be going painlessly. Thinking ahead, Gale was also checking out condos for Cheryl to buy when the finances were settled. We weren't exactly sure where Cheryl stood emotionally, but we knew she needed our support.

"I get so angry sometimes … I scare myself," Cheryl went on. "Sometimes I start shaking so badly I can barely keep it together." I wasn't sure she was as free of Frank's influence as she wanted to think she was, but I was hoping for the best. "In fact, tomorrow morning after he leaves for the office, we're going over to the house to get the rest of my stuff."

"You mean you still have things at the house? Who's 'we'?"

"Gale and me. There are some things . . . I just didn't have any place to store anything till now. When Gale found out my things were still there, she insisted I use the storage space in the back of the shop until I get settled again. I don't want any of the furniture or anything. Just my mother's china, my favorite books. You know, personal things and the rest of my clothes. When I left, I packed two suitcases and that's what I've been living on for the past year. As hard as this is, you and Gale were right. I never realized how really miserable I was. Never thought I'd say that when this first blew up, but, well . . . you predicted it . . . here I am." She turned and slipped her key into the car door. "I'm bushed. I'm heading home to my tiny cell and putting my feet up with a glass of wine. Want to join me?"

"Thanks, no. I need to get back to Gloria's and pick up Wizard and get home."

"Wish me luck in court this week. Can you be there?"

"I'm not sure. I'll have to check my calendar. But if I can, I will. In any case, I'll keep my fingers crossed for you." We hugged and Cheryl clambered into her car. I watched from the sidewalk as she pulled away and headed toward Montgomery. Retracing my steps, I returned up the hill to Castle Alley, where I'd once again have to relive the events of the last forty-eight hours.

When I arrived, my grandmother was ensconced in the kitchen with a cup of tea, waiting to hear all about the wedding. I took a deep breath and summed up the events of the prior night as gently as I could. When I finished, she sat still, her face pale. "How could that have happened?"

"Happens more often than you think," I said.

She shook her head. "Thank God you're all right. Staying in that house. You could have been shot. What was Moira doing in the garage? And why did she shoot at her brother-in-law?"

"They don't know for sure that she did. Rob believes there was someone else there with her. The police aren't talking. We were up all night while they asked questions and searched the house and the garage."

"Well, dear, I'm so sorry for that poor family. And Geneva, how awful. How terrible for her. No nice wedding memories for that family. Here I was, hoping you might have met someone. And now I'm just so grateful you're safe and sound."

I ignored her comment about meeting someone. So far, I'd forestalled all her efforts to pair me up.

"Are you sure you don't want to stay here another night? We could watch a movie?"

"That sounds really nice. But maybe another time. I really feel the need to be home."

"Well, I'll miss you. It's been so nice having you around a little. Wizard can stay with me. He's a sweetie."

"No way. He's getting too fat."

By the time I had Wizard's litter box cleaned up and packed, with his bowls and cans of cat food in the car, it was almost nine o'clock. I returned up the stairs, grabbed him as he tried to escape, and put him, protesting, into his cat carrier. He howled all the way home, quieting only when we stopped at red lights.

"Shut up, Wiz. You're driving me crazy." I turned on the car radio and hit the button until I found a station playing soothing classical music, hoping this would calm him down. I drove through the Broadway Tunnel to Van Ness and picked up California Street. Crossing Park Presidio, I drove straight into the fog. Droplets of moisture obscured my view all the way to 30th Avenue. Wizard resumed his howling every time I accelerated.

I pulled up in front of the garage door at my duplex and hit the brakes. A dark figure was huddled on the stairway of my building. A frisson of fear ran up my spine. Then a pale face turned toward me. It was Geneva, bundled up in a dark coat.

I climbed out of the car, leaving the engine idling. "How long have you been here?"

She stood up. "Not long. I decided to wait a bit. Thought you might be home soon."

"Come on up. I'll unlock the front door. Just have to pull the car in and grab my stuff. You go on up."

I let Geneva in through the front door and pulled the car into the garage. Wizard was silent. He knew he was home. I unzipped the carrier and released him. He bounded away through the door leading to the backyard and left me to haul his necessities and my stuff up the side stairs to my kitchen. I called out to Geneva and put a kettle on for tea. She'd turned on a lamp in the living room and was sitting in the big club chair, still huddled in her coat. From the windows I could see the fog that had moved in from the Pacific. It hung over the tops of the pine trees in Lincoln Park, lending an eerie glow to the night. I shivered and closed the drapes, then turned on the gas jets in the fireplace. The room started to warm up immediately.

"Tea will be ready soon."

"Thanks." Her face was pallid under the lamplight.

It struck me that our positions were now reversed. Two and a half years ago, it was Geneva who was strong and I who'd sat lifeless in that very chair.

When I heard the kettle shriek, I ran back to the kitchen and prepared a tray with two large mugs of tea. I carried it to the living room and placed it on the table next to Geneva. Something was on her mind, something important, or she wouldn't be here.

She cupped her hands around the hot mug. "It seems like a lifetime ago we were living in the Sunset above that crazy antique store, wondering how our lives would turn out. Making our plans."

"Antiques?" I laughed. "That's really stretching it. Junk shop is more like it."

Geneva smiled for the first time and took a sip of her tea. "I really needed to talk to you tonight and I didn't want to phone. Mom's finally asleep. David's with her right now, so I had a chance to get away for a few minutes. I need your help."

"Anything. You've got it."

"I need you to do something for me." Geneva hesitated for a moment as if gathering her thoughts. "I need you to search Moira's apartment, if not tonight, then first thing tomorrow. I've brought a key." She reached down and rummaged in her purse, pulling out a single key on a ring attached to a large silver M. "I'd do it myself, but I'm afraid I'd fall part. And tomorrow will be hard, with my mom and all the arrangements we have to make. Dan and I plan to empty out Moira's apartment in the next day or so—the end of the month is coming soon—but I need you to have a look around right away. You're the only one I trust to do it. I've written the address down." She slipped a Post-it note under the key.

I felt uncomfortable about her request but wasn't sure why. "I'm not sure I like the idea of this, Geneva. And I'm not sure exactly why."

"Nothing can hurt Moira now."

"Why not ask David? Surely you trust him?"

"I could ask him, and I'm sure he would do it, but I'm not certain he wouldn't miss something important that you would spot in a second."

"What exactly are you looking for?"

"Anything that would cause the police to jump to any wrong conclusions."

I shook my head. "That's a little vague. Can you be more specific?"

Geneva sighed. "Look, Moira had her problems. She's abused drugs and she's caused a lot of trouble for Brooke in the past. She needed to stay straight and keep up with her AA meetings, but she started drinking again. Her behavior had become more and more unpredictable. You saw that during the wedding. But that's not what worries me. What worries me is that even though she was working only occasionally, she had an awful lot of money to spend. Andy was angry with her, and, I think, maybe even jealous. They were fighting a lot. There were things going on that worried me."

"Was he violent with her?"

Geneva shook her head. "I don't know. I hope not, but I wouldn't rule it out. I just need to know what she was up to, because whatever she was up to got her killed. She must have been meeting someone last night. Down in the garage. Maybe Rob was right when he said there was someone else there."

Geneva took a sip of her tea. "Julia, they searched our house today."

"What? Your and David's house? Whatever for?"

69

"I don't really know. We were at my mom's. They served the warrant on us there." She laughed mirthlessly. "David headed over to keep an eye on things."

"What were they looking for?"

"They're certainly not going to tell us. That's why I need you to do this as soon as possible. Rob fired his gun because he was shot at and terrified. I don't want to believe that Moira fired at him. And if it was Rob's bullet that killed my sister, then whoever shot at Rob is responsible for her death too."

"I'm sure the police have a warrant to search Moira's apartment. I'd be accused of interfering with an investigation if I remove anything."

"I'm not asking you to take anything, unless... I'll leave that to your discretion. But just tell me whatever you find. I have to know what she was doing, and I don't trust the police not to write her off as some drug-addled crazy who deserved what she got." Geneva dropped the key on the tea tray. "It just chilled me to the bone when they handed me that search warrant, Julia. David and I don't have anything to hide. We would have given them permission to search our house."

I wanted to reassure her. "You don't have anything to worry about. You and David are in the clear. You weren't even at Brooke's house last night."

"That's just it," Geneva cried. "David *was* there."

TEN

♈ ♉ ♊ ♋ ♌ ♍ ♎ ♏ ♐ ♑ ♒ ♓

I STARED AT HER in surprise. Geneva struggled to pull herself together. "When the limo took us home, I crashed. I was completely
exhausted. But David couldn't sleep—he was still wired from the
wedding—and he didn't want to wake me. In all the commotion of
the day, he'd left our tickets and cruise information in an envelope
in his car. It's parked in Brooke's garage, you know, 'cause we only
have space for one at home. So he had to go back to get the package
for our trip." Geneva sighed. "What irony. We actually thought we
were leaving for our honeymoon."

"How did he get in?"

"Brooke gave us a key a while ago, since we were spending so
much time there getting ready for the wedding."

"What time was David there?"

"About ... maybe one o'clock or so."

"Why didn't he let anybody know he was there?"

"He figured everyone would be asleep. He didn't want to ring
the bell. He parked in the access alley behind the house and let himself in."

"At the front door?"

"No. Through the gate and the garage door in the back. I told you he didn't want to wake anybody up. I'm afraid, Julia," she whispered. "What should we do? Should we tell the police? I mean, it looks funny now because David hasn't told anyone he was in the garage. Of course he didn't have anything to do with this, but I'm afraid the police will suspect him if we tell the truth." She pulled a tissue from her pocket and swiped at her eyes.

I had to agree with her there. "You gotta admit, it looks pretty bad. A man on his wedding night leaves his wife asleep and goes back to a house where someone is murdered. And he hasn't told anyone but you about this until now?"

"What are you saying?" Geneva stopped wiping her nose and looked up at me.

"Well, it's kind of strange. It was your wedding night, after all."

Geneva stiffened. "We've been living together for more than a year. It's not like either of us was driven by an insane passion. I told you we were exhausted."

"I'm not saying I think he's guilty. I'm just saying it's funny he never mentioned it when we were at breakfast."

Geneva's face flushed. "I don't know why he didn't! But how can you talk like that about David? I thought you were our friend?"

"I am your friend! I'm just laying it out the same way the police will."

Two bright red spots appeared on Geneva's cheeks. "Thanks for the tea." She stood up and belted her coat around her.

"Please don't leave like this!" I stood too. "I'm just looking at it the way the cops will."

She glared at me. "Well, at least I know where *you* stand."

"That's not fair, Geneva! Look, can you get me the birth information for everyone, including Moira? Maybe that will give me some ideas."

She laughed mirthlessly. "Oh yeah, right. Astrology's really gonna help us now." The hurt must have shown on my face. "You know I've never been a believer."

"I don't care if you are or you aren't. I'm just asking for my own information."

"Forget it. You obviously think David's guilty of something. I'm sorry I told you. I'm sorry I came to you. I thought you of all people would understand how I feel." She walked quickly to the top of the stairs and headed down. I heard the front door slam before I was able to move.

Open mouth, insert foot. A Sagittarian trait if ever there was one. When would I ever learn to be more tactful? I try. I really do.

My head was pounding and frankly, I felt terrible. Of course, Geneva was upset and super sensitive. I should've seen that and not been so quick to offer an opinion. On second thought, the cops would be a lot less tactful. That is, if they found out.

I heard Geneva's car pull away as I checked the lock on the door. I walked back up the stairs and picked up the tray with the teacups. The slip of paper with Moira's address and the key was still on the tray. Geneva had been so upset she'd forgotten to take it. Or had she? Was she still counting on my searching Moira's apartment?

I turned off the gas jets in the fireplace and closed the damper, hoping to retain some heat. What should I do? Should I keep my promise and search Moira's apartment? Actually, I hadn't really promised to do anything. I'd just told her it didn't feel right. How could searching a dead woman's apartment, even at the request of her sister, possibly feel right? The whole idea made my skin crawl. I decided to try to talk to Geneva tomorrow and hopefully calm her down. After some reflection, she'd realize I hadn't meant to upset her.

I carried the tray back to the kitchen and checked the clock over the sink. It was late, almost eleven. I could head over to Moira's first thing tomorrow, but by then it could be too late. If the police hadn't already searched her place, then they surely would soon. They'd probably been busy all day at Geneva's and David's house. And if the police hadn't yet realized David was in the garage close to the time the murder took place, then why search his home first? I figured maybe they knew more than they were saying. If there really had been someone else in the garage with Moira, who'd shot at Rob, then whoever it was must have taken off with their gun. Was Moira's wound consistent with Rob's Glock? Or was Rob innocent and Moira shot by someone else? The police had to be searching for a missing gun.

I realized that if Moira's apartment hadn't been searched yet, this really might be my only opportunity. I could understand Geneva's concern—if the police learned Moira's history, they might very well write it all off as a drug deal gone wrong. Discovering her contacts could be difficult if not impossible, and if so, how hard would they really investigate? It wasn't Rob who'd been killed, after all.

I downed two more aspirin and gulped some water. The altercation with Geneva hadn't helped my head. I rinsed out the cups and left them on the dish strainer. Then I set up Wizard's cat box and bowls and emptied my tote bag, separating laundry from fresh clothes. I pulled a heavy cable sweater over my T-shirt, grabbed my purse, Geneva's note, and Moira's key, and headed down the back stairs to the garage.

ELEVEN

♈ ♉ ♊ ♋ ♌ ♍ ♎ ♏ ♐ ♑ ♒ ♓

THE BUILDING ON GUERRERO was a once-proud Victorian with bow front windows. It had since been broken up into six small units and fallen into disrepair. I drove around the block several times before I managed to find a parking spot a few doors down. The shops on the main street were long closed, and the neighborhood streets deserted. I shivered and let the car heater run another minute to warm up before I left the comfort of my little metal box. There was something about this chore that made my stomach go into knots. Rummaging through a dead woman's possessions was bad enough, but what if I found something that implicated Moira in a crime? Drug-related or otherwise? Should I even tell Geneva? She said she'd leave it to my discretion. It was tacit approval to do what I thought best, but I really didn't like the idea of searching a dead woman's apartment, much less risk the police finding out.

I climbed out of the car, careful to lock it behind me, and approached the long stairway leading to the front door. The wind had died down and now fog danced around the streetlights. It was eerily quiet. No lights shone from any of the windows. I hoped all the residents were safely tucked up in their beds. I climbed the cracked granite stairs to the entrance. The weathered door stood ajar, listing slightly on its hinges. I grasped the handle and twisted it, but the lock mechanism was out of commission. Inside, a bare overhead lightbulb hung from a chain. It cast a meager glow down the long corridor, cannibalized from a once grand entryway. The hallway smelled of dirty cat litter, moldy vegetables, and cigarette smoke. I followed the corridor to the end, and stopped at the last door on the right.

I slipped the key Geneva had given me into the lock. It offered no resistance. The door opened immediately. Had it not been locked? I caught a slight scuffling sound and cringed. I hoped no furry longtailed creatures were waiting inside for me. I reached around the doorway and felt along the wall. My fingers hit the switch. A rusting chandelier with two bulbs missing illuminated the one large room that was both Moira's living room and bedroom. I tested the key with the door open, locking and then unlocking it. Now I felt the resistance. The door had definitely been unlocked. I stepped inside and shut it behind me, making sure the lock was secure. Was it possible someone had been here before me and left without locking the door? Or had Moira simply been careless?

I had to make sure I was alone in the apartment. There were no hiding places in this sparsely furnished room. I checked under the bed just to be certain and opened the closet, terrified that someone or something might jump out at me. The closet was narrow and filled with a jumble of clothing, half of it on the floor. I walked into the kitchenette and spotted a doorway that led to the back stairs and the yard. I tested the handle on the door. Locked. I checked the space between the refrigerator and the wall, and then the shower stall in the bathroom. I was alone. I'd been holding my breath and finally let it out in a great sigh.

I started with the drawers in the kitchen and checked the counter, looking for any notes with names or phone numbers. There was nothing. The kitchen was surprisingly clean, as if Moira had never used the room. Inside the refrigerator were a few condiments, a half-eaten unwrapped apple, and a loaf of whole-wheat bread. I quickly rummaged through the drawers and the freezer to make sure there were no bundles of cash disguised as frozen meat.

The main room housed a collection of hand-me-downs and broken furniture, ripped curtains, and piles of clothing in various spots around the floor. Had Moira really lived like this? I heaved up the mattress, first on one side and then the other, making sure nothing was hidden between it and the box spring. Under the bed, I spotted only dust bunnies. I pulled open each of the bureau drawers, checked their contents, and pulled them all the way out to make sure nothing was behind them. Then I opened the small drawer in the spindly nightstand. Amid a loose pile of clutter was a dark blue velvet box embossed with the letter *R* in cursive gold script. Could it be from Rochecault? I was fairly certain it was—Rochecault is an infamously expensive jeweler on Maiden Lane downtown. But how could Moira have shopped there? Was this what Geneva had meant when she said her sister seemed to have a lot of money to spend?

I opened the box and gasped. An amazing bracelet, heavy with blue stones in varying colors, rested inside. The setting had the slightly matte, industrial sheen of platinum. Moira couldn't possibly have afforded this. Shoving the box into a side pocket of my purse, I decided I was definitely not leaving this for the police to find. I slid the drawer shut.

I scanned the room. Moira hadn't been much of a housekeeper, but there wasn't much furniture to hide things in. I headed for the desk, a rickety affair with two drawers and a computer on top. I clicked and waited a moment. The screen came to life and asked for a password. It would take someone much more talented than I to unearth its secrets. But under a jumble of papers and unopened bills, my eye caught a small black notebook. This looked promising. Perhaps it was an address book that would give us all of Moira's contacts. I dropped my purse on the floor and reached for the book.

A searing pain shot through my skull. Blinded, I fell to the floor.

TWELVE

♈ ♉ ♊ ♋ ♌ ♍ ♎ ♏ ♐ ♑ ♒ ♓

I WAS SWIMMING FOR all I was worth, using my arms and legs to reach air from a great depth of murky water. Rotting green vegetation had caught in my hair and my legs, so heavy it was pulling me down. I struggled to free myself. When I woke, groaning, my head was throbbing and I was lying on a hard wooden floor in the dark. I gasped with terror, not able to remember where I was or how I'd arrived there. When I tried to sit up, a sharp pain in my skull took my breath away. Where was I?

Memories filtered back. Moira's. That was the last place I remembered. But why was it so dark? I lay very still on the floor and noticed that a gray light was coming from somewhere behind the dingy shades. Daylight. How long had I been out? Slowly, I managed to roll over and, pushing against the floor, reached a crouching position. My arms were stiff, but I could wiggle my toes. Gingerly, I reached around to touch the back of my head where it hurt. A good-sized egg had formed there. Someone had knocked me out.

The notebook. The black notebook. I remembered now. I'd been reaching for what I hoped would be the Rosetta Stone of Moira's life. I was sure of it … and that was the last I remembered.

Grasping the edge of the desk, I pulled myself up and sat on the rickety chair. I reached over to the window and flicked the plastic shade. It flew up to the top. Outside, dawn had come, but a gray dawn that might just as easily be sundown. Had I lost a whole night? Who had been here? And where had they been hiding? I'd checked the whole apartment, even the back door in the kitchen, making sure it was locked. Someone had to have entered through the back door. Someone else had a key to Moira's apartment. I'd been so busy rummaging through drawers, I hadn't been aware of any sound as my assailant crept up on me.

Had they taken anything? My purse? My car keys? On the floor, my purse was exactly where I'd dropped it, but someone had pulled out my wallet, leaving it open to my driver's license. Now someone knew where I lived. More importantly, someone wanted me to know they knew where I lived. I shivered, realizing how vulnerable I'd been. I rummaged through the papers on top of the desk again. The black notebook was gone. I mentally cursed my lack of attention. That notebook could have told a lot. All of Moira's contacts, perhaps even her recent activities.

I dragged my purse onto my lap and replaced my wallet. I checked the time on my cell phone—six thirty in the morning. The screen on the computer was dark. At least the intruder hadn't taken it. I debated unplugging the whole arrangement and taking it with me, but then I'd definitely be accused of interfering in a police investigation. If Geneva's house had been searched, Moira's had to be next on the list.

The bracelet, I thought. Had the bracelet been taken? I unzipped the side pocket of my purse and reached in, feeling the velvet surface of the box. I breathed a sigh of relief. I could deliver the bracelet to Geneva. Geneva! I had to talk to her. I'd planned to call her this morning anyway, but first I needed to pull myself together.

I stumbled to the bathroom and splashed water on my face. I felt a roiling in my stomach and was afraid I was going to be sick. I sat heavily on the toilet seat cover and took deep breaths until the feeling passed. Then I grabbed a clean facecloth, soaked it in cold water, and dumped ice cubes from the freezer into it to make a compress. I found a bottle of ibuprofen in the kitchen cabinet and gulped four of them with a glass of water. Remembering the back door, I hurried across the room and grasped the handle. It opened immediately, to a back stairway leading down to an overgrown yard. Whoever had been here had left by the same route, not bothering to lock the door behind him … or her.

My hands were shaking as though my blood sugar were low. I needed food and strong coffee as soon as possible. Another rush of nausea swept over me. Did I have a concussion? My skin felt cold and clammy. I returned to the bathroom and lifted my eyelids to survey each eye, making sure both of my pupils were evenly dilated. Somewhere I'd read that one normal pupil and one dilated was a sign of concussion. They were both the same, and both responded to the bright bathroom light.

I checked the cabinet, looking for any meds that would be out of place. I found the usual things—toothpaste, antacids, Band-Aids, not even a prescription med. Nothing unusual had been wrapped in tinfoil in the refrigerator, either, unless something had been cleverly hidden inside a mustard container. I'm rather naïve about drugs.

I'm not sure I'd even know enough to recognize illicit substances. Maybe Geneva was wrong. Or maybe I was totally the wrong person to be searching Moira's apartment. Obviously I was, or somebody wouldn't have clunked me on the head and left me on the floor, grabbing what was probably the best clue to Moira's life.

My hands were still shaking badly. I didn't trust myself to stay there any longer. If I passed out, who would find me? The police, when they arrived with a search warrant? Wouldn't that be just dandy. How would I explain what I was doing? I dragged the chair over to the closet and climbed up to check everything on the shelf. Several sweaters were piled up. There were two boxes, one with a pair of shoes, the other filled with several scarves. Otherwise, the closet held no secrets. I climbed down, grabbed my purse, brushed my hair away from my face and headed out the door, making sure the key with the silver *M* was in my purse and both doors were locked behind me.

The noises of a city coming awake greeted me as I walked to my car. At the end of the block, I heard the whine of a garbage truck's mechanism and the clicking rails of a streetcar passing by. My car was still safe. Parked exactly where I'd left it. No windows smashed and thankfully no tickets stuck under the windshield. I glanced up at a street sign that warned *No Parking* on Wednesdays from ten in the morning to noon. What day was this? I had to make a conscious effort to remember. Monday. This was Monday. I had a client coming this afternoon. I really would have to pull it together.

As I stood on the curb, I spotted a bright yellow sign over a plate-glass window at the end of the street. *Nate's Early Bite*. Just what I needed. I hitched my purse over my shoulder and headed to the corner.

The restaurant had just opened. Four men in work clothes sat in a booth while a waitress in jeans and a denim shirt headed in their direction with a large tray. The whole place smelled of frying bacon, toast, and coffee. The same waitress arrived at my table with a large mug of coffee. I ordered a fried egg with toast and hash browns. Somehow my stomach had come back on line. I tried to remember when I'd last eaten. Oh yes, the Twin Dragons, Chinese food with Cheryl the night before.

When my order arrived, I slathered ketchup and salt over the hash browns and wolfed everything down, mopping up the last bits of egg yolk with a piece of toast. My hands had stopped shaking even though the back of my head was still throbbing. The waitress slapped a bill on my table. I left some cash for the meal and a tip and checked the time. Seven thirty. Too early to call Geneva at her mother's house, and too early to make an unannounced visit.

I left the diner and headed back to my car, parked midway between Moira's apartment building and the corner. As I walked, I noticed a light-colored, nondescript sedan pull up in front of the building. An alarm bell went off in my head. The car was a little too conservative for the neighborhood. Police?

I slowed my steps and finally halted. I moved closer to a large van parked on my side of the street and peeked around it to get a closer look at the occupants of the car. Two men I didn't recognize. The passenger door opened and one of the men stepped out. The driver exited next, and together they headed up the stairs to Moira's.

Once they were safely inside, I hurried to my car and hopped in. I revved the engine and headed home. I'd never seen these two men before, but just to be on the safe side, I didn't want the police to see me in the neighborhood.

THIRTEEN

♈ ♉ ♊ ♋ ♌ ♍ ♎ ♏ ♐ ♑ ♒ ♓

WIZARD WAS SITTING AT attention by his food bowl when I walked into the kitchen. He looked up at me and meowed piteously as if to say, *Where have you been?* I reached down, ignoring the sudden pain at the back of my skull, and rubbed his tummy. "Hey, big guy. I'm here. I'll feed you." I plopped a huge scoop of Fancy Beast in a clean bowl and placed it on his tray. He ignored my presence and made purring sounds as he dove into his food.

I stripped off my clothes and dumped them in the laundry basket, then climbed in the shower and let water as hot as I could stand pour over my back and shoulders. With fresh clothes and clean hair and makeup I felt a thousand times better. I downed two more aspirin to hopefully forestall the pain in my head. Was my liver going to fall out from all these meds? At this point, I didn't care. I just wanted my head to stop hurting.

At nine o'clock, I dialed Mary Leary's number hoping someone would be awake by now. The phone rang six times but no one answered, not even a machine. Were they all out? Or just not answering? Maybe they'd unplugged the phone so they wouldn't be bothered. My hand hovered over the phone as I tried to decide if I should drive over and ring the bell. Surely they were there. Even if they didn't want to be disturbed, I still very much needed to talk to Geneva. Grabbing my purse and jacket, I headed down the stairs. I pulled the door open and came face to face with Detective Paolo Ianello— or the Wolf-Faced Man, as I now thought of him.

"Going somewhere, Ms. Bonatti?"

"Uh, well ... yes, I was."

Ianello remained silent. What is it about cops? They stare and remain silent and somehow I feel compelled to fill the silence, blabbermouth that I am.

"Just to visit a friend."

"I see. Could I have a few minutes of your time?"

"Now?" I yelped.

"Yes. That would be convenient."

I nodded. "Fine. Okay. Please come up." A rush of guilt swept over me. I was glad Ianello climbed the stairs behind me and couldn't see my face. Did he know I'd entered Moira's apartment last night and searched it? Could the SFPD have the manpower to watch a murder victim's apartment? Somehow I didn't think so, at least logically, but I was reacting emotionally. Not only that, but Moira's very expensive bracelet was still in my purse, and her black notebook had been stolen. There was absolutely no way I could admit to being there last night.

I led the way down the hall to my living room. Ianello strolled slowly, taking in everything. He turned in a full circle in the living room and finally sat in one of the chairs. I noticed he wasn't wearing his patent leather shoes. Today he wore a pair of black leather loafers.

"I'd like to go over the events of Saturday night and Sunday morning with you again, if you don't mind." He removed a small notebook from his breast pocket and clicked a silver pen.

"Not at all." Did I have choice? I reiterated everything I could think of, careful not to mention the fact that David had gone to Brooke's house that night.

"I'd like to clear up a few things with you. You said you were asleep when you heard the shots?"

"Yes."

"And you said you heard three shots?"

"Yes."

"Did you notice any gap between those gunshots?"

I had to think a moment. "There was the first one—the one that woke me—and then a second one right after that. Maybe there was a gap between the second and third shot, but I know I heard three in all.

"Did Mrs. Ramer come down to the garage immediately?"

"Brooke? I ... don't really know for sure. She was there when we discovered it was Moira on the floor, but exactly when she came in, I don't know."

"Are you sure no one left the group or did anything unusual?"

"Well, we were all in the garage at some point. Brooke left with the ambulance. She didn't even change out of her robe. Geneva and David were at their house, of course."

Ianello looked up from his notebook suddenly. I managed to keep my expression neutral. Did he already know that David had been in Brooke's garage near the time of the shooting? Had Geneva or David broken down and informed him?

"Matt and I followed Rob down into the garage. Brooke came down next and then Mary. Andy was the last to arrive. When the paramedics got there, Brooke asked Matt to take her mother upstairs. Later, Matt went up to the third floor to make sure Ashley was still sleeping and that the shots hadn't woken her."

"Why did Matt do that?"

"Mary Leary was in a state of shock, but she was worried about Ashley. Matt volunteered to check on her."

"How long was he upstairs, do you recall?"

"I don't remember, really. Not long. He came downstairs before you arrived."

"Anything else?"

"Dan Leary got to the house just before you did, and then he went to the hospital to be with Brooke. Andy wanted to go too but the officer stopped him from leaving."

"What was Mr. DeWinter wearing at that time?"

It took me a moment to realize he was referring to Andy. "Uh … jeans. I guess at the time I thought he'd pulled them on when he left his room. And a jacket."

"You're sure about that?"

"Yes. Now that you mention it. I remember he offered me his jacket when we were in the garage. It was pretty cold that night."

"Were you aware there was a gun or guns in the home?"

"No. I had no idea. I never even thought of anything like that. Why would I?"

"So you had no idea that Mr. Ramer possessed a gun?"

"No."

"Did you see any other gun at any time in the house?"

"No. But then I'm not that familiar with the house. The only reason I was there was because of the wedding."

"I understand that you were the first to reach Moira Leary as she lay on the floor of the garage."

I shuddered, remembering her body and the pool of blood oozing around her head. "Yes."

"Was she able to speak at all?"

I shook my head no, unable to banish the memory.

"What was the next thing that occurred?"

"I . . . I think Rob approached as I pulled back her hood. He cried out. He was horrified when he realized it was Moira."

"And then?"

"I've answered all these questions before, Detective."

"Please humor me, Ms. Bonatti."

"Julia, please." I forced myself to go through the event step by step. "Rob rushed over with a blanket—a car rug I guess—and covered her."

"Why did he do that?"

"I don't know. Instinct, I guess. If she'd had a chance of surviving, it might help in case of shock. It just seemed like the right thing to do. It didn't strike me as strange at the time." I hesitated but decided to take the plunge. "Maybe you could tell me something?"

Ianello's face shifted to a lopsided smile. He waited.

"I heard the police searched Geneva and David's house. What are you looking for?"

"I can't tell you that. It's an ongoing investigation."

"When will the autopsy be finished?"

He remained silent.

"Have you found any shell casings?"

"That's not something I can discuss either." Ianello squirmed.

I was annoying him but I couldn't shut my mouth. "You think Moira was shot with a different gun, don't you? That's what you've been searching for, isn't it?"

"I'm not at liberty to say," he replied.

What else did I expect?

"That's it for now, Ms. Bonatti. We may have more questions for you in the future. Please stay in touch if you think of anything, and make sure you're available."

He rose with a serpent's grace from the deep chair, probably hoping I wouldn't ask him any more questions. I followed him down the stairs. As we reached the front door, he turned back to me, looking puzzled.

"Bonatti... I know that name from somewhere. Where are you from?"

"I grew up in North Beach. My grandmother still lives there."

Ianello didn't respond, just stared at me for a long moment before he turned and walked out the door.

He hadn't volunteered any information, but it was obvious to me that they were searching for a gun other than Rob's. Maybe it was foolish not to tell him about being attacked in Moira's apartment last night, but I didn't want to incur his wrath, or worse. I certainly wasn't about to tell him that David had gone to Brooke's house in the wee hours. I'd promised Geneva. She was upset and grief-stricken, and having her husband under even more suspicion wouldn't help her at all. Besides, what possible motive could David or anyone else in the family have to kill Moira?

I looked out the living room window and watched Ianello's car pull away from the curb. As soon as I was sure he'd gone, I dialed Mary Leary's number again. Still no answer.

My client Adele was due in an hour and a half. Mary's house was only eight blocks away from mine, at the corner of 35th and Anza—five blocks up the hill and three blocks over. I could get there in five minutes. There was still time. Once again, I grabbed my purse and headed down the stairs to my car, annoyed that Ianello had delayed me and hoping against hope Geneva wasn't still angry.

The Learys' home is a two-story stucco house, painted white with three arched windows facing the street. It had been remodeled years before to create more bedrooms for their large family, now grown and gone. Geneva's dad, an electrician, died five years into his retirement. Mary Leary had stayed on, living alone in the house. It was Mary who opened the door when I rang.

"I hope I haven't come at a bad time. I'm just here to see Geneva for a few minutes."

"Come in, dear. There is no good time right now." Mary's complexion was gray. Her movements were slow.

Geneva rushed down the hall toward me. I shed my jacket and dropped it on a chair by the front door. Mary turned away and shuffled down the long hall toward the kitchen.

Geneva hugged me. Her eyes were swollen and red-rimmed. "I'm so sorry. You were right to say those things last night. It's exactly what the police will think too, about David."

"Can we sit out here so we can talk privately?" I gestured toward the living room.

Geneva turned and followed me. "Have you had a chance to…" She left the rest of the sentence unsaid.

I nodded in response and pulled the velvet box out of my purse. "What's this?"

I handed it to her. "Open it."

Geneva turned the box over, her expression puzzled. She clicked it open and gasped. "What *is* this?"

"I found it in Moira's apartment. In a drawer."

"Oh, dear God, where did she ever get this? It must have cost a fortune." Her complexion paled and she looked up at me. "Do you think it's stolen?"

"I don't know. But I have no doubt it's terribly expensive."

"Where would Moira get something like this?"

"Could Brooke have given it to her, or maybe Moira took it from her house?"

"Anything's possible. It could be Brooke's, but I've never seen it. If she had something like this, I think I'd know about it. And as much as she loved Moira, I can't imagine why she'd give her something like this. Like I said, Brooke and Rob make a great deal of money, but they do have a huge mortgage and expenses. Brooke's very practical—I can't imagine her spending money on something like this when she could have made some house payments. Just not like her."

"Where's Brooke today? At home?"

"No. She had to go into the office, but she'll be home later. Julia, hang on to this for now. Just keep it in a safe place. I don't want my mother to see it, in case I'm wrong and it does belong to Brooke. Or worse, it doesn't belong to Brooke." We heard Mary's footsteps in the hallway coming toward us. "Here." Geneva shoved the box at me. "Don't say anything to my mother."

I hastily shoved the box into my purse just as Mary rounded the corner.

"Julia, would you like some coffee or tea? I'm just heating the water now."

I smiled at Mary. "Thanks, but no thanks. I have to take off in a few minutes. I have an appointment to get to." Mary nodded and returned to the kitchen.

I turned back to Geneva. "That's not all. I spotted a black notebook, probably an address book or maybe a journal."

"Did you bring that with you?"

"I was knocked out before I could get a look at it. I woke up on the floor just as the sun was coming up."

Geneva's eyes widened. "I'm so sorry, Julia. Someone was in the apartment when you got there?"

"No one was there. I checked. I was alone and the back door was locked. But somebody must have come in through the back door while I was searching in the living room, and they had a key. I would have heard if they'd used the front door. Which, by the way, was unlocked when I got there."

"Moira would never have left her door unlocked. That's one thing I know about her," Geneva said. "She was always careful about that, even locking all her car doors when she was driving. It was a real thing with her."

"I thought about taking the computer, but that would have been a red flag to the police. Besides, I didn't know her password. If I hadn't been attacked I would have gotten her notebook."

Geneva sighed heavily. "What's going on, Julia? If anything had happened to you ... especially since I asked you to go there."

"I'm glad I did, in spite of how my head feels. After you left last night, I thought about it. I realized it might be the only time to have a look before the police arrived. Obviously, somebody else had the same idea."

"I really have no idea what was going on in my sister's life." Geneva sighed. "But whatever it was, it wasn't good. Dan and I have to go over there to clean it out tomorrow. Her rent's paid till the end of the month, but that's only a week or so away. I certainly don't want to owe her landlord a month's rent, especially for that place."

"Listen, I've got to get back—I have a client coming soon. I'll check in with you later."

Geneva rose and walked me to the door. I slipped my jacket on and pulled the front door open. Ianello stood on the doorstep, his finger hovering over the doorbell. Another plainclothes officer and two uniforms stood on the steps below him.

"Ms. Bonatti. We meet again."

Geneva looked at me questioningly. I saw a flicker of fear in her eyes.

"Detective Ianello stopped by to see me earlier," I said. I hoped Geneva would intuitively know that I'd never have betrayed my knowledge of David's whereabouts to him. She nodded, and I was sure she grasped my meaning.

Ianello stepped aside as I walked out the door. When he had Geneva's full attention, he pulled an envelope out of his breast pocket and handed it to her. "This is a warrant to search the premises."

Geneva's face went white. "You can't be serious. My mother can't handle any more upset."

"I'm very sorry for your loss, but I have no choice." Ianello stepped inside, the other officers following him. I turned to speak to Geneva, but the front door was slammed in my face.

FOURTEEN

♈ ♉ ♊ ♋ ♌ ♍ ♎ ♏ ♐ ♑ ♒ ♓

I STOMPED DOWN THE stairs, mentally cursing Ianello's insensitive timing, and climbed into my car. I pulled a U-turn and headed up the steep hill to Geary. I was home in under ten minutes. There was just enough time to change my clothes and straighten out my desk. I aired out the apartment, put a kettle on the burner, and prepared a tray for tea. I needed to clear my head to be able to focus on my client's reading. And speaking of my head, it still hurt. I swallowed two more aspirin and placed a cone of incense in the belly of my bronze Buddha in the hallway.

Adele's appointment was set for noon, but she's a very nervous and particular woman and always arrives early. I used to find this unsettling, but by now I was familiar with her habits and always made sure I was ready well ahead of time. The doorbell rang exactly at 11:45. I said a silent little prayer as I trotted down the stairs to open the door for her. I always do this—I pray that I won't put my foot in my mouth, and that I'll always have a positive message even if the transits are terrible, and that I'll do my best to support and not harm.

94

Adele is in her seventies and had been a very successful accountant before she retired. In spite of her life experience, she was an emotional teenager in many ways. On her first visit, she confided that she'd been carrying on an affair for ten years with a man named Melvin, who was twenty years her junior and married, no less! After all that time, she still knew almost nothing about him. It takes a lot to surprise me, but Adele's first visit caused my jaw to drop. She didn't want to get married, but she did want her lover to leave his wife. There was just one teeny problem—his wife was his sole support. In addition, his wife was quite wealthy, and I was willing to bet anything that Melvin would never voluntarily leave her. His Sun sign was conjunct Neptune in his birth chart, so it was likely he was somewhat prone to fantasy, at worst dependent and deceptive. It was far more likely that his wife would leave him under a coming Saturn transit to her chart.

Adele wanted a companion. I'd reminded her that Melvin couldn't possibly be a companion. He had a wife. I asked her if she wanted to live with him. She said, "No, I don't want to live with him."

"So you don't want to marry him, you don't want to live with him … you just want him to be available to you?"

"Well, yes. And I want him to leave his wife," she replied.

I heaved a sigh, hoping that by now she'd moved on from this position. My file folder contained notes from a year before, when Adele had first come to see me, and the notations for her transits, progressions, and solar arcs were still valid for the next six months. I had pretty much covered this time period for her and I couldn't help but wonder why she was coming back, besides the fact that she probably wanted to hear a different answer than the one I'd given before.

Right now, Adele's progressed moon was conjuncting her natal Uranus. Perhaps she *had* had a change of heart. I figured she might be planning a trip, since her natal Uranus ruled her ninth house of long distance travel. I double checked the work and set her file to the side. I checked everything else—the tape recorder, tape, and a box of tissues.

I ushered her to the client chair in the office and returned with the tea tray.

"Thank you, dear. This is just what I need." Adele seemed, if possible, a little more nervous than the last time I'd seen her.

I sat behind the desk. "Well, I see you're planning a trip."

"Oh, Julia, how did you know? You must be psychic."

I laughed. "No, I'm not, believe me. It's really very simple. Are you taking a cruise perhaps?"

"Yes, my daughter's taking me. But I feel bad about not being able to see Melvin for three weeks."

"Mmm," I responded noncommittally. I was in the position of having to give the best advice I could, but quite frankly I disapproved of this little arrangement and thought Melvin was a real turd.

"Now, Adele, I'd like to make a prediction. You're about to meet someone new."

"What?" Adele said. "That would be wonderful. I'm so tired of this whole situation."

"Actually, I think it will be someone who shares the same work as you—or once shared the same work—because the ruler of your sixth house, the house of daily duties, is moving by solar arc progression to conjunct your Venus in the ninth house, the house of long-distance travel. You might even meet someone on this cruise. He could possibly be a foreigner."

"Oh, that's wonderful, Julia. I have to admit I was so scared to come see you today. I've been so nervous about taking this trip."

"Oh, you shouldn't be." I squeezed her hand. "I think you'll have a wonderful time. Now this is what you need to think about." Common sense advice was always the best. To myself, I prayed that when I reached the ripe old age of seventy-two I wouldn't be quite so foolish, or I'd ask a friend to shoot me in the foot. Then, of course, I felt immediately guilty for judging my client. "You're in your seventies. You're healthy, and you'll more than likely live another ten or fifteen or possibly twenty years, given the average life span of women. You need to think about what it is you want for the rest of your life." I pitched my voice deliberately to a more soothing tone. "You're looking for someone who will be a companion, who you can play golf with, go to the theater and concerts and plan vacations with. Someone who's really there for you."

"I know, Julia."

I watched Adele's face carefully. "I don't mean to lecture, but you want someone dependable, not someone who isn't providing you with much time or comfort or emotional support."

Her eyes grew very large. "Oh, I know you're right. That's exactly what my daughter says." Thank heavens the daughter was more sensible than the mother. I couldn't help but think of my grandmother—what if she were to get involved with someone unsuitable? No, I thought. She's way too sensible. But what if she did? After all, what did I really know about her daily life? I should pay more attention and ask questions, even if Gloria didn't want me to. She was the only family I had, and Kuan and I were the only people who could really look out for her.

"There's just something so exciting about Melvin. I've never found anyone quite like him."

"Well … that's not quite true. I have to point something out to you." Adele looked at me expectantly. "There are very similar things in Melvin's chart to the man you were married to."

"Oh, him!" Adele grimaced.

"You realized he was a jerk because you spent so many years with him and you were required to carry the entire ball—support and raise a family. You have to remember that Melvin, like your ex-husband, has a Sun-Neptune conjunction. In that sense, they are very similar people."

My client was quiet a moment, staring at me, and then said, "I never looked at it that way."

"They're both men who depend on women for their strength and support. After all, isn't it Melvin's wife who supports him?" I'd said these very things to Adele several times before, but nothing had really penetrated. She seemed much more open to what I was saying today than she had been previously. Maybe she'd finally turned a corner with this romance.

Ten minutes before the hour was up, I said, "Well, I think that's it. Do you have any questions?"

Pulling out a check, Adele said, "Julia, do you really think I might meet someone new? I'd be so happy."

"Yes, I really do." I smiled. "There's a very good possibility. Just keep an open mind." I slipped her check under the big amethyst crystal on the top of my desk. Amethyst, in the world of gems, stands for humility, and I was very aware of the dangers of wanting to be right about my predictions. I always remind myself to remain nonjudgmental. Sometimes I have to mentally bang my head against the wall, but I honestly try my best to clear away my own preconceived notions. Sometimes I'm successful, sometimes not. "I look forward to seeing you again, because I'm sure there'll be someone new in your life!"

Adele slipped her jacket on and I walked her down the stairs to the front door. I gave her a gentle hug and a brush on the cheek. "You'll have a wonderful time. Don't worry about that." The door closed behind her.

As soon as my client was safely on her way, I dialed the Leary house yet again. The phone rang several times. And once again, no one answered and no machine picked up. They really must have unplugged the phone. An hour had gone by while I was with Adele. I was worried about Geneva and her mother, but hesitant to return in case the police were still there.

What were the cops searching for at Mary's? They had Rob's gun. A Glock. Would it be too much to hope for that Moira truly hadn't been shot by Rob's gun? Could they tell from the wound? Did they have the fatal bullet even though they hadn't completed the autopsy? I assumed they'd dug the bullets that had been fired at Rob out of the garage wall. If it was obvious the bullets weren't from a Glock, then they must be looking for another gun. If no gun was discovered in Brooke's and Rob's house, then someone else—someone other than the family and the wedding party—had been in the garage with Moira that night and escaped, undoubtedly with that gun. None of us had left the premises except for Dan, who hadn't been there at the time of the shooting anyway. Well, as far as anyone knew. And of course, Brooke who left in the ambulance and returned later. And who in that group would have wished to harm Moira? Andy was angry with her, of course. But while her family had been driven to distraction, no one would have wished her death. Did the police think that one of us could have managed to spirit a gun away under those circumstances? I couldn't think of any other reason they would be searching Geneva's and Mary's homes.

The rest of the day stretched in front of me. I wandered around the apartment, unsure what to do next. I gave Wizard a bit more food and poured a cup of coffee. Was there anything I could do to help Geneva? If I had the family's birth information, perhaps it would tell me something and I could use the one skill I did have.

Work had been piling up on my desk for the past week or so. Wedding rehearsals and dress fittings and such had cut into my schedule. If I didn't get to it soon, I'd fall behind on my astrology column for the newspaper, something I'd been hired to do about seven months before and still really enjoyed. Some weeks were slow in my private practice and I'd come to rely on the money from the column more and more. When I was first writing it, of course, the column turned into the bane of my existence—a well-meaning response on my part had led to being targeted by a fanatical religious group. Thankfully, that was behind me, and I was enjoying my *AskZodia* job more and more.

Plus, I was feeling guilty and anxious that I wasn't accomplishing more on my next research project. My book on love triangles was quite thrilling, but I wanted to research parent-child astrological connections, both between biological parents and their children and adoptive parents and their children. The universe works in strange ways, and my working hypothesis was that perhaps adoptive parents have closer ties to their children than biological parents do. It was just a thought, but an area that had begun to interest me. Unfortunately, I hadn't gotten past collecting data. I needed even more, and I barely had the time to do it.

I opened the first *AskZodia* email forwarded to me by Samantha, my contact at the *Chronicle*:

Dear Zodia:

I'm a single woman in my 40s. After a very early disastrous marriage, I've been looking for Mr. Right for almost ten years, and still no luck. I'm a fairly bright, attractive woman but just don't understand why nothing seems to work out for me. My birthday is March 13th, 1973, at 5:30 a.m. in Syracuse, New York.

—Lost and Lonely

I groaned inwardly. Not a letter I could ignore and so many of the letters to *Zodia* were along the same lines. So many lonely people. I was tempted to write back and tell Lost and Lonely that if she found an answer, to please let me know. I fed her information into my program and generated a natal chart.

Dear Lost and Lonely:

You're feeling particularly vulnerable now because of your current transits. These will pass. May I suggest that because of your natal Saturn conjunction at the fourth house cusp, you are very self-protective and fearful of connecting with others. This may be due to an unresponsive father or parent figure in early childhood. The men you are attracted to represent some aspect of this, and in turn these disappointments generate even more self-protection and fear. Please think about these things and, perhaps with professional help, delve into these childhood issues. I truly believe this is the way out of your dilemma. There is a time coming in approximately four months that indicates a major emotional epiphany. I believe if you work on these issues now, a bright future is ahead of you.

—Zodia

I'm always nervous about sending these messages into the void. I have no doubt that astrology works and will point the way if we're just smart enough. What worries me is my concern that the messages do no harm and can help someone find their way.

I worked my way through nine more letters, five from males and four more from females with diverse ages and problems, before I felt I'd accomplished enough for the afternoon. I returned ten other letters to Samantha that I thought wouldn't be the best for the column, asking her to provide a list of local astrologers to the readers whose letters I couldn't answer.

It was almost six o'clock. Surely the police would be done with their search of Mary Leary's house. I picked up the phone. No answer, again. I decided to return uninvited for the second time that day.

FIFTEEN

♈ ♉ ♊ ♋ ♌ ♍ ♎ ♏ ♐ ♑ ♒ ♓

GENEVA WAS OUT OF breath when she opened the door. "Julia!" Her shoulders slumped and her face fell. She was obviously disappointed to see that it was me.

"I tried to call. I hope it's okay I came back?"

"It's fine. Come on in."

I could smell something meaty and delicious cooking. "I was worried about you. Sorry I had to run off earlier." I followed her into the living room, where she flopped down on the sofa.

"That horrible detective…"

"Ianello?"

"Yes, the thin creepy one. They searched the house for hours, and then when David came in, they took him downtown."

"Did they say why?"

Geneva shook her head. "They said they wanted to question him further. Julia, I can't take anymore. When the doorbell rang, I thought it might be David coming back." She glanced furtively down the hallway and whispered, "Do you think they know?"

"About David being at Brooke's house? No. Not unless you told someone else, or somebody saw him."

"I don't want the police to know. They'll think the worst."

"By the way, where's Rob?"

"He was released from custody late yesterday. Brooke called to let me know." Geneva peeked down the hallway and lowered her voice. "There's something else…" She hesitated, making sure her mother wasn't within earshot. "David owns a gun, a .22. He's had it for years. I didn't know this, actually—I wasn't thinking about anything like this—but he was nervous about leaving it in the house while we were away and the workmen were there. A few days ago, before the wedding, he made sure it wasn't loaded and hid it with the box of bullets in the spare tire well in the trunk of his car, under the carpeting. We knew we were going to leave his car in Brooke's garage, and he thought it would be safer there."

"Where is it now?"

"It's gone. We have the car now, here at Mom's. The gun's gone and there are bullets missing from the box. David's really in a panic."

"Ianello specifically asked me if I'd seen any guns at Brooke's house. Obviously they know something they're not telling you. Why else would they search your house and your mother's house? They're looking for another gun, and this could mean that it wasn't Rob's shot that killed Moira."

Geneva groaned in response. "What if someone used David's gun?"

"You've got to tell the police. What if David was seen, anyway? Those houses are right on top of each other. And now there's another gun on the premises and it's missing? They need to know."

"Julia, I just feel paralyzed. I don't know what to do."

I could see how drawn Geneva's fine features were. Her hair is a beautiful pale honey color, and she has perfect skin and a clear complexion, but now there were dark circles under her eyes and red blotches on her cheeks.

"I'm doing my best to keep my mother calm. The doctor has her on sedatives. And I have to make the arrangements for Moira whenever they release her body. Brooke's a mess too. Rob blames himself for not realizing it was Moira in the garage, but he still says he thought there was an intruder."

"If the bullet that missed Rob was the same bullet that killed Moira, then someone else was there. They had to have taken off with that gun or disposed of it somehow. And unless they find David's gun, they can't prove those bullets came from his gun. Has anyone come up with any idea what Moira was doing in the garage that night? Why she wasn't upstairs in the guest room with Andy?"

"Andy says he had a lot to drink, and he was so tired, he just passed out. Didn't hear Moira leave the room at all." Geneva's lower lip started to quiver and she took a deep breath to regain control. She pulled a tissue from her pocket to cover her nose. "But Andy could have known the gun was in David's car. We were all in and out of the house before and after the rehearsal. Julia, if anyone had a motive to kill Moira, it was him."

"Andy? Well, obviously, they weren't getting along, maybe he was feeling jealous. I picked up on that, but that doesn't mean he'd want her dead." I watched Geneva carefully. "Look, if they don't release David right away, maybe Rob could help him? Brooke mentioned he does criminal defense work now."

"He does. Since he left the district attorney's office."

"Why did he leave? Money?"

105

"I'm sure that was part of it, but I think it had more to do with the death of his first wife."

"He was married before? I didn't know that."

"Yes. Sondra was his first wife. She died in an accident, a fall. I've only heard about it recently, but I guess it was awful, and he said he just couldn't continue. He didn't want to do the same kind of work. He needed a change. Brooke and he met about a year after Sondra's death."

"I've heard about the problems between Rob and Moira."

Geneva shrugged. "She was always doing crazy things, but she was absolutely nuts about Ashley. She loved to spend time at their house, and it helped Brooke out a lot because of her work hours. Ashley had a nanny, but she also had her Auntie Moy. That's what she used to call her."

"That sounds like a plus."

"Rob didn't like it. He didn't think too much of Moira because of her track record, and because she dropped out of school. He just didn't trust her. He can be kind of a control freak, and he thought she might be a bad influence on Ashley. But Brooke's attitude was always 'That's my sister. She's welcome in my home any time.' Brooke was very protective of Moira."

"Was Moira working?"

"She was. A dive bar called the Alibi over on Waller. Waitressing."

"If you like, maybe I can talk to the people she worked with. Maybe they know something your family doesn't. And maybe they'll tell me things they wouldn't tell you."

"Would you? Thank you, Julia. It's a lot to ask ... "

"I owe you. Big time. I'll talk to the people she worked with at the Alibi, and I'll try to find out what I can about that bracelet. I'll do whatever I can do to help you through this."

"You don't owe me. Don't be silly. We're friends."

I shook my head. "I'll never forget. If it weren't for you, I don't think I'd be in one piece today."

Geneva held a finger to her lips. We both heard Mary's footsteps in the hallway. "Here comes Mom. Why don't you stay for dinner? My mother's been in the kitchen all day. She just doesn't know what else to do with herself."

I had to admit my stomach was growling. "Can't say no. Can I help you with anything?"

"Nope. Just grab a seat. She's got everything's ready. Hope you're hungry."

"I wasn't till I walked in."

The dining room table was set with two place settings. Geneva added a third with silverware and a napkin. Mary had cooked a roast, with mashed potatoes and green beans. A real home-cooked meal. I probably hadn't had one since the last time I ate at my grandmother's. Geneva and her mother carried dishes from the kitchen and set them down in the center of the table. Mary's face was pale and devoid of makeup. I wondered where she found the strength to stay on her feet.

She sat heavily in her chair and turned to me. "I guess Geneva's told you. They're questioning David. I can't imagine why. I just wish there was something we could do about all this, but I feel so powerless. If we knew what Moira was doing that night…" She put down her fork and looked across the table at Geneva. "I'm not sure I can eat anything."

"Try, Mom."

Mary turned to me. "If I could understand what was going on, it would help." Tears sprang into her eyes. She put her face in her hands and took a deep breath. "I'm sorry, dear. It's just so hard."

Geneva jumped up and grabbed a tissue, passing it to her mother. As she returned to her seat, we heard the front door open and close. Geneva glanced at her mother, and Mary fell silent. We heard Dan call out.

"We're in here," Geneva responded.

Dan appeared in the archway of the dining room and headed to his mother. He leaned over and kissed her on the cheek. "Hi, Mom. Sorry I couldn't get here sooner. He looked at his sister. "Any word from David?"

"Not yet."

"I'll wait with you till you hear. What did you cook? Smells great."

"Just roast and mashed potatoes—let me get you a plate, there's plenty."

Dan came to my side of the table and kissed me on the cheek as well. "Glad you stopped by, Julia. We need all the friends we can get right now." He sat in the empty chair next to me as Geneva placed a heaping plate in front of him. Dan devoured his meal while Geneva and her mother picked at their food and fell silent, as if afraid to speak of the obvious while Dan was in the room. His anger was palpable. I was sure they didn't want to set him off and were doing their best to keep the meal calm.

I managed to make a serious dent in my serving. "Mary, this is delicious. I can't thank you enough. Let me help you clean up."

"That's okay, Julia, don't worry," Geneva replied.

I ignored her and started to clear the plates.

"Thanks," she said.

"For what?" I asked.

"For just being there. For being a friend."

"Like I said ... You were always there for me." A clear memory flashed before my eyes. Geneva standing in the kitchen of our old apartment in the Sunset District, asking me when I'd last eaten. I couldn't answer her because I couldn't remember. I'd unplugged the phone and unscrewed a fuse so the doorbell wouldn't ring. Geneva had forced the manager to let her in, and she stayed for two weeks. She fed me and forced me to go on daily walks with her and refused to go home, no matter how much I insisted she leave.

Dan and Mary moved into the living room, where Dan placed some kindling and a log in the fireplace to warm the room. Geneva and I washed the dishes and cleaned up the already neat kitchen. The phone rang. Geneva grabbed it on the first ring. I dried the dishes while trying not to eavesdrop. I heard her making affirmative noises and she finally said, "Okay, thanks."

She hung up and turned to me. "That was Marjorie, Rob's attorney. Rob asked her to help David out, and she's with him right now. She's giving him a lift home. They'll be here any minute. I'll know more when I have a chance to talk to him."

Dan stuck his head into the kitchen. "Was that David? He's on his way home?"

"Yes."

"Good. I'll head out then. Just wanted to make sure you and Mom were okay." He shrugged into his jacket and walked down the hall to the front door. "'Night," he called as he left. "See you tomorrow."

Geneva followed Dan to the front door and then returned to the kitchen. "Listen, Julia, there is actually something you could help us with."

"Sure, anything." I wiped my hands on the dish towel.

"This is so awful. I told you how Dan and I have to go over to Moira's apartment. Her rent's paid for another week, but I doubt it'll be any easier if we wait. We'd love your help cleaning it up. After what happened to you there, do you think can you handle going back?"

The idea sounded excruciating, but I didn't want to turn her down. "Of course. I'm happy to help you with anything. And I'm sure you can use the moral support, if nothing else."

"You have the address. Can you meet us there around ten-ish? Dan'll have his truck and some empty boxes. I don't think Moira had much in the way of furniture, but we'll have to empty the apartment somehow."

"I'll be there."

We heard the front door open and then slam shut. Geneva rushed out to the hallway. I peeked around the corner and saw her hugging David tightly. His hair was sticking up in places where he'd run a hand through it. He followed Geneva into the kitchen and slumped into a chair. Geneva placed a plate of food she'd kept warm in the oven in front of him.

"Honey, I don't think I can eat."

"What did they want you there for?"

"I feel like such an idiot. They found out." David looked over at me. "I guess Geneva's already told you. Brooke's neighbor is an insomniac and awake most nights. I drove Geneva's car over and the neighbor saw me in the access alley. He watched me go into the garage."

"Oh no!" Geneva cried.

"It's just as well. I told them about my missing gun too." David removed his glasses and wiped them on a handkerchief. "It was pretty stupid. I should have talked to them and told them about going to Brooke's right away. But in all honesty, I didn't even remember about the gun or look for it until late yesterday. When I got the car, I remembered I'd hidden it in the trunk.

I was thankful for Geneva's sake the police weren't making any moves to arrest David. "Did this neighbor happen to see anyone else entering or leaving the garage?" I asked.

"That I don't know. They don't exactly share information," he replied caustically.

It was obvious Geneva wanted to be alone with her new husband. I made my excuses. "It's getting late. I should get going."

Geneva nodded and followed me to the front door. I peeked into the living room. Mary had dozed off in her chair in front of the fire.

"Julia, I want to apologize again about last night. I didn't mean to hurt your feelings about astrology." She reached into her pocket and retrieved a folded piece of paper. "Here's everyone's birth information. I wrote it all out. I still need to ask David for his time and find Dan's time . . . I think he was born in the morning. I know Rob's a Libra, and maybe I can even find Andy's information. My mother has some papers in a file cabinet in the garage, and I think Rob's birth certificate is there. I'll call you."

I slipped the paper into my purse. "I'm really not trying to make a believer out of you. I just know it works."

"Maybe you could have a good look at Moira's chart? It might give us something."

"I definitely will. Don't get me wrong—I'm happy to do anything—but it might not provide any clarity." I hesitated. "I guess part of me is a little afraid that you might not like what you hear."

"I don't care. I just want you to be straight with me. Tell me what you see. You know the Catholic Church forbids astrology, don't you?"

I laughed. "I guess. But I don't believe any religion has a monopoly on the unknown. Human beings are wondrous creatures, terribly complicated, and amazingly creative, and whatever's beyond our physical reality can't be neatly put into a form of dogma."

We hugged and said our goodbyes and I descended the stairway to the sidewalk. Outside, the fog had thickened. I turned up the collar of my jacket and hurried to my car. The Avenues were socked in, and I could hear the foghorns in the straits. As I drove over the hill to my apartment, I remembered today's date. Midsummer's Eve, the longest day of the year. In my neighborhood it looked more like winter solstice.

Once inside, I locked my front door and called out to Wizard. His bell tinkled as he jumped off a chair in the living room and came to greet me on the stairway. I picked him up and carried him to the kitchen, where I closed the kitty hatch. I dumped my purse in the office and checked the answering machine. Nothing new. I stripped off my clothes and slipped into my thrift shop Chinese robe and flip-flops. I felt better immediately. My head had stopped throbbing and the lump on the back of my head was slightly smaller.

I was relieved Geneva had gotten over her snit of the night before, but I still thought David's behavior the night of the wedding was a little strange. Maybe he'd had post-wedding jitters and really couldn't wind down. Maybe it was absolutely true that he'd simply wanted to make sure their cruise tickets and info didn't get misplaced. It was a moot point now anyway. He and Geneva weren't going anywhere. I pictured him in my mind's eye, with his fair hair and wire-rimmed glasses. He certainly seemed like a gentle soul. Geneva's family loved him, and frankly I couldn't imagine his ever hurting anyone. And what possible motive would he have had to kill Moira?

No matter what, we were all under suspicion. Other than Rob, who was already in the garage, anyone in the house could have left an upstairs bedroom, shot Moira, and returned by the back stairway. The real question was, what would the autopsy reveal? Did Moira die from a bullet fired by Rob's gun? And how could anyone who hadn't left the premises make another gun disappear?

SIXTEEN

♈ ♉ ♊ ♋ ♌ ♍ ♎ ♏ ♐ ♑ ♒ ♓

IF POSSIBLE, THE BUILDING on Guerrero looked even more dilapidated in the morning light. The front door stood open, still listing on its hinges. Dan's electrical truck, loaded with side tool boxes, was parked in front, blocking the driveway. Large red lettering proclaimed *Dan Leary Electrical Contractor—39th and Cabrillo, San Francisco.* The bed of the truck was empty in anticipation of hauling Moira's possessions away.

I climbed the stairs once again and followed the corridor to the end. I knocked on the door. Geneva opened it immediately. Her eyes were puffy and red-rimmed. Clothes on hangers were stacked on the single bed, and the drawers of the small bureau stood open, almost devoid of their contents.

"Julia. Come on in. We're close to done. There wasn't as much stuff as I thought there'd be. I feel bad now that I dragged you over."

"Don't. Just tell me what you'd like me to do. The faster we get through this, the easier it'll be. You can always go through the things later when it's not so difficult." I glanced around and shivered at the memory of waking up in this room.

114

Dan emerged from the tiny kitchen with a box in his arms. "Hey, Julia. Thanks for coming by."

"No problem. Dan, seeing your truck reminded me—could I give you a call sometime? I'd like to get a timer put on the light outside my front door. I hate to bother my landlady about it."

"Sure, I can stop by. In fact, I'll be in your neighborhood today finishing up a rewiring job."

"You're sure it's not inconvenient?"

"Not at all. Probably only take a few minutes." He returned to the kitchen.

Geneva stood in the center of the room surveying the piles of clothing on the bed. I dumped my jacket and purse on a chair by the door.

"Where should I start?" I asked.

"Why don't you start on the desk. Go through it and pack everything in this box—if it looks like garbage, just dump it."

The same layer of dust I'd noticed the night before was still visible on the desk, but I spotted a clean spot where Moira's computer had been. "What happened to the computer?"

Geneva held a finger to her lips and pointed in the direction of the kitchen to indicate she didn't want Dan to overhear that I'd been there the night before.

"Take a guess," she replied. "I'll give you three, but you'll get it in one."

"Ianello?"

"Yup. I'm not going to argue with them about it. Maybe it's normal for this kind of investigation. Dan was the one who set the computer up for Moira." She came closer and whispered, "It's too bad I didn't think to ask him if he knew her password. You could have accessed it last night."

"Too late now, I guess." I grabbed an empty box and started methodically going through the drawers. I found several unpaid bills and a few collection notices. I bundled these up separately and placed them to the side to give to Geneva. The other drawers contained odds and ends—pencils, pens, scraps of paper, paper clips, matchbooks, all the usual detritus of a messy desk. The bottom drawer was broken and stuck. I pulled on it and the front piece came away from one side. Peeking in, I could see papers sticking up behind the drawer as though accidentally jammed. I reached in and pulled the rest of the drawer out, careful not to rip my finger on a jutting nail. There were several crumpled pages. I smoothed them out on the desktop. Tax forms. Three pages of a Schedule E of Moira's tax return for the prior year.

"Hey, look at this," I said.

Geneva put down the sweatshirt she was folding and walked across the room. She picked up the rumpled pages, scanning them carefully. At the top was Moira's full name and social security number. The form listed three properties—one in Arizona, one in Oregon, and one in Florida.

Geneva looked confused. "This doesn't make any sense. Moira didn't own any real estate. She didn't have any money. Why is she declaring real estate on her tax return?"

"Maybe she had a windfall of some sort and invested the money?"

"I'm sure she didn't. I hate to say this, but if she'd had a windfall, she'd have been more likely to blow the money." Geneva handed the papers back to me. "Hold on to these. I don't want Dan to see these right now. He's upset enough as it is."

I folded the crumpled papers and stuffed them in my purse. Moira worked as a waitress and drove her sister's car—she didn't even have one of her own—and lived in a low-rent apartment. Unless she was some sort of financial wizard, how could she have purchased real estate?

I finished with the desk and started on the nightstand. The lamp on it had seen better days; the light socket hung to one side and looked like a fire hazard. I added the lamp to Geneva's throw-away box. The one drawer in the nightstand—the same drawer in which I'd discovered the sapphire bracelet—contained a few loose pieces of costume jewelry and one or two earrings missing a mate. I also spotted a matchbook covered in red silk with *Macao* lettered in a black Art Deco style. I knew the place, although I'd never been there. It's a pricey bar with live music that opened a few years ago on the Embarcadero. I held up the matchbook to show Geneva.

"Did Moira work at this place too?"

"Oh, yeah. Occasionally. Catering private parties, that sort of thing. Andy got her in there. She liked the people and she was friendly with one of the bartenders. She made some good tips, too."

I tucked the matchbook into my pocket to think about later.

Geneva had accomplished quite a bit in the time she'd been in the apartment. Most of Moira's clothing was packed in bags to be taken to the local Goodwill. The odds and ends of the kitchen were jumbled into boxes with a large *FREE* marked on the side, to be left at the curb next to the garbage cans. Dan had dismantled the bed and loaded it with the bureau, nightstand, and a few other odd pieces into his truck to be donated to charity as well.

"I'm only taking her photos and papers, and personal bits and pieces with me," Geneva said. "As hard as this is, I think it's better if we get rid of as much of her clothing and furniture as possible. I really don't want my mother to have to deal with this stuff. Oh, look, Julia." She held up a photo that had been stuck in the mirror frame. "I have this same one at home too." It was a well-worn photo of the three sisters lined up on their mother's front stairs. They ranged in age from perhaps five to twelve years old, all dressed up for a special event.

Geneva covered her face with her hands. I could see she was struggling not to break down. I put my arm around her shoulders.

"What happened to us, Julia? We were such a happy family."

We heard Dan opening and closing cabinet doors in the kitchen, making sure that everything had been removed. He called out to us. "Geneva, this fridge, does it belong to the apartment?"

"I don't want Dan to see me like this," Geneva whispered. "He'll just get upset." She straightened her back and took a deep breath. "Yes it does," she called out. She turned back to me. "I can't believe how difficult this is. I'm so glad my mother isn't here."

I heard a footstep at the doorway and looked up. Rob Ramer was standing on the threshold.

SEVENTEEN

♈ ♉ ♊ ♋ ♌ ♍ ♎ ♏ ♐ ♑ ♒ ♓

ROB SMILED HESITANTLY AND moved into the room. His face was pale and he seemed more careworn. It took Geneva a moment to register his presence.

"Rob! What are you doing here?"

"I'm sorry. I didn't mean to surprise you."

"How did you find us?"

"Your mother gave me the address. I wanted a chance to talk to you."

"This really isn't a good time." I could see the conflict in her face, aware that Dan would come out of the kitchen at any moment.

Rob spoke quietly. "Brooke and I want to bring Ashley to the memorial service, whenever it's finally arranged. I think it's important for her, and I wanted to tell you in person."

"I see," Geneva replied.

"I know this is a terrible time. I just wanted you to know Marjorie's been able to get some information from the police. Now they're unofficially saying they don't think Moira ..." He took a deep breath.

"They found the bullet I fired in the wall. They don't think it was my gun that…" He trailed off.

"Oh, I appreciate that, Rob. I know you never meant any harm. I'm just having a very hard time with all of this."

Dan, hearing voices, looked out from the kitchen. He stared at Rob. "What the hell is *he* doing here?"

"Dan. I wanted to tell you and Geneva that we'd like to bring Ashley to the service you arrange. I've tried to explain things to her as well as I could, but she wants to say goodbye to her aunt."

A flush rose in Dan's face. "I don't give a damn what you want. And it's definitely not a good idea to bring Ashley to any wake."

"Look, I didn't mean to upset you. Any of you." He included me in his gaze. "I just wanted a chance to talk to you."

"Yeah, well, under the circumstances, you've got a hell of a nerve." Dan's face was suffused with blood.

Belatedly, I realized maybe I should be the one leaving. "Look, why don't I wait outside?"

"Stay right where you are, Julia." Dan stomped across the room and grabbed Rob by the coat jacket. "Get the hell out of here. How dare you come around here after what you've done." He shoved Rob backwards toward the door.

A warning flared in Rob's eyes and Dan stopped in his tracks. Rob held up his hands. "I'm leaving." He took a deep breath and calmed himself. "There's new information. Geneva can tell you. You know I never would have deliberately hurt Moira." He turned and walked quickly down the hall. The front door slammed behind him.

"Dan." Geneva walked over and took her brother's arm.

He pulled away angrily. "How the hell did he know we were here?"

"Mom told him."

"I can't believe that guy. The nerve of that bastard coming here now." Dan shook his head and took a deep breath. "I'm sorry. I shouldn't have lost my temper like that."

"Apparently Marjorie has information from the police. It wasn't Rob's gun."

Dan stared silently at his sister. "I'll believe that when I see the report with my own eyes." He turned to me. "Julia, look, I just never liked the guy, and I certainly don't now. Always had a bad feeling about him."

Geneva spoke up. "Let's get out of here. We don't have to finish everything today. This is the bulk of it. I can come back later this week and sweep up and double check everything."

"What about the curtains and the curtain rods?"

"Just leave them. I don't care about them. We need to get back to Mom's."

Dan's truck was already loaded with the few pieces of furniture. We carried two boxes downstairs and piled them into Geneva's trunk. We left four more boxes on the sidewalk next to the garbage cans. Someone would definitely rummage through and take what they needed. If not, they'd be picked up the next day on the regular garbage run.

Dan called out, "I'll meet you at Mom's tonight." He climbed into the cab of his truck and Geneva watched as he pulled away.

I opened one of the nearest garbage cans and dumped the contents of a wastebasket in and shut the lid. I headed toward the stairs, and then stopped. Something from the wastebasket had caught my eye. I lifted the lid of the garbage container again and looked down. A small blue cardboard box was sticking up out of the trash. I reached in and gingerly pulled it out.

It was the container from an over-the-counter pregnancy test kit. Had Moira been pregnant? Or thought she was? Geneva came up behind me.

"What is it, Julia?"

I held the box up for her to see. Her eyes opened wide.

"Was my sister pregnant? Oh dear God," she groaned.

"We don't know that. Not yet. If she was, you'll find out eventually."

"Sorry. Somehow that really threw me for a loop."

"Don't think about that now. This doesn't mean she was."

"Maybe not, but she was worried enough to buy one of those kits."

I took her by the shoulders. "Listen to me. Lots of people do. It doesn't mean she was pregnant."

"You're right. You're right. I shouldn't jump to any conclusions."

We walked back up the stairs and down the hall to the apartment. Geneva took a long look around. "I guess I've had this crazy idea that I'd find something here that would give me some answers. Something that would tell me what Moira was going through."

I thought the things we'd found had only raised more questions.

"It just doesn't make any sense."

I put an arm around her shoulders. "Let's go. This is all we can do today anyway."

We locked up and walked down the front steps of the apartment building. Two of the cardboard boxes by the garbage cans had already vanished.

Geneva looked at the boxes that remained there. "Maybe Dan should've just unloaded the truck and left it all here. Not waste gas driving to the Goodwill." She opened her car door and climbed in. Then she rolled down her window and leaned over. "Thanks, Julia."

"It's nothing. I'll talk to you later." Geneva nodded. "And I'll spend a little time setting up those charts."

She revved her engine and drove away. I turned and started walking along the sidewalk to my car parked half a block away. I was rummaging in my purse when I felt a presence behind me. I turned quickly and came face to face with Rob.

I took a step back. The surprise must have shown on my face.

"Please. I don't mean to alarm you. I just wanted to talk."

"Where were you? Were you waiting here all this time?"

"Yes. Well, actually I was across the street at the café. I decided to grab a cup of coffee and I hoped I'd catch you on your way out. Away from the family. Do you have a minute? Can I buy you a cup?"

"Thanks, but no thanks. I've got to get going. Besides, I don't know what to say. I mean, I'm not a member of the family. I don't have any influence over anyone." I couldn't help it. The guy had put my back up.

He was quiet a moment. "Put yourself in my position. One day, I'm happily married, in love with my wife. We have a beautiful daughter and a future in front of us. The next, my sister-in-law is dead in our garage. I know I fired a shot, but I'm hoping to God that Marjorie's right, that it wasn't my gun that killed her. Julia, I know there was someone else there. If it does turn out my bullet killed her, do you think I'd ever be able to patch my life back together?"

"I'm sorry too. Sorry for you and Brooke and the Learys. But I'm really only involved for Geneva's sake."

"Dan never liked me. I know that. But Brooke's mother did. Mary was very happy when Brooke and I married."

"And Moira?" I watched him closely.

He shook his head. "Moira and I were oil and water. I resented the way she used Brooke, and I didn't like having her around. I was up front about it, but Brooke wouldn't hear anything negative about her baby sister."

"Hadn't Moira cleaned up her act?"

"Yeah, right. That's the official story. I never bought it. I don't think she really straightened out. Besides, you saw her behavior at the wedding. Look, I didn't hate her or anything, but I just didn't want her hanging out at our house all the time. That night, I never suspected it was Moira in the garage. Believe me, I would never have fired my gun if I hadn't been shot at and panicked. I told the police this too. I know I heard whispering when I went in. Then I heard a gunshot. It was loud, and then I heard a second shot, and somehow I knew, I just *knew*, the bullet had hit the wall behind me."

"What do the police say?"

"Nothing. They won't give me or my lawyer any more definite information. In fact, I have to go downtown with Marjorie and talk to Ianello again tomorrow. Ask yourself this—what would you have done if someone fired at you in your own house in the dark and you couldn't see a thing? Don't you think you'd fire back if you thought your life was at stake?"

"I hope that's a decision I never have to make."

EIGHTEEN

♈ ♉ ♊ ♋ ♌ ♍ ♎ ♏ ♐ ♑ ♒ ♓

As I DROVE AWAY, I glanced in my rearview mirror. Rob stood on the sidewalk looking after me. I'd planned to head home, but when I reached the corner of Market Street, I had second thoughts. I pulled over to the curb and popped the trunk. Rummaging around, I found my notebook with a list of contact numbers for everyone in the wedding party. I slammed the trunk and climbed back in the car. I'd promised Geneva I'd do everything I could to help her. We could speculate forever, but Andy was the person closest to Moira in the last days of her life.

I dialed his number. His home phone rang four times and finally his voicemail picked up. I disconnected. I didn't want to send a signal without reaching him directly. Next, I tried his cell and heard his outgoing message after one ring. I decided to try again later.

Geneva had mentioned that Moira worked at a bar on Waller in the Haight. I headed out on Castro and cut through the Panhandle, the thin strip of greenery that extends like the handle of a pan eastward from Golden Gate Park. In the drugged-out days of the sixties and seventies, the Haight was a mecca, but by the eighties, it had achieved a certain level of respectability as a tourist stop with small shops full of paraphernalia reminiscent of its original fame. The area's been tarted up, yet a certain shabbiness still prevails. The street is lined with shops, thrift shops, coffee shops, head shops, bookstores, and a couple of tattoo parlors.

I got to the corner of Waller and Cole and pulled over out of traffic. I looked up and down the street but still couldn't see the place where Moira had worked. I drove around the block, slowly this time, and finally spotted it.

The Alibi was a hole in the wall, more a sports bar that had seen better days. I turned down an alleyway and parked near a back entrance. Inside, the place was dim and virtually empty. One customer, a lone gray-haired man in a checkered jacket, sat at the bar nursing a beer. He didn't look up. The walls were covered with dingy Masonite molded to look like pine paneling and stained with years of grime and cigarette smoke. The floor was checkered linoleum, dull and cracked in spots.

It took a minute for my eyes to adjust to the interior. A young woman was listlessly wiping tables and setting up menus in holders on each of the five tables the place boasted. She was a little over five feet tall and slightly chubby, with a mass of dark curly hair. She wore a black T-shirt and denim skirt, both covered with a long white apron. Her name tag said *Rita*.

She looked up when I walked through the back door. "Hi. Can I get you a menu?"

"No thanks." I walked over to the bar and sat on a barstool. The TV in the corner was tuned to a baseball game but the sound was muted.

Eventually Rita reappeared behind the bar. "What'll you have?"

"Just a Coke." I waited while she poured the drink.

"Anything else?" she asked as she plopped the glass with a napkin in front of me.

"Actually, yes. There is." That caught her attention and she took a closer look at me.

"My name's Julia. I'm a friend of Moira Leary's family."

Her eyes opened wide. "I heard what happened to her. It's awful. The cops were even here. Look, I really don't want to talk about this."

"Wait, please. Her sister sent me." That wasn't exactly a lie. "Her family's devastated, and they're trying to find out anything they can about what was going on with her."

Rita hesitated, her expression shifting slightly.

"Can you imagine how they must feel?" I pleaded with her.

She gave a resigned sigh. "Okay, look, let's sit over here at one of the tables. I'll take a quick break, but that's it."

I left a few bills at the bar, picked up my glass and napkin, and followed her to a table near the wall. The man at the bar stared blankly at the mute television, oblivious to our presence.

Rita sighed and sat heavily in a chair. "I don't know what I can tell you. Moira was nuts. She was always in some kinda trouble, and the owner here was ready to fire her anyhow."

"Why?"

"I don't know. I think she mighta been doin' drugs, speed maybe. Some days she'd show up, some days she wouldn't, or she'd be late. She was a flake."

"Where'd she get her drugs?"

Rita laughed. "Just walk the block."

"Anybody special?"

"Oh, prob'ly Zims."

"Zims?"

"Yeah, he hangs out down the street, near the church. He's an old messed-up vet on disability. Legs blown off somewhere but he's got more money than a lot of the straight people I know." She laughed. "Guess he supplements his disability income."

"What about men hanging around? Was there anyone like that?"

"Well, she used to have that boyfriend Steve, the mechanic. I mean, I didn't know her all that well, it's just that we both worked here together. He used to show up sometimes. He seemed all right. Although the cops kept asking me if I knew a guy named Andy."

"Did you?"

"Nah. Never met him."

"Where does this mechanic work? Do you know?"

"Some Honda repair shop on Geary. I'm not sure. I was talking to him once about where to get my car fixed. I have a Honda, and I think that's the place he said he worked at. Do you know it?"

"I've seen the sign. Is it the one going out toward the Avenues, past Masonic?"

"Yeah, that's the place, but I live over here, so it's kinda out of my way. I never took my car there."

"Was she seeing anybody else?"

Rita didn't answer right away. I saw her lips twitch slightly.

"I don't know this for sure. I've never told this to anyone, 'cause I didn't want to tell the cops. Screw them, anyway." She pulled a cigarette and a lighter out of her apron pocket. "I think there was somebody else. I overheard her fighting with Steve about it one night. He was jealous about something. Whatever it was, judging from the way she was acting, it was really hot. She never said any-thing or mentioned any name. Guess it was a big secret."

"Had you ever seen her with this other guy?"

"No, nothing like that. For some reason, she wouldn't talk about him, but I think he mighta been buying her presents and stuff. She had on some nice earrings one day." I flashed on the bracelet I'd found in Moira's apartment. "I know he picked her up here one night, 'cause she was all dolled up and rushed outta here in a hurry and she didn't have a car to drive then."

"And you never saw the guy?"

"Just a glimpse. I saw her getting into a big car, black, looked expensive. I peeked out the bathroom window. You can see the parking lot from there." She grinned sheepishly. "I was curious."

"And there was nobody else? Just this Steve and a guy in a black car?"

Rita shrugged and flicked a cigarette ash on the floor. Something had closed down in her face. I had the impression I'd hit a nerve and there was something she wasn't willing to tell me.

I tried a new angle. "Did you ever meet her sisters or her brother?"

"No, never. Moira kind of hinted they were too snooty to walk into a place like this. I think there was some trouble with one of the sisters or her husband, something like that. I kinda gathered that from something she said."

"Like what?"

Rita was warming to her subject. "Something about she couldn't see her niece whenever she wanted. She kinda implied her sister's husband was a dick." Rita shrugged her shoulders. "But you know they were pretty good to her. She told me her sister used to pay some bills for her and they gave her a car to drive when her engine blew. That was pretty nice of them, so why she thought they didn't like her, I don't know."

I sipped the Coke and wondered what Moira's chart would show. Was there a romance or an affair no one knew about? Was there a transit activating her fifth house?

"Thanks, Rita. I appreciate your talking to me."

"No problem. It's terrible what happened to her." Rita rose from her chair. "Can I get you another?" she asked, indicating my empty glass.

"Thanks. No. I should get going."

Rita nodded and walked back toward the bar.

I returned to my car and pulled out to the street, cruising down Waller. Then I drove around the block and passed down the street one more time. I flicked on the car radio. An oldies station was playing a seventies song, probably popular when this neighborhood was the place to be. I didn't see anyone hanging out on the street in a wheelchair, but I spotted the church Rita had mentioned. If Zims the dealer was so well known, I'd find him eventually. I gave up the hunt and followed Masonic up the hill to Geary. At the top, I turned west looking for the Honda repair shop that I remembered. It was in the middle of the block, wedged between an electrical supply store and an apartment building. I pulled over at the first parking space I could find and hoofed it a block back to the garage. This had to be the place Rita meant. It was the only repair shop I knew of in the area.

The bay door was open but no one was in sight. Inside, a car was on a lift with another parked next to it. At the rear was a door with a small glass window that housed an office. Engine oil assailed my nostrils. I entered and walked carefully around equipment, stepping over hoses and avoided passing under the lift. At the rear wall, a man in a dark blue greasy coverall stood pouring a soapy solution over his hands at a sink. He was tall and rangy, maybe early thirties, with stringy blond hair. He rinsed his hands under the faucet and grabbed a paper towel from a dispenser. He ignored me as he walked back toward the lift. This had to be Steve. He was the right age.

"I'm closing for lunch, lady." He still hadn't looked directly at me.

"Are you Steve?"

The man stopped and turned. "Yeah, I'm Steve." He continued to wipe his hands on the paper towel. "What can I do for you?"

"My name's Julia. I'm a friend of the Leary family."

He hesitated. "So? Is that supposed to mean somethin' to me?"

"You were Moira's boyfriend, weren't you?"

"Was. Past tense. I guess I was her ex-boyfriend when she died."

"So you heard about it? How?"

"I got friends."

"She broke up with you?"

"I don't know if I'd say that. I guess she did, without telling me. I told her to get lost. I think she was fooling around with drugs again. I told her to take a hike."

"Where was she getting her drugs from? She didn't have any money."

"Probably that brother of hers. They used to hang out together a lot."

That took me by surprise. Dan didn't strike me as the type of brother to enable his sister. But then I really didn't know anything about their relationship.

"That's why you broke up with her?"

"That and the fact she was cheatin' on me."

"How can you be sure?"

He was silent a moment, staring at me. "I just knew."

"Do you know who the guy was?"

"Nah. I don't know and I don't care. I just wanna forget the whole thing, okay? The cops have already been here and they bugged the shit out of me. I didn't have anything to do with her anymore. Crazy bitch." He threw the towel into a bucket and walked to the front entrance. "I'm closin' now."

He still avoided looking at me. Reaching up, he grabbed a chain attached to the door mechanism. I can take a hint. I stepped out to the sidewalk as Steve released the overhead door. It clanged as it hit the concrete. This guy wouldn't win any prizes for looks or charm. Even if Moira's life had been a train wreck, I wondered what she'd ever seen in him.

When I got home, the message light on the answering machine was blinking. I hit the play button and groaned when I heard Celia's voice asking if I had Michael's things ready to return to her. The woman had a one-track mind. What had set her on this current course I could only imagine, but I knew I'd have no peace until I had searched, packed up anything in my possession, and sworn there was nothing further. I decided to do the mature thing and ignore her for now.

I was starving. I washed my face and hands and threw my T-shirt in the laundry basket, exchanging it for a fresh sweater. I stuck a tortilla in the toaster and when it was hot, slathered it in mayo, making a big wrap with lettuce, tomato, and some croutons. I wolfed it down, cleaned up the counter and washed my sticky hands. Then I went into the office and flicked on the computer. It was time to do the charts.

I plugged in the birth information I had for every member of the family—Geneva, Brooke, Moira, and Mary. I didn't have Dan's or David's birth times, but I could set up solar charts for them. I didn't have Rob's information at all. Hopefully Geneva would be able to get that for me. With luck, she might also find out Andy's birth date and time, or maybe I'd be able to discover that when I caught up with him.

I quickly set up the charts for Geneva, Mary, and Brooke. I noted that Brooke's progressed Moon was about to move into her twelfth house. The twelfth house represents a lot of things, but one thing that always comes to mind is secret enemies. It can imply a form of imprisonment. Modern, psychologically oriented astrologers look upon the twelfth house as forces of the unconscious, and if one wants to take an esoteric point of view, planets placed there represent unfinished business from a former life. The movement of Brooke's progressed Moon into this house would signify a period of being bound to a situation, resulting in a feeling of imprisonment.

Brooke's natal chart showed a lovely Sun and Venus conjunction in Libra in her eleventh house. She would be a charming, ethical person, blessed with love and popularity. All three charts showed current difficult transits from Saturn and Pluto to various points in each chart. No small wonder, given the murder of a family member.

I left Moira's chart for last. I said a silent prayer for her and hoped she'd forgive me for prying into her life and her death. She'd only been twenty-eight years old. She'd seemed older, but I knew, given Brooke's and Geneva's ages, that the year of her birth was correct. She was born near dawn in late November, a Sagittarian, with three planets in Sagittarius—her Sun, Moon, and Mercury—clustered near a Sagittarian ascendant. Full of personality and a zest for life, but a Mars-Pluto conjunction in Scorpio in the twelfth house painted a different sort of picture. At the time of her death, Pluto was transiting her natal Venus. Was her love life out of control? Had she not cared? Aries was on the cusp of her fifth house, ruled by Mars and affected by the Pluto conjunction. A secret love affair? A heavy sexual and romantic involvement in her life?

Who was her real lover?

NINETEEN

♈ ♉ ♊ ♋ ♌ ♍ ♎ ♏ ♐ ♑ ♒ ♓

I GRABBED A LARGE pad of paper and began to make a list of what I'd learned over the last few days. Moira drank too much. She could still have been doing drugs, and those drugs or the money for them might have been provided by her brother. I wrote Dan's name with a big question mark next to it. Maybe Rita was right and Moira had had a local dealer, or maybe Rita was just spreading dirt about a coworker. Andy was Moira's current boyfriend, Steve was her ex, and perhaps she was cheating on both of them. If so, she'd been a very busy girl.

It still didn't explain why Moira had been in the garage in the middle of the night, or who had taken shots at Rob. There had been no gun near Moira's body and the police were undoubtedly still searching for one. Rob had heard one shot and then a second before he fired his gun. I struggled to remember what he'd mentioned earlier: *I heard a gunshot... then I heard a second shot, and I knew the bullet hit the wall behind me.* If Marjorie's information was accurate and Rob's bullet *wasn't* the fatal shot that had killed Moira, then she had been shot by an unknown intruder.

Moira had been fighting with Andy. Was that the argument I'd overheard when I was near the creek at the wedding? Or had she been arguing with her brother, even though Dan denied it? Or with someone else altogether? Moira had sulked all the way back to the city, definitely unhappy about something. Had she been in the garage planning to take off in Andy's car? I hadn't seen any keys near her that night, but they could have been in a pocket of her hoodie. And why had the lights been out? Who knew the house well enough to unscrew the fuse?

When the doorbell rang, I jumped. I'd been so engrossed in my musings, I'd lost all track of time, completely forgetting that Dan might stop by. I hurried down the stairs and peeked through the glass of the front door. Dan was there, wearing the same outfit— jeans, boots, plaid cotton shirt, and a windbreaker. A tool belt hung around his hips loaded with screwdrivers, pliers, and various other implements.

I opened the door. "Hey, Dan. Come on in." There was a stoop to his shoulders. His face looked strained. "Are you sure this is okay?" I asked. "I didn't mean to put any pressure on you at a time like this."

"Nah. It's no problem. Just take a few minutes." He climbed the stairs behind me and stopped in the hallway. "Is this the switch you want a timer on?"

"Yes. For the outdoor light. It's a dual switch. I can turn it on up here or at the bottom of the stairs."

"Well, let's get a timer installed right here." Dan dropped a workbag next to the banister and pulled out a screwdriver to remove the light switch cover. "Show me where your fuse box is and I'll just unscrew those. Don't think I need to shut off the power completely."

"It's in the laundry room off the kitchen. I'll do it—I know which one it is. Dan, I really appreciate this. When you're finished, have a cup of coffee with me?"

True to his word, fifteen minutes later, Dan peeked around the corner of the kitchen door. "It's all set, Julia. I set the outside light to turn on around eight o'clock at night and off at five-thirty in the morning for right now. How's that?"

"That's perfect. I hate not having a light on when I come home, and I can never get my key in the lock in the dark. Let me pour you a cup."

Dan pulled out a kitchen chair. "I'm really glad you're staying close to Geneva right now. She needs your support. You can't believe how weird some of our relatives have been through all this."

"Oh, I can imagine," I replied grimly, thinking of Celia.

"I apologize for losing my temper today at Moira's place. It's just..." He trailed off. "I just never liked the guy, at the gut level, you know what I mean?"

"Well, he seems like a sensitive, thoughtful guy. I'm sure Brooke really fell in love with him. If this hadn't happened with Moira, would you feel the same way about him?"

"Like I said, I never really took to him. Just something about him. But I never said anything because... hey, she's my sister and I love her, and it really isn't any of my business."

"Did Brooke know how you felt?"

"Not in so many words. I think maybe she suspected. I think Rob turned into a control freak. And... don't repeat this... but I wouldn't be surprised to find out he was cheating on her."

137

"Really!" I thought about that one. "What kind of trouble did they have?"

"He wanted to have another child. He wanted a son. After Ashley was born, Brooke decided one child was enough. She didn't want any more. It caused a lot of problems between them. Typical, isn't it? Macho man isn't happy with a daughter, he wants a son. It got pretty serious, the fights between them. Brooke finally told him if he wanted a divorce, he could have it. If he was so set on having a son, then they could split everything up and go their separate ways."

"Dan, the night of the wedding, Moira said something about Sally Stark. She was convinced that Sally's drink was meant for her."

Dan shook his head. "Julia, I honestly don't know. I thought about that too. But here's the reality. First of all, we have no idea what caused that woman to collapse. It might have nothing to do with anything she ate or drank. As much as I love my sister, Moira was drunk and maybe taking other substances. Don't forget, I was pretty upset with her. She passed out and claimed she'd only had two drinks, which was probably a lie. She could be a twenty-four-karat drama queen when she wanted to be. I wouldn't lend too much credence to what she said. It was likely an attention-getting device." Dan sighed and took a sip of his coffee. "My mother and sisters are lovely women, but they're people who have a hard time telling the plain unvarnished truth. They don't want to see the dark side in people. I think that's the real reason Moira was always acting out. There was a certain lack of emotional reality in our house."

"I heard that Moira caused some trouble for Brooke in the past."

"Yeah. I'm sure it all stemmed from resentment toward Brooke. Don't get me wrong. She loved Brooke, she really did, but some-times … it was like the monster would come out. That's the best way

I can put it. Everything Brooke did was perfect. She was a hard act to follow, and Moira would alternately resent her and admire her. I guess that's what a shrink would say."

"How did Moira meet Andy? Through you?"

Dan nodded. "Yeah. I met Andy a few years ago when I was in computer school. They hooked up much later. Maybe the end of last year, I think."

"What does he do for work?"

"He's a bookkeeper. He's doing well, lots of clients. He does some real estate deals for people and takes a commission, but he's not licensed. Kind of under-the-table stuff. I don't really know any details. To tell you the truth, I never paid much attention. Not my thing at all."

I thought about the partial tax form I'd found in Moira's desk. If her name was on real estate records, I wondered if it was connected to Andy. "Dan, what do you really know about Andy? Do you think he'd have any reason to hurt Moira?"

"Not a chance. Listen, Julia, if I thought for a second Andy had anything to do with this ... well, let's put it this way. I'd take care of him myself. I can't see that. Andy doesn't have a violent bone in his body."

"I had to ask."

"It's okay. We're all on edge. Anyway, thanks for the coffee. I'm beat. I'm heading home."

"Dan, how did you manage to get to Brooke's house so quickly that night? Don't get me wrong, I'm glad you showed up, but ..."

Dan shrugged. "That's okay. The cops asked me the same thing. Actually, Andy called me. I'd stopped at a bar on California Street on my way home and got talking to one of the guys I know there.

We ended up hanging out well after closing time. That's where I was when the call came in. Just a few blocks away."

"Listen, before you go. What do I owe you for today?"

"Forget it. You paid me. A cup of coffee."

"Come on, Dan—I don't feel right about that."

"No, really. It's nothing. I'll talk to you later."

"There's something else I have to ask you." I hesitated. I didn't want to have to deal with Dan's temper if he blew up.

"Okay," he replied, a puzzled look on his face. "What is it?"

"I don't know how to say this…" I took the plunge. "Did you supply Moira with drugs?"

"Whaaat?"

"Did you get drugs for her?"

"Absolutely not." Dan's face turned red. "What the hell kind of question is that?"

"Someone told me that."

"Who? Who said that?" His voice rose.

"Steve. Moira's ex-boyfriend."

"Ah! That jerk. I'd like to put his lights out. I would never do anything like that. I don't do drugs and I sure as hell wouldn't give any to my sister."

"Do you have any idea where she'd get drugs, or where she got the money to buy them?"

Dan continued as if he hadn't heard my question. "I can't believe that guy. See, he knows I told Moira to dump him. And besides, I don't think Moira was fooling around with anything. She really wanted to get sober. She even went to some AA meetings, even though she was still drinking. I guess they don't throw you out if you're not totally sober. But I can't believe that guy would put that story around. Christ!"

"I had to ask."

"Why, Julia?" Dan shook his head. "You've known us for years. I can't believe you'd even listen to that creep." He looked like he wanted to put his fist through the wall. "Moira had terrible taste in guys. That's why I wanted her and Andy to get together."

I'd known the Learys for years, but now their sister was dead. Everybody needed to be scrutinized. Somebody had murdered Moira. "Like I said, Dan, I had to ask."

He took a deep breath. "I'm glad you told me. I think I'll go have a word with Steve myself." Dan turned down the stairs and was out the front door before I could follow him, slamming it behind him. I watched through the glass as he put his canvas bag in the front seat of his truck and climbed in the driver's seat. He slammed the door hard and pulled a U-turn, revving his engine as he headed toward Geary. It was a safe bet he was going straight to the Honda shop.

Maybe he was right. Maybe Steve was just bitter about being dumped and wanted to spread rumors about Moira and her brother to anyone who'd listen. I returned to the kitchen and rinsed out the coffee cups in the sink, mentally kicking myself that I'd forgotten to ask Dan for his birth time. I wandered into the office and sat at my desk. The conversations I'd had the past few days were spinning around in my head. I'd learned a few things, but I wasn't sure it was anything that would help the family. Before it all slipped away, I grabbed the notes I'd started. I made a list of everyone connected with Moira, jotting down abbreviated notes outlining what each had said or thought of her.

I replayed the events of the wedding in my mind. I recalled Moira's disappearance just before the ceremony, her claim that something was wrong with her drink. We'd all dismissed that as her covering up her alcohol intake, but what if she wasn't lying? What if someone had spiked those drinks? It hadn't killed her, but it had taken her out of commission for a while. Yet I couldn't argue with Dan. He knew his sister very well, and what he'd said made logical sense. But it nagged at me nonetheless.

We'd initially assumed Sally collapsed because of exhaustion or some other condition, perhaps even a heart attack. Had Moira's drink somehow ended up in Sally's hands? Would Sally recover? Would they check for poisons or barbiturates? Only Dan and I had heard Moira's comment in the car. Perhaps Detective Ianello should know about it. Maybe I'd ask Geneva what she thought.

When I finished my notes, a couple of things raised more questions. Rita had claimed Moira was very tight-lipped, but Rita was nevertheless sure that someone new was in Moira's life. Someone who showed up in a dark expensive car. Moira had fought with Andy, and Steve thought she was cheating on him. Was she seeing Andy before she and Steve broke up, or was there another man even then? Maybe Geneva would remember the chronology of Moira's love life.

I glanced at the clock. It was only seven and I was free for the night. The more I thought about Andy, the more questions I had. I called his home number again but there was still no answer. I dialed his cell and he picked up on the first ring.

"Andy, it's Julia."

"Who?"

"From Geneva's wedding."

"Oh, yeah. I didn't recognize your voice." His words were slurred. Noise in the background. It sounded like a party.

"Did I call at a bad time? I wanted to talk to you."

"Let me guess. About Moira. Everybody wants to talk about Moira. Sure, what the hell."

"Where are you?"

"I'm at the..." I imagined him looking around and trying to remember. For all I knew he was on a bender that had started days ago. "I'm at the Plough."

"I'll be down." The Plough and Lyre is a boisterous Irish pub on Clement Street, half a mile from my apartment. I suspected most of its denizens still had former IRA connections and the other half were eager to play the role. Disguised as a friendly neighborhood pub, it was in fact a virulent meat market. I didn't particularly want to deal with a drunken, bereft boyfriend, and certainly not at a loud Irish bar, but I also didn't want to take the chance I wouldn't be able to connect with him again.

I grabbed my jacket and purse and headed out. I found a parking spot on a side street and walked to the front door. Inside, the aroma of fish and chips assailed my senses. My stomach growled in response. What is it about grease and salt, my two favorite food groups, that's so tempting? The place was packed. The crowd surrounded three musicians playing an upbeat Celtic tune with instruments I couldn't name.

I fought my way through a gauntlet of guys hanging by the front door and located Andy at the bar. I signaled the bartender and ordered a basket of fish and chips. He nodded and held up his hand to indicate a five-minute wait.

"Andy."

"Hey." He turned blurry eyes toward me.

I leaned on the bar, hoping someone would give up a seat. Finally a young woman with choppy blonde hair slid off her stool and headed for the ladies room. She looked as if she was about to up-chuck. I grabbed her stool, betting she'd never remember where she'd been sitting—assuming she didn't pass out in the john. The band stopped playing, but no sooner had the decibels dropped than more loud music blasted from a jukebox.

"How long have you been here?"

"What day is it?"

"I need to talk to you."

"Not again. The cops had me downtown already."

The bartender slapped a woven plastic basket in front of me filled with hunks of fish and potatoes aromatic with grease. "Come on, let's get out of here. It's too noisy," I said.

Andy didn't seem to object. I left some money on the counter and half supported Andy out the door, carrying my basket of food. The fog had rolled in and the street was slick with mist. I led Andy down the block and maneuvered him into my car. I really hoped he wouldn't be sick.

"Have some." I passed the basket toward him.

"Nah. Not hungry."

I picked up a large piece of fried potato and munched on it. It was delicious.

"Whadya wanna talk about?" He leaned his head back on the headrest.

My ears were still ringing from the noise in the bar. "I want to know what was going on with Moira. What were you arguing about at the wedding?"

Andy crumpled forward and started to cry. "God. I accused her of cheating on me. She kept denying it, and now she's gone."

"You have any idea who it was?"

"I had my suspicions." He spoke slowly, slurring his words. "There's a bartender at the Macao—Asian guy. Moira did some catering a few times for private parties there."

I remembered the silk-covered matchbook I'd found in Moira's apartment. "What's his name?"

"How the hell should I know?" Andy snorted. "Snotty guy. Thought he was too good for everybody 'cause he's getting some advanced degree at Berkeley. What the hell does it matter now?"

Geneva had mentioned Moira's friend at Macao. Maybe Andy was right. Maybe the bartender was more than just a friend.

"What do you know about Moira's ex-boyfriend Steve?" I asked.

"Him? God, what a jerk!" Andy laughed mirthlessly. "He was still calling her months after they broke up. You'd think the guy could take a hint."

"When exactly did they break up?"

Andy turned his head to look at me. He was having trouble focusing. "You sure have a lot of questions. I don't know. I don't know when exactly they broke up. Why are you asking?" He spoke slowly, forming his words with difficulty.

"I'm just trying to help Geneva. She wants to know what was going on with her sister."

"Ya better watch out. You stick your nose into other people's business, you never know what's under some of those rocks." I shivered, remembering Zora's words: *You don't know this yet, but you're in danger. Keep your nose out of other people's business.*

Andy's head lolled back against the car seat. He seemed close to passing out. "I wondered if she wasn't in some kind of trouble," he murmured. "It woulda been just like her to do something dumb and think there'd be no consequences."

I was still curious about Andy's supposed real estate dealings that Dan had mentioned, but I didn't want to tip my hand about the tax forms I'd found in Moira's apartment, not yet at least. "What kind of trouble are you talking about?"

I waited, but Andy volunteered nothing more. I finished off the last piece of greasy potato, licked my fingers, and dug some tissues out of the glove compartment. I handed a few to Andy and he wiped his eyes and blew his nose.

"Sorry. I'm a mess."

"I'm going to drive you home, since you're in no shape to get behind a wheel. Where do you live?"

"In the Haight. On Cole."

"Okay. Let's go. Put your seat belt on."

I pulled up in front of the large Victorian Andy pointed out. He climbed out of the car slowly and walked away without shutting the door. I reached over, pulled it shut, and watched him stagger up the stairs and hopefully into his apartment. I sighed. I hadn't learned a thing. Nothing I didn't already know, at least. My trip was a waste of time.

Since Andy's building was only a few blocks from the Alibi, I decided to cruise down Waller one more time. Hopefully I'd even spot Zims, the man in the wheelchair. A few people wandered along the street, but most of the shops, with the exception of the Alibi and the tattoo parlor, were closed. I made two more passes but didn't spot anyone conducting illicit business, or any business for that matter, on the street.

I wasn't sure how far my loyalty to Geneva would take me, but there was no doubt in my mind that David's visit to Brooke's that night, and his missing gun, had raised some flags with the police. What was lacking in David's case was a motive—and if anyone had a motive for killing Moira, I wanted to know what it was. I decided I'd search for Moira's possible drug dealer another day and headed home.

I left my car on the street and trudged up the stairs to my apartment. My fingers still reeked of potato grease and I hoped I hadn't dribbled any over my jacket. I washed my hands at the kitchen sink and felt Wizard rub against my leg, patiently waiting for some attention. I dried my hands on a dish towel and picked him up before he had a chance to skitter away. He pushed his head against my forehead and I returned the pressure.

"Hey, Wiz. I'm not really ignoring you." He yawned in response as if to say, *Yeah, right!* He squirmed away and I lowered him gently to the floor. He sat by his bowl, his back to me. I was getting really good at reading his body language. Translated, this meant, *I'll forgive you if I get a treat.* Blackmailed by my cat. I fished out a pellet from his pouch of kitty treats and dropped it in his dish.

The light was flashing on the answering machine in the office. Two new messages. The first from Celia, the second from Gale. Celia wanted me to call her back. I groaned. I'd managed to procrastinate long enough. I would dig the boxes out tonight and get whatever I found over to her first thing in the morning. Otherwise I'd have no peace.

I returned Gale's call.

"Thank God you're there!"

"What now?"

"She's signed over the house."

"What?"

"Cheryl. She signed a quitclaim to the house. That jerk showed up on her doorstep and sweet-talked her into signing over the house to him."

"Did he bring a notary?"

"Oh. No. I don't think so."

"Well, then, don't worry about it. Doesn't mean much if it's not notarized."

"You're right. I'm so upset I can't think straight. That son of a bitch turned up with wine and flowers and a line of crap about how they could work things out, and you know her, she talks big but she's scared of her own shadow, and she agreed to sign the paperwork. And she didn't even think to call me or at least call her lawyer, you know that nasty little short man I found for her. The ex-Mafioso."

"I don't think you should keep calling him 'ex-Mafioso.'"

"Why not? That's what he looks like. He wears those terrible sharkskin suits. Nobody wears those outside of South Philly."

"First of all"—I heaved a sigh—"if he's a Mafioso, then I doubt he'd be able to become an 'ex.' And besides, you've got to stop making derogatory comments about my people."

Gale laughed. "Honey, this guy ain't your people. I'm calling Sam right now. He needs to know about this. The hearing is tomorrow morning."

Sam Giovanni was the attorney Gale had retained to help Cheryl through her divorce. If you happened to be one of his clients, he was

148

actually a terrific guy. He was Satan if you were the opposing party. He was a short, swarthy man who'd been in trouble with the police when young and then had his juvenile record expunged so he could be admitted to the bar. His specialty was family law, and his second specialty was sleeping with all of his clients. He had money and lifts in his shoes and the world was his oyster. Gale was probably right. He was exactly what Cheryl needed right now.

"I'll see you there tomorrow?" she added.

I sighed. "You think I should come?"

"Yes." Gale hung up.

I heaved another sigh. There was no avoiding this. I couldn't procrastinate any longer. I opened the closet door and stared at its contents. On one side were garment bags full of dresses, coats, and seldom-worn items. Most of these were samples from my grandmother's shop before she retired. Boxes I'd never unpacked when I moved into my apartment were stacked on the other side. There were six. I hauled them out one by one and lined them up on the living room floor, then sliced through the tape on each with a pair of scissors. Chances were, anything of Michael's would be in just one box, but I'd packed in such a hurry before the move, I couldn't be absolutely certain. Now I just wanted to satisfy Celia and be able to tell her I had nothing in my possession that technically belonged to her.

The first box was full of old kitchen utensils and mismatched dishes. I remembered going shopping to replace a lot of this stuff after my move. I rummaged through and discovered a couple of items that could be useful now—a lemon squeezer and a small colander. I pulled them out and re-taped the box. This was a charity donation. Three of the boxes held high school and college memorabilia and old books. I separated the books I no longer wanted and added them to the giveaway pile. The rest I shoved into a half-empty bookshelf in the living room.

I found Michael's things in the fifth box. There were a pair of hiking boots, gloves, and an olive green all-weather jacket with a hood and big pockets. I had such a clear memory of Michael wearing that jacket. A wave of longing swept over me. I buried my face inside the jacket and inhaled. I ached for him. Whether it was a lingering scent or my imagination, he was physically with me for a fleeting moment.

Reluctantly, I placed his boots, gloves, and jacket in a large shopping bag. I rummaged through the rest of the items. There were three books related to his studies. I added these to the shopping bag. Underneath the books, I found two fat notebooks from the work he'd been doing in Guatemala. He'd shipped them to me just prior to his return. A note clipped inside said, *Julia—hang on to these for me. They're important. I'll fill you in when I'm home. See you soon. Love, Michael.*

I ran my fingers over his handwriting. It was debatable whether Celia had a right to these or not. Technically, Michael's possessions belonged to his next of kin, but these had been sent to me for safekeeping. One part of me was aware of Celia's obsessive behavior and wanted to rebel, and the other part of me clung to Michael's memory as fiercely as she did. These were mine. I was keeping them. There was absolutely no reason for Celia to ever know about his notes. And as for the rest—cards we'd given to each other, a shoebox full of photos—those were mine as well.

Most days, I never gave these things a second thought. But sometimes when I needed to pick at old wounds, I read his letters. Tonight I couldn't bring myself to do that. We'd thought we were invincible, looking forward to our life together, never anticipating that there'd be no future for us. Ever since, I'd built a protective wall around myself, and I wasn't sure how to tear it down. When Brooke had asked if there was anyone in my life, if I'd been honest I would have said I wasn't sure I even wanted someone. It wasn't a risk I could take again. Maybe never.

I replaced the photos, cards, and notebooks in the box. Celia could have the rest.

I rose from the floor and retaped the remaining boxes, stacking them once again in the closet. The day would come when I'd go through all of this more thoroughly. Another day. In the meantime, I could drop the giveaway stuff at a charity shop and deliver the shopping bag to Celia at Cold Comfort Farm, as I'd dubbed her house. I was sure I wouldn't be thanked or invited in for a visit. Fine with me.

I turned off the lamps and put some water on for tea. Wizard had disappeared through the kitty hatch before I could lock him in. When the tea was ready, I shed my clothes and slipped on a nightie. I climbed into bed and grabbed my book on chart comparisons, snuggling under the comforter. Wizard meowed from the hallway. He ran into the bedroom and hopped up on the little slipper chair. He made two counter-clockwise turns and finally curled into a fetal position. I climbed out of bed, closed the kitty hatch, unplugged the bedroom phone, and did my best to concentrate on my book. I shivered, remembering that this was the same one that had lulled me to sleep the night of the shooting, but the foghorns reminded me I was safe in my own bed tonight.

TWENTY

♈ ♉ ♊ ♋ ♌ ♍ ♎ ♏ ♐ ♑ ♒ ♓

SAN FRANCISCO SUPERIOR COURT is housed in the Civic Center complex. Its main building is an ornate French Renaissance edifice, topped with a golden dome, that also encloses City Hall and the main library. After the last big quake, that dome required an expensive application of gold leaf. Today it glowed in the morning light.

I made sure I was there by eight o'clock. I didn't want to be late for Cheryl's final divorce hearing. I passed through the security check and took the wide marble stairs to the second floor. Courtroom 405 was at the end of the hallway. Hard wooden benches occupied the spaces between recessed doors leading to each courtroom. I spotted Cheryl and Gale seated alongside many other supplicants. Sam Giovanni was nowhere to be seen.

"Where's your lawyer?" I asked as I approached.

Gale looked up. "He'll be here. Don't worry. Glad you could make it." Then, with a stage whisper, she leaned toward me. "She needs some hand-holding. She's a mess."

"No I'm not," Cheryl piped up. "I'll be fine." Her lips were white and she clutched her purse and a large envelope with both hands.

I felt a presence behind me and turned. "Ladies, ladies, how lovely you all look." Sam Giovanni was almost five four, with dark curly hair. He was dressed in an expensively tailored suit. Without the Cuban heels, he was probably five two. He swayed continuously from one foot to the other while he spoke.

"Listen, honey," he said to Cheryl, "don't worry about a thing. You're in Sam's hands now."

Cheryl nodded mutely and tried to speak, but no words came.

"By the time we're done, this guy won't be able to find his balls. Hah!" Sam chuckled.

Cheryl's face turned a ghastly green. "I think I have to go to the restroom." She rose from the bench and raced down the hall, running with tiny steps on her high heels.

"Oh God," Gale groaned. "Go with her. Make sure she comes back."

Sam had placed himself by the door to the courtroom. Standing on his toes, he peered through the small round window, tapping on the glass to get the bailiff's attention.

I whispered to Gale, "Are you sure about this guy?"

"Don't worry." Gale waved her hand vaguely in the air. "He just drinks a lot of cappuccino."

I followed Cheryl to the ladies' room. Sounds of retching came from one of the stalls. I took a safe position by the sinks. I have a very sympathetic stomach and didn't want to end up hurling and gagging right along with her.

"Cheryl, are you okay?"

More gagging sounds. "I'm … okay. Ugh … I'm okay."

Eventually I heard the toilet flush and Cheryl came out of the stall with mascara running down her cheeks.

"God, Julia, I'm not sure I can go through with this."

"Of course you can. It'll be over very quickly and we're here with you. Don't worry. Gale knows what she's doing." I didn't mention I wasn't so sure about the lawyer, but I bit my tongue.

"What's wrong with me? What was I thinking last night? Frank showed up with wine and flowers, and I just signed the quitclaim." She moaned. "Julia, am I an idiot or what?"

"Let it go. You're not the first woman to make a mistake. Let's get back. They'll be opening the doors any minute."

"I caaaan't," Cheryl bawled.

I grabbed her by the shoulders and spoke sternly. "Yes, you can, and you will. Now come on, let's wash your face and we'll put some more makeup on."

"Okay," she responded meekly.

We emerged from the ladies' room, Cheryl looking quite a bit better than she did when she ran in.

Gale was at the end of the hall, waving to us. "Hurry up, you two."

It was eight thirty exactly and the bailiff had promptly opened the doors to the courtroom. Everyone filed in to take seats. I looked at the list posted outside the door and realized Cheryl's case was the fourth one up. This might take a while.

A wooden railing separated us from the front of the room. Inside the railing were two long tables at either side of the center aisle, with the clerk's enclosure near the side wall. The judge's raised bench was empty. The bailiff stood in the center aisle watching everyone carefully as we filed in. The clerk glanced up from her desk, stood, and gathering files together, placed a stack at the side of the judge's bench.

As we took our seats in the row behind the banister, I turned and saw Frank push through the padded double doors into the courtroom. Although I'd never met the man, he conformed to my mental image. Somewhere in his mid-forties, partially bald and extremely portly, he wore an ill-fitting sports jacket and slacks. His face was red and flushed. He was accompanied by a twenty-something woman wearing a miniskirt, cowboy boots, and a low-cut tank top that displayed her mammary charms. The tank top didn't quite cover her definitely extended and likely pregnant belly.

I nudged Gale and rolled my eyes. She turned to look. "Oh dear God," she hissed. "Can you believe that?"

At that moment, the bailiff asked us to all rise as the judge exited his chambers and stepped onto the bench. As we stood, I did my best to block Cheryl's view. I was too late. She'd spotted Frank. As we sat back down, Cheryl stayed standing. Her face took on a deep flush and she screamed in a high-pitched voice across the courtroom, "Did you really have to drag that underage slut here?"

Frank stood up too. "Shut up, Cheryl. Shut your friggin' mouth."

"Is she pregnant?" Cheryl screamed. "God damn you." She attempted to climb over Gale's lap.

The judge banged his gavel on the bench. "All right, everyone. Calm down. And you, madam, please sit down immediately or I will have you removed."

I could have sworn steam came out of Cheryl's ears. It was as if she'd run into a force field. Torn between leaping over us to attack Frank and sitting down as the judge had instructed, she became paralyzed. Gale stood up, took Cheryl by the shoulders, and plunked her back into her seat. "Shut up or I'll smack you silly."

Cheryl meekly replied, "I'm sorry. I'll be good."

Frank's face was now beet red. As he sat down, his girlfriend did a quick little flounce and wiggle of her shoulders in Cheryl's direction and settled into her seat.

The first few cases dragged slowly. Cheryl's jaw was set. She had lapsed into a boiling silence. I was sure any remnant of affection she felt for Frank had vanished. Finally, the judge called both Frank and Cheryl up before him. The bailiff swore them in. Sam Giovanni took his place next to Cheryl and began recounting the events of their separation, making clear the terrible emotional duress his client had suffered.

"Your Honor, I'd like to present this so-called quitclaim deed as exhibit one, which, I'm sorry to say, my client was manipulated into signing in the belief that it would facilitate a reconciliation. She signed this un-notarized document *without* consulting an attorney."

Gale leaned forward, listening intently to every word. I glanced over my shoulder at Frank's girlfriend. She'd stretched her legs out, cowboy boots jutting into the aisle. The contents of her purse were strewn on the empty seat next to her while she filed her nails. At that moment, I almost felt sorry for Frank. The operative word here is "almost."

I turned back to the main action. The judge, his glasses halfway down his nose, stared at Frank.

"Mr. Pitzmahr, you are without an attorney, so you may not be fully aware that California is a community property state. This means that when a couple divorces, the assets and the liabilities are split equally, unless one or the other party claims responsibility for any of those liabilities. I'm not the slightest bit interested in hearing about your marital woes, or complaints about Mrs. Pitzmahr.

It was a shock to hear Cheryl's married name. It certainly didn't suit her. She didn't look like a Mrs. Pitzmahr.

"But, judge—"

"You may address me as 'Your Honor.'"

Frank took a deep breath, a deeply confused look on his face. "Your Honor. It was my income that purchased and maintained the Berkeley house. I can't possibly afford to give my... Cheryl... half the value of it."

The judge nodded. "Your income ceased to be strictly your income upon your marriage. At that point, half of your income belonged to your spouse. I'm ordering that within thirty days after entry of judgment, you will pay to your spouse half the value of that home. You may do so either by refinancing or by selling. I see that your income is certainly more than adequate to follow this Court's orders. Mrs. Pitzmahr, are you quite certain you do not wish this Court to consider spousal support?"

Cheryl nodded affirmatively. "Yes, Your Honor. I want to cut all ties with my former husband."

Frank's face had become more flushed. He shouted at the judge, "You can't do this. This isn't right. I'm not going to give that... one red cent."

The judge's look became even more severe. "You most certainly will follow my orders or you will be in contempt of this Court." He glanced at his wristwatch.

Frank howled and, running around the table, attempted to rush to the judge's bench. The bailiff stepped forward to block his path.

"You can't do this," Frank yelled. "I've worked my whole life for this house and this money. You're not gonna do this to me."

The judge nodded to the bailiff to physically remove Frank from the courtroom. Frank struggled against the bulkier man, still shouting and resisting the bailiff's efforts. Cheryl took several steps backward, against the railing. Gale's mouth hung open as she watched Frank's antics. The bailiff lifted Frank up bodily and speed-marched him toward the door to the corridor. Frank's girlfriend leaped up and, rushing in their direction, kicked the bailiff in the shins. She raised her purse high in the air and swung it at the bailiff's head. The terrified clerk was on the phone calling for reinforcements.

The judge banged his gavel repeatedly. Two uniformed police pushed through the courtroom door, grabbed both Frank and his young girlfriend, and hustled them out to the corridor and down the hall. Cheryl turned to us, her face white. Gale waved her hand, indicating Cheryl should stay exactly where she was.

Peace in the courtroom was quickly restored. The judge looked at Sam and Cheryl. "You will receive my final orders by mail or you can have your attorney service pick them up when available."

Sam nodded and gathered up his paperwork. He led Cheryl through the gate in the railing and indicated to us that we should meet them outside.

"Next case," the judge shouted.

Gale and I headed out to the corridor. Cheryl's hands were over her face and Sam was patting her on the back.

"You did just great, honey."

"But it was so horrible. I've never seen Frank so mad. Is he under arrest?"

Sam smiled. "I'm sure they're holding him. He'll be charged. This couldn't have gone better. Ladies." He nodded to us. "Can I leave her in your good hands?"

Gale thanked Sam profusely, shaking his hand, and turned to hug Cheryl.

As Sam headed in the opposite direction, I said, "Wait here for me. I have to ask Sam something."

I caught up with him at the end of the corridor. He looked puzzled when he turned to me. "I have a favor to ask," I said.

He smiled in a very suggestive way. "I'm at your service."

I was temporarily taken aback. Did he think I was asking him out on a date? The top of his head barely reached my shoulder. "I was wondering if one of your paralegals has the software to do real property searches?"

He nodded. "We sure do. Have to do asset checks all the time, believe me. You wouldn't believe what some of these guys try to hide from their wives."

"I need to check the ownership of some out-of-state properties."

"Stop by any time." Sam smiled again in that intimate way. "I'll call Carol, my assistant, and let her know. She can run those for you, and then maybe we can have ..."

"Thanks." I said, quickly backing away. "I really appreciate that."

"Anytime. Does this concern a divorce action?"

"No. It concerns a ... murder."

Sam's jaw snapped shut. "Okay then."

I hurried back down the corridor.

"What was that all about?" Gale asked when I reached her. "Was he coming on to you?"

"I don't think so," I lied.

"Oh, please. I could read his body language from forty feet away. What did you ask him?"

"For a favor. I'll explain later."

Cheryl looked glassy-eyed.

Gale nodded in her direction. "I'm taking our girl here out to a fancy three-martini lunch. Want to join us?"

"Love to, but I've got stuff to take care of."

Gale smiled and blew me a kiss. "I'll see you later."

TWENTY-ONE

♈ ♉ ♊ ♋ ♌ ♍ ♎ ♏ ♐ ♑ ♒ ♓

I HEADED FOR THE parking lot and was just about to climb into my car when I heard my name called. I looked around, thinking for a moment I'd imagined it. Then I heard it again. I shut my car door and turned in a full circle. Rob Ramer was waving to me from two rows away.

He cut through the parked cars, leaving a woman standing by a red sports car.

"Rob! What are you doing here?"

"Meeting Marjorie, my lawyer." He indicated the woman who'd just climbed into the red car. "She had a hearing this morning. We're heading downtown together to see Ianello now. Believe me, I'm not looking forward to this visit."

"There's something vaguely sinister about him, isn't there?"

Rob laughed. "Good way to put it. But I have some excellent news."

"Really? What?"

"Marjorie has a friend at the coroner's. It's not official yet, but I think I can pretty much bank on it. Moira couldn't possibly have been shot with my gun. Thank God."

"Really? I don't mean to rain on your parade, but how can they tell?"

"The autopsy hasn't been completed, but apparently they're sure the bullet was much smaller, more likely a .22 caliber. A bullet from a Glock would have left a very different wound. If it lodged in her skull she'd have died instantly, but if she was hit from a short distance and at an angle, she might have survived at least for a while. Sounds like she did, if the paramedics felt there were signs of life. The cops maybe guessed that at the time. If they can find the gun, they might be able to do a ballistics test."

"What would stop them?"

"If the bullet bounces around inside the skull, it can be so damaged, ballistics might be difficult. Just depends."

My stomach did a few flip flops. "Okay, that's enough. I get it."

"It doesn't make any of this less terrible, but at least I can live with myself." He hesitated a moment. "Uh ... I wanted to ask if you've had a chance to talk to Geneva or Dan since yesterday."

"About?"

"About this whole situation. About their feelings toward me." As if he could read the expression on my face, he said, "I'm sorry. I'm putting you on the spot."

"Rob, like I said, there's not much I can say to them right now. They're in the depths of grief. It's all they can do to get by day to day. I just don't think it's the right time. Maybe this would be better coming from Brooke, anyway."

He nodded. His face showed his disappointment. "She doesn't want to put any additional pressure on her family. I'm just anxious to be vindicated, I guess, and I want to do whatever I can to defuse the situation with Dan. He's such a hothead."

"Just give it time. I really do wish you the best."

"Thanks." He jogged back to the sports car and waved once more before he climbed in.

He hadn't mentioned again his belief that there was someone else in the garage. But if his gun didn't kill Moira, and no other gun was found, Moira must have met someone in the garage that night. I shuddered and climbed into the warmth of my car.

———

Giovanni & Associates occupies a small but sleek office in the Embarcadero Center with a breathtaking view of the Bay and Treasure Island. I found Carol in a tiny office that was breathtaking in a different way. Every surface and every square inch of space was covered with files, black binders, and boxes. It was meticulously organized but claustrophobic. Carol's strawberry-blonde hair was the only bright spot in the room. Her complexion was so fair, I wondered if she ever saw the sun. She was wearing jeans and a short-sleeved flowered shirt, and small red-and-blue butterflies were tattooed on her arms. She was munching on a turkey sandwich while she stared at her computer screen, sandwich in one hand, mouse in the other.

"I've interrupted your lunch," I said after introducing myself.

Carol waved the half-sandwich in my direction. Her mouth full, she said, "What lunch? I don't call this lunch."

"Don't they ever let you out?"

"Oh, I'm free to go, but if I do I'd never get home in time to see my husband or kids. Grab a seat if you can."

There were two chairs, both occupied by boxes. "Just throw those on the floor if you can find a space." I picked up a box that had to weigh thirty pounds and looked around for a vacant spot of floor. "Sorry. Somehow no matter how often we remodel, there's never enough room." Carol jumped up and took the box from me, placing it behind her desk. "Sam told me you needed some searches done?"

"Yes. I have the addresses right here." I dug in my purse, fished out the rumpled copy of Moira's tax return, and passed it to Carol.

"Okay, let's look these up." She turned back to her screen.

"What kind of programs do you use to run these searches?"

"We have several. Most of our searches are for assets in western states. Sometimes we have to check out other places, like back east, but we can access records there too."

She typed in some information. "Let's see, the one in Arizona is Maricopa County. I'll start there." She hummed softly as she moved the mouse from place to place.

"Okay, here it is. I'll print it out for you. Purchased eight months ago for $359,500 and then transferred two months ago to Western Benefit Mutual, LLC, for the exact same amount." The printer whirred softly as Carol clicked on more sites.

"Oregon ... Oregon ... Portland's in Multnomah County. Hmmm. A condo. Purchased seven months ago for $216,000 and then transferred two months later to an individual, Don Woo, even money transfer." Once again, the printer clicked into action.

"Now, Florida ... I'd have to call a guy we work with at a title company for that one. Want me to give him a buzz?"

"No, thanks. You're a doll. I don't need to know who the owner is as much as I needed to know this property is just moving from hand to hand." I took the two printouts that Carol had obtained.

"Something funny going on with these transfers?"

"Something funny indeed. For what purpose I'm not sure."

I waved goodbye and headed back to my car. It was pretty clear Moira wasn't sitting on a secret fortune and buying real estate for investment purposes. Given her lifestyle, someone was fronting the money and the property was transferred after several months with no profit to her, except maybe a cash kickback. Andy had to be the connection to all this activity. There'd be mortgage brokers and real estate agents involved as well, although they might be innocent of any wrongdoing. Andy had to be using Moira's identity, with or without her knowledge. Was this because he couldn't do it in his own name? Or was it something more sinister? The real question was, where was the money coming from?

TWENTY-TWO

♈ ♉ ♊ ♋ ♌ ♍ ♎ ♏ ♐ ♑ ♒ ♓

SINCE I WAS ALREADY downtown, I wondered if there might be a chance I could catch Brooke at the magazine's offices. I was nervous about still carrying Moira's Rochecault bracelet around in my purse, but I wanted to know who it really belonged to. If it turned out to be Brooke's, then problem solved. If it wasn't, well … I'd worry about that later. Moira could merely have helped herself to her sister's jewelry, but I had to find out for sure.

The *Eccola!* offices are housed in an expensively remodeled and updated brick building on a narrow section of Jackson Street. Once part of the notorious Barbary Coast, the area's pirates today are architects, ad agencies, decorators, and antique dealers. Amazingly, I snagged a parking spot as a white Bentley pulled slowly away from the curb just two doors down from the magazine's main entrance.

I sat in the car and drummed my fingers on the steering wheel. I wanted to be a friend to Geneva, I wanted to keep my promise to her, but now I was really getting worried. Everything I'd learned seemed to be leading to something bigger and darker than anything

I'd anticipated, and I had no idea where this might end. Geneva could barely cope at the moment. She'd never be able to ask the questions I could ask. But whatever I found out might only cause her more grief. I'd volunteered for the job, and as much as I wanted to walk away, I couldn't. I just couldn't leave her hanging. I was in a unique position. There were people who would talk to me but might not talk to the police.

I climbed out of the car and looked up at the building. Like its neighbors, its façade was old brick. I hoped it had been retrofitted and reinforced to comply with earthquake standards. The main door was heavily etched glass. Inside the narrow lobby, magazine covers peopled with extremely young, very thin women lined the walls. Compared to them, I'd be considered old at thirty-six and fat at a hundred and eighteen pounds.

A small directory by the elevator door listed departments and individuals by room and floor. Brooke's office was in the sixth floor penthouse. I stepped into the waiting elevator and pressed the button. It rose and the doors slid silently open to reveal a reception area dominated by a semi-circular counter. The walls here were graced with more framed magazine covers, and cushioned banquettes lined either side of the area.

I gave my name to a slender black man at the reception desk and asked for Brooke. He was wearing dark slacks, a tightly fitted black T-shirt that displayed well-cut abs, and a diamond earring in one ear. I'd kill for his abs.

He hesitated. "Do you have an appointment?"

"No. I'm a personal friend, a friend of her family."

167

"Oh. I see. Well, please have a seat." His eyes followed me as I retreated to a perch on the banquette. He spoke quietly into his headset. As I watched, he looked up and smiled.

"Someone will be with you shortly."

I nodded in reply.

A few minutes later, a discreet door opened in the back wall and a tall red-haired woman stepped out. I heard the door lock as it shut behind her. She was close to six feet tall, in four-inch heels, and wore a pantsuit in a textured material. A vintage fifties broach glittering with green stones was pinned to her lapel. Her hair was pulled back in a stylish chignon close to the nape of her neck. She seemed familiar but I couldn't immediately place her.

She walked toward me and held out a hand. "Hello. I'm Lana, the Assistant Editor. I understand you were asking for Brooke Ramer?" She hesitated. "Oh, we've met, haven't we?"

Then I made the connection. I remembered her from Geneva's wedding. She was the tall redhead in the green clingy dress Matt had stalked around the dance floor.

I laughed. "Oh, yes. I'm sorry. I didn't recognize you at first either. I'm Julia. Julia Bonatti."

"You were wearing mauve, weren't you?"

"Not my favorite, I'm afraid."

"Nor mine." She laughed in return and sat next to me on the banquette.

"I just stopped in to see Brooke ... if she's here." I lowered my voice, aware that the receptionist was watching us closely. "Geneva asked me to talk to her about some of her sister's things."

"I'm sorry, you just missed her. She's gone for the day. Anything I can help you with?"

I hesitated. I wasn't willing to display the bracelet to anyone outside of the family. "No. Thanks. It's not urgent. It can wait actually. I'll see her very soon. I'm sorry if I interrupted you. I was nearby and I thought I might catch her."

"No problem. It's been pretty hectic, and I for one will be glad when she's back on a regular schedule. Can I offer you some coffee? Or wine perhaps?

"I'm fine, really."

Lana stood and picked up a glossy magazine from a stack at the reception desk. "Well, in that case, please take this with my compliments. It's the current issue, just about to hit the stands."

"Thank you." Was she trying to give me fashion hints?

She leaned closer in a conspiratorial attitude. "This is so terrible, isn't it? How is the family doing? I talked to Brooke this morning very briefly, but I didn't want to pry."

"As well as they can under the circumstances."

"From the way Brooke has always spoken, I gather they're very close."

"Yes. Very."

"We're so upset and sad here. I just wish there was something I could do for her." Lana followed me to the elevator bank. I pressed the down button on the gray concrete wall. The elevator doors slid open and I stepped inside. Lana held up a hand in goodbye as the doors slid shut.

I sat in the car and mulled over the real estate information I'd gleaned from Sam's office. I have to admit to a certain naïveté about finances.

I've never owned real estate and can barely balance my checkbook every month, but I knew one person who could enlighten me. I rummaged in my purse for my phone book and dialed Adele's number. She'd just been to see me, so I was hoping she wouldn't mind my call. She answered right away.

"Julia! Of course. What do you need?"

"I'd like to pick your brain."

She laughed. "Such as it is these days."

"I'm sure it's quite sharp. I can't really explain why right now, but can you tell me what you know about money laundering? How it works?"

"Oh! Well ... I've certainly never been involved in anything like that, but I do know generally how it's done. Do you know it was perfectly legal until 1986? After that, the laws were changed, primarily to track drug sales." Adele paused. "You see, the problem with illegal activities that bring in cash is how to funnel that cash into legitimate areas without arousing suspicion. Sometimes bank accounts, legitimate ones, are opened in various names, or sometimes with stolen identification. Smaller amounts are deposited, never over ten thousand dollars, of course. That way it isn't questioned by bank officials or reported to the government. After the funds sit unused for maybe six months, they're considered 'seasoned.' Then, those same funds are used to purchase expensive items, like boats, real estate, what have you. After the dust settles, the real estate is sold or transferred back to the person who provided the cash, or another middleman, usually with a fee being paid to the person who did all the legwork."

"So real estate *is* used in that way?"

"Oh yes. Big-ticket items are the best. Some countries have bank secrecy laws, like the Bahamas or Bahrain or Hong Kong, to name a few. And then there are countries with alternative banking systems, trust-based systems that leave no paper trail and operate outside of government control. One is the *fie chen* system in China, and I've heard about one in India and Pakistan, but I can't think of the names of them just now. And then, sometimes shell corporations are set up..."

My head was starting to spin. "Thanks, Adele, I just wanted to run something by you. I really appreciate the information. Someday soon I'll explain why I'm asking."

"Well if you suspect your identification has been stolen, you should notify all appropriate consumer agencies. I can give you a list if you like."

"Thanks, but no, that's not it. We'll talk soon. Thanks again."

I hung up. Having money, legit or not, sounded like more of a headache than not having any at all. I thought about Dan's reference to Andy's real estate activities. What had he meant when he said "under the table"? Had Moira been a willing partner? Or had she discovered that her identity was being used in this way and threatened to blow the whistle? We'd all assumed that her and Andy's arguments were based on Andy's jealousy, but perhaps jealousy had nothing at all to do with it.

TWENTY-THREE

♈ ♉ ♊ ♋ ♌ ♍ ♎ ♏ ♐ ♑ ♒ ♓

THE SHOPPING BAG IN my trunk was calling to me. It's amazing how easily I manage to forget unwelcome chores. I dialed Celia's number in an effort to get that errand taken care of.

"Celia, it's Julia."

"Don't tell me you've been too busy to go through your things!" she exclaimed.

I bit my tongue. This woman could infuriate me in a nanosecond. "Not at all. I called to tell you I did find a few things of Michael's, some clothing and books. I can drop them off this afternoon, if you'll be home."

"This is very inconvenient. I'm on my way to a doctor's appointment."

"Well, I could leave the bag on your front doorstep."

"That won't do. Call me tomorrow." She hung up. Maddening. Was she playing a deliberate control game? Her doorway was very sheltered. Surely no one would climb the steps to steal a paper bag.

Bottom line was, I just didn't want to have to think about Celia one more day.

I debated what I could do next. I still hadn't found the owner of the bracelet. I'd talked to Rita, Moira's coworker; her ex-boyfriend Steve; and Andy. But none of my efforts explained why I'd been attacked or who had stolen Moira's notebook from her apartment that night. Other than my suspicion—call it more than a suspicion—that Andy was keeping himself busy laundering money for someone, and had probably used Moira's name to do so, there was really no further information I could give to Geneva. And I was fairly certain the police still had no idea who'd killed Moira.

There was only one person I hadn't talked to yet.

———

Macao was at Pier 3 at the Embarcadero. I knew it was a jazz club at night, but I wondered if it offered lunches. And if so, maybe Moira's friendly bartender would be on duty.

I spotted the place immediately when I reached the Embarcadero. It was a renovated one-story building on the water side, with a long awning extending from the front entry to the edge of the sidewalk. A sign above the roof proclaimed its name in the same Art Deco lettering as on the matchbook I'd found in Moira's apartment. The valet kiosk was unattended and there were no signs of activity at the front door. I drove past, and half a block away pulled over to the curb at a meter. I didn't know what I was looking for, or what I might find, but in the best of all possible worlds, I might locate the man Andy was jealous of.

The entryway was paved in stone, with a wide pathway outlined in glass block. A sense of vertigo suddenly washed over me and I wasn't sure why. I looked down. Under the glass, there was movement. I gasped as a large fish swam by in an underground pool. Unnerving. Like discovering a spider under your skirt. I followed the pathway and peered through the glass front doors. A sign at the entryway told me Macao was open for lunch, but closed from three to seven o'clock. No one was in sight. I tried the door handle. Unlocked. I pushed it open and stepped inside. I called out but no one answered.

Inside, ceramic urns held potted palms. A long mahogany bar ran the length of the spacious room. The plate-glass windows were covered with shutters and bamboo fans hung from the ceiling. The interior suggested French villas of the Dien Bien Phu era. The main room was deserted. I walked to the end of the bar and saw a padded swinging door marked EMPLOYEES ONLY in small lettering. I pushed through and entered an anteroom leading to an industrial kitchen area. Three Asian women were pushing mops around the floor but didn't immediately notice me.

"Hello. Can you help me?" I said. The three looked up, stood stock still, and didn't answer.

After a moment, one of the women turned to the other two and spoke in an Asian language that didn't sound like Chinese. Vietnamese? She indicated with her hands that I should wait where I was. She left the kitchen in a hurry, propping her mop at the counter. I smiled at the other two, but they continued to stare at me with stony expressions. After a few minutes, when no one returned, I became impatient. I headed for the door that the first woman had exited through and found myself in a hallway. The two women behind me whispered to each other and returned to mopping the floor.

The hallway I'd entered led in one direction to an open door that faced a small pier and the water of the Bay. In the other direction, the corridor made a sharp right turn. I headed that way. An engine from an outboard motor coughed and came to life. If anyone questioned my presence, I'd say I'd lost... what?... a wallet... no. Some item of clothing. A scarf. I mentally rehearsed my excuse. I'd lost a scarf and thought I might have left it here. Rounding the corner, I pushed open the first door on the left and stepped into a large room that appeared to be an unused kitchen facility. A long counter in the center topped stainless steel cabinets almost four feet high. A huge cooktop was built into the wall. Otherwise, the room was empty.

I heard a man's demanding voice and a woman's higher-pitched response. They weren't speaking English. The footsteps stopped in the hallway, outside the door. Panicked and not wanting to be caught snooping, I ducked behind the counter, between it and the cooking range. The door opened. The man was barking orders. I pulled open the door of one of the stainless steel cabinets and crawled inside. The cabinet opened to the opposite side too, and that door was cracked open slightly. If I stayed crouched down, I had a slit through which I could view the empty side of the room.

I heard the squeaking of wheels from a large dolly. The man with the harsh voice was giving more orders. Another man in work clothes entered, pulling a flatbed carrier behind him loaded with wooden crates. Next, two more men entered, and following them, a huge man in a black suit, over six feet tall and built like a refrigerator. He was the one giving orders. The workers immediately started stacking the crates at the other end of the room. They pulled each crate off the carrier and placed them three high.

As the men lifted the last crate from the dolly, it slipped out of their hands and crashed to the floor. The wooden top came loose and several packages fell to the floor. One of the men swore. Each package was a rectangle, tightly wrapped in plastic. I sucked in my breath. Somehow I doubted they held noodles. I didn't want to be caught snooping now. If this was what I thought it was, I didn't know what these people would do if they found me here.

The workers pushed the damaged crate against the wall and re-placed the plastic bundles, laying the broken lid on top. Refrigerator Man stood in the doorway until the men finished their work and left. He took a last look around, then turned and slammed the door shut behind him. I waited until I heard their voices move further away. The outboard motor revved again and then silence. Was it safe to crawl out of my hiding place? I let perhaps fifteen minutes go by before my heart returned to its regular rhythm. Finally, I crawled out of the cabinet and tiptoed to the door. I couldn't hear a thing. The door was steel and the doorknob had a serious lock. I reached for it and very carefully tried to turn it. It didn't move. I was trapped.

TWENTY-FOUR

♈ ♉ ♊ ♋ ♌ ♍ ♎ ♏ ♐ ♑ ♒ ♓

I FELT PANIC RISE in my chest and did my best to quell it. I looked around. A small amount of daylight filtered in through dusty windows near the ceiling. Bars covered the windows. There were no other doors. I was good and trapped and couldn't imagine how I could get out other than banging on the door and screaming for help. That is if anyone could hear me. And for obvious reasons that was something I really didn't want to do. Would anyone come back to this room? Today? Tonight? Tomorrow? I felt sweat break out on my forehead. I took a deep breath to stay calm.

I pressed my ear to the door and prayed I wasn't locked into long-term storage. I examined the rest of the room for ventilator shafts, or hatches that might lead into another unused kitchen. But the door was the only way out. Surely sooner or later, someone would open it.

I moved over to the wooden crates. The cover that the workmen had dropped wasn't tightly secured. I lifted it and saw layer upon layer of the rectangular packages secured in plastic coverings. Each package was marked with an insignia like an elongated spider. I dropped my purse on the floor and dug out my makeup case. Rummaging around, I found an eyebrow tweezer. I pulled my address book out of my purse and ripped out a blank page. Slipping off my jacket, I used it to pick up one of the bundles, fearful of leaving fingerprints on the plastic. With my tweezers I punctured a tiny hole in one corner of the package and wiggled it until a very small amount of white substance sprinkled onto the paper. Then I very carefully turned the edges of the paper in and wrapped it up, being careful not to spill any. I tucked the paper packet into my makeup case, along with the eyebrow tweezers, and replaced the rectangular brick in the crate. I made sure not to touch anything else. If I ever escaped from this storeroom, I wanted to be able to prove what I saw.

As I turned away, I spotted a workman's glove lying on the floor next to the one of the crates. One of the men must have dropped it and forgotten to take it with him. I slid down the wall and sat on the floor. I waited. Far away, I thought I heard voices, but no one was approaching. Even if I banged on the door it was possible no one would hear me. And if I did, how could I explain what I was doing there? I didn't dare. Not after seeing those crates. I took a deep breath, wishing I could put myself into some sort of altered state. I tried several times, but each time I managed to relax, my heart would once again start pounding against my rib cage. I couldn't afford to panic.

I decided it was safer to return to the stainless steel cabinet. In case someone did return, I didn't want to be discovered. I just wanted to escape. I pushed the thought out of my mind that it could be days before someone opened that door. I crawled back into the huge cabinet, leaving the door open a crack. The angle of the sunlight slanting in through the barred windows had shifted. How much time had elapsed? I checked my cell phone. Only forty-five minutes. It felt like three hours. I tried deep breathing again to quell the panic. I could call someone to let them know where I was, just in case something happened to me. Who could I call? And what good would that do? I could call 911 and tell the police I was being held captive. That was if worse came to worst. I thought of my friend Don Forrester. He was nearby, at the *Chronicle*—the newspaper's star researcher who had access to all kinds of information, most of it not in print. I wasn't sure how he'd get through the restaurant and find this door, but the thought of calling him cheered me. That would be my last resort, I decided. I didn't want to put anyone else in potential danger if there was another way.

I must have dozed off, because the next thing I heard were voices. Two men. I woke with a start. The room was pitch black. The sun had set but a tiny amount of light from the street was visible. I squeezed my eyes shut, trying to adjust to the darkened room. The men were in the hallway. They were approaching the door. Half crawling, I pushed open the cabinet door and scrambled across the floor in the general direction of the door to the corridor. My foot had fallen asleep. Limping, I forced myself to move, ignoring the pins and needles. I hoped I was close to my mark. My eyes had adjusted somewhat and I was able to make out the outline of the door. It opened into the room, that much I was sure of.

I reached the door and felt along the edge with my fingers. The voices were louder now. I felt the hinges. I heard a metallic sound as a key was inserted into the lock. I pressed myself against the wall so I would be behind the door when it opened. It was my only chance.

I pressed my right foot against the floor, willing it to come back to life. If I had a chance to escape, I'd have to be able to move quickly.

The door opened. Two men stood inches away from me on the threshold. One sounded as if he was chastising the other. The second man replied in a higher pitched tone, as if explaining himself or making an excuse. Suddenly the room was flooded with light from overhead neon racks. I squinted to protect my eyes. One of the men made a final remark and walked away. The second man came into the room. I could hear his footsteps. He cursed softly and moved slowly around the crates. I took a chance and peeked out from behind the door. He made an exclamation under his breath and stooped to pick something up from the floor. It must be the heavy glove he'd left behind.

Now was my chance. I prayed my feet could move fast enough. Before he straightened, I slipped around the edge of the door and in a flash ran down the corridor. At the bend, I turned and kept running. The hallway was empty. As I passed the first kitchen I heard several people talking at once and smelled something delicious, but I didn't dare head out that way. The restaurant must have opened by now. Even if the front doors were unlocked, I didn't want to alert anyone to my presence. I headed straight for the end of the corridor where the door led to the small pier. I pushed it open, stepped outside and quickly closed it behind me. I leaned against the wall of the building, praying I hadn't been spotted. My heart was thudding and adrenaline was coursing through my veins. Fear was causing me to hyperventilate.

Inky water lapped several feet beneath me under the pier. I peeked around the corner of the building. No path or walkway gave access to the street. Had I escaped one trap only to find myself in another? I heard the clinking of dishware and glasses, then voices and laughter from somewhere above. I looked up. At a neighboring restaurant, perhaps eight feet above where I stood, was an outdoor dining area, the railing outlined in small white lights. A wooden ladder ran up the side of the Macao building. I wasn't sure it would hold my weight, but I had no choice. I wouldn't last long out here in the freezing wind coming off the bay. The motorboat I'd heard earlier could return and I'd be discovered.

I hung my purse around my neck and started climbing. When I reached the level of the neighboring restaurant, I clung to the far side of the ladder and leaned over. The distance between the buildings was about six feet. Close, but still a risk. I'd have to take a chance. I'd have to let go of the ladder and leap, hoping to reach the other railing. If I made the jump, I knew I could easily clamber on to the deck. I took a deep breath and tried to ignore the black waters below. If I fell I might not be able to swim to safety. Even in the sheltered part of the Bay, people have been washed out to sea if the tide is turning. I had to make it across.

I closed my eyes, imagining myself making it successfully across the gap. Just stay focused for those few seconds, I thought. Taking a deep breath, I launched myself from the ladder, reaching out with both hands.

My foot hit the edge of the wooden flooring. I slipped. Panicking, I grabbed for the railing. It creaked loudly, as if about to break in two. I looked up. I'd missed the heavier top rail. My feet were flailing below me, searching for something to stand on. Splinters had lodged in the palm of my hand. Painfully I clung on, grasped the top railing with my right hand, and pulled myself up. I struggled to get one foot on the edge of the deck, then the other.

A group of diners were seated around a large table, wineglasses raised, about to make a toast. One woman's eyes grew wide. She pointed at me. The others turned to stare. They didn't utter a sound. I ignored them and climbed over the railing onto the restaurant's deck. I pulled a small piece of wood out of my palm, brushed myself off, and, managing a weak smile, walked through the restaurant and out to the street.

Once on the sidewalk, I jogged back to my car, passing the front entrance to Macao, half afraid someone there would see me and sound an alarm. With shaking fingers, I managed to get my car door open and fell into the driver's seat. I hit the door locks and took deep breaths until my heart rate returned to normal.

TWENTY-FIVE

♈ ♉ ♊ ♋ ♌ ♍ ♎ ♏ ♐ ♑ ♒ ♓

AS CALMLY AS POSSIBLE, I pulled out into traffic and drove several blocks away from Macao, then parked in a red zone. I dug my cell phone out and dialed Don's number. He's a large teddy bear of a man and I often find myself crying on his shoulder. My hands were still shaking as I hit the buttons on my cell phone. I took a deep breath and told myself to speak calmly. Don answered on the first ring.

"Hey, I thought you'd still be at the office!" I said. "Can I buy you a late dinner?"

"Oh God, what does she want *now*?" He laughed a deep belly laugh.

"You've got my number, huh?"

"Your timing is impeccable. I'm starving. I want the most expensive steak you can afford. None of that PC yuppie vegan garbage, the stuff that food eats. I'm having a bad day. I need to eat meat today, great hunks of dripping bloody mammal flesh. Where are you?"

"Near the end of Broadway by now, I think."

"Turn around and meet me at Market and Stockton. There's a great steak place there."

Twenty minutes later, we were seated in a plush booth with huge menus. Don, true to his word, ordered a large porterhouse, rare. I ordered the tomato bisque soup with croutons. At one time, Don had dated my college roommate, and we'd became close friends when she dumped him to join a commune up north. In those days, Don would hang out at my apartment, spending time with Michael and me, but eventually he recovered from his heartbreak and married his high school sweetheart.

He was watching me carefully. "You look like hell. Hope you don't have a date later."

"Thanks a bunch."

"Speaking of dating, are you?"

"Don't change the subject."

Don narrowed his eyes and glared at me. "I didn't know we were on a subject. Oh, let me guess, you want some information. You're paying for this dinner, I hope you know."

"To answer your question, no, I'm not dating anyone. You sound like my therapist." Several months after Michael's death, I'd started seeing Paula. It helped a lot to be able to talk to someone, and it pulled me through a bad time. Unfortunately, those sessions were also very expensive and, I felt, no longer necessary.

"What does *she* have to say about your single state?"

"I don't see her regularly anymore." I mumbled.

Don reached across the table and gripped my hand. "Julia, for heaven's sake, look in the mirror. You should be fighting them off with a baseball bat."

I took a deep breath. My friends all meant well. It just wasn't a subject I wanted to get into, especially at that moment. "Don, you're a true dear. But can we talk about something else?"

"Fine. Okay. I won't nag you anymore."

"What do you know about a place called Macao?"

"Macao? That place on the Embarcadero?" Don narrowed his eyes. "Owned by a guy named Cheng. Luong Cheng—Vietnamese."

"Is he a big guy, dark-skinned?"

"No. Slight, slender guy. Believe it or not, always dresses in white and has a very nasty female bodyguard, and Dobermans too."

"How do you know all this?"

"Newspaper articles, stuff on government investigations. Saw them once getting into a limo. Caught my eye and somebody pointed them out to me. She was scary, the bodyguard. I could feel my you-know-whats shrivel right up. I don't know why you're asking about him, but you shouldn't even be asking. What are you messing with?"

"Trying to help a friend find out what was going on in her sister's life and maybe why she was killed." I filled Don in on the night of Moira's murder.

His eyes widened and he was speechless for a moment. "Julia," he finally said, "this is not a nice guy. He was a real bad guy in the old country, and I'm sure hasn't seen the error of his ways in the good old USA."

The waiter returned and placed a huge piece of dripping beef in front of Don. My soup came a moment later. Don punctuated his speech with his steak knife. "There was a federal inquiry into Cheng's gambling practices. He's set up some clubs down south. They were looking to nab him on smuggling, but it wasn't enough to shut him down. They'll probably eventually trip him up on tax evasion. The feds keep their eye on him, believe me."

Don poured a generous helping of steak sauce on his dinner plate and scooped some up with a piece of meat. "What does this have to do with your friend? This was the Laurel Heights murder, right?" I nodded without speaking. "Well, let's put it this way. If this sister was in business with Cheng, I'm not surprised she's dead."

"I don't know that she was, but there's a connection. She worked there off and on. Have a look at this." I pulled the small packet of paper out of my makeup case and slid it across the table.

Don looked at me questioningly. He put down his fork and inconspicuously opened the tiny packet. He touched a small amount to his finger. "Where did you get this?" He hissed. "I don't know enough to be sure, but this looks purified, what they call 'number four.'"

"There are crates of this stuff in a storeroom at Macao."

"What the hell were you doing *there*?"

I didn't answer. Don wrapped up the packet and passed it back to me. "If you're smart, you'll head for the ladies room and flush it down the toilet. Don't walk around with this stuff in your purse. What are you going to do?"

"What do you think I should do?"

"Absolutely nothing. Forget you were ever there. Forget you ever saw a thing. I'm not kidding Julia. This is heavy stuff."

"Don't you think I should report this?"

"No!"

"What?"

Don sighed. "Tell you what. I have some contacts. I can make a phone call and keep you out of it"

"Don, if drugs are bringing in huge profits, then wouldn't there be a need for the dealers to get that cash into circulation—to launder it?"

"I'm sure Cheng has a whole team of smart people working on that." Don reached across the table and grabbed my hand. "Julia, I'm your friend. Take my advice and stay the hell away from this. I know you mean well, but these are not the people to mess with."

It's a bad trait of mine, but I have to admit I hate being told what to do. I've been told I have a mind like a bear trap. The best way to get me to do something is to tell me not to do it and vice versa. If that makes me contrary and ornery, well, I guess I am. Don knew me well enough to know that. I didn't answer.

"And wipe that stubborn look off your face. I mean it. Stay the hell out of this and let the cops worry about Cheng and this woman's murder."

TWENTY-SIX

♈ ♉ ♊ ♋ ♌ ♍ ♎ ♏ ♐ ♑ ♒ ♓

THE NEXT MORNING, I woke with a start. I was dreaming I'd fallen into black ocean waves so thick and viscous I couldn't move my arms or legs. A hangover from the night before no doubt. I dragged myself slowly out of bed. My right side ached. I'd pulled muscles clambering onto the deck of that restaurant. I wasn't complaining—the other option would have been far less appetizing. I shivered when I thought what might have happened if Refrigerator Man, as I'd dubbed him, had discovered me hiding in the storeroom. If these people were as bad as Don seemed to think, my chances of getting out of there wouldn't have been good.

I put the kettle on to boil, downed two aspirin, and dumped a large amount of espresso coffee into a filter. Wizard was circling my legs waiting to be fed. I scooped some Fancy Beast into a clean dish. When the water boiled, I poured it through the filter, inhaling the aroma. My drug of choice in the morning. The night before, I'd taken Don's advice and flushed the contents of the tiny packet down the toilet. If Moira had been mixed up with these people, it opened a Pandora's box of possibilities.

The phone in the office began to ring. I glanced at the clock: 7:15. An uncivilized hour for anyone to call. Even my grandmother wouldn't call this early. My head was pounding. I trotted down the hallway and checked the caller ID. Not a number I recognized. Heaving a sigh, I picked up the phone, hoping I wouldn't sound like something that had almost washed up in the Bay the night before.

"Julia? Hi." A man's voice.

"Hi." I hesitated, not sure if I was correct. "Is this Matt?"

"Listen, sorry to call so early, but I was just wondering . . . " Matt hesitated. "Have you heard if they've questioned David? The police, I mean."

"Yes, they did."

"Well, I don't believe he had anything to do with this for a second. I've known him for years and he's just not capable of hurting anybody."

"I'm glad to hear that." Erring on the side of caution, I wisely kept my mouth shut and offered no information. There was something about Matt right now that didn't feel quite up front, as if he were the type to throw out a tidbit of information, hoping to reel in more. Maybe it was just his stockbroker's personality revealing itself, talking up an investment to an uncertain client, or was there more to it?

"I'm wondering . . . actually . . . um . . . I'd like to make an appointment with you. You know, for a personal consultation, like we talked about. Could we arrange that?"

"Oh. Of course. Let me check my calendar. What day is good for you?"

"Later today would be great. That's if you have the time."

"Today?" I squeaked. I quickly reviewed what I'd planned for the day. I still hadn't caught up with Brooke to ask her about the bracelet I'd found at Moira's apartment. She might or might not be at her office today. Other than that, I had to prepare some Zodia responses for the column, although I could do that at any time. I was well ahead of my deadlines, and my client scheduled for today had cancelled—an attack of cold feet for the second time. I was relatively free. Why turn a new client away?

"I know it's somewhat short notice, but … I just happen to have some free time …" he continued.

I was surprised by his eagerness, and generally I'm very careful about new clients coming to my home, at least until I get to know them better. I always ask who referred them, and if my client is male, I tend to be even more cautious. When in doubt, I arrange to meet them in a private room at the Mystic Eye. I don't mean to sound paranoid, but there are lots of crazy people out there. And most victims are done in by someone they know, even someone close. Family, friends, neighbors. The human race can be quite disgusting.

It's also been my experience that whenever a client calls with a sense of urgency couched in a casual excuse, it's often urgent. They just don't want to tell you what the real issue is. Whether from an unwillingness to be open or a test of the astrologer's ability, I've never figured out. "Well then, today it is," I said. "Much later today—I'll need some time to do the work. My fees are—"

"Oh, money's not a problem, Julia. Whatever you charge is fine with me. How about five o'clock this afternoon?"

"That'll work. I'll see you then." I gave Matt my address and he said goodbye, sounding genuinely relieved. What could be on his mind, I wondered. Did it have anything to do with Moira's death, or was it something more personal? Whatever it was, I'd find out very soon. I'd intended to do some more work on all the Leary family charts, but now that would have to wait.

I devoured some toast, hopped in the shower, dressed in a presentable outfit, and straightened up the apartment. Then I spent the next two hours with Matt's chart, making notes and preparing for his visit. When I finished, I stood up and stretched, stiff from sitting in one position too long. I felt a bad twinge in my side, but the good news was that my headache was gone. Maybe I was getting soft and needed regular exercise. But the prospect of joining a gym appalled me. I despise gyms. The equipment confuses me and everything looks like a torture device. Most of all, I hate the smell of sweat and dirty socks.

When all was ready for Matt's appointment, I called Brooke's office only to learn that she wasn't in and the receptionist had no idea when she might be available. The bracelet was burning a hole in my consciousness, but it was easier to worry about the bracelet than dwell on Macao and what Moira's involvement in that place might have been. I tried Brooke's home number, but an answering machine picked up. I left a message that I had a quick question for her but it was nothing urgent. Given what she was going through, I certainly didn't want to pressure her. It was always possible Geneva had had a chance to talk to her about the bracelet by now anyway.

There was one other person who might know if the bracelet was Brooke's. Rather than calling Rob first, I thought I'd go straight to his office for an unannounced visit. I was curious to see him in his own environment. It was slightly presumptuous of me, but since he'd lain in wait for me outside Moira's apartment, I didn't see any reason why I couldn't beard him in his own den.

Rob's law firm occupies two floors of a high rise at 600 California Street, in the heart of the financial district, just south of Grant. I wasn't about to open a vein to pay for parking there, so I pulled into a public lot a block up the hill. I rode the elevator up to street level and cut through a small park with kiddy swings and a sandy play area. I didn't spot any kids, but a homeless man was enjoying the slide. Across California Street, the bells of Old Saint Mary's chimed the noon hour. The inscription on the tower reads, *Son, observe the time and fly from evil.* I shuddered. A dire warning aimed at the fearful.

The plaza in front of Rob's building was crowded with people rushing out for an early lunch. I pushed my way through and stepped into the elevator. With a slight sensation of upward movement, it deposited me on the twenty-eighth floor. The interior lobby was dominated by a desk that rivaled the Starship Enterprise. The receptionist looked up as I approached. I gave her my name and asked to see Rob Ramer. She smiled and gave me a curious look but buzzed his office immediately.

I sat near the control deck. The waiting area was enclosed with layers of floor-to-ceiling green translucent glass. Shadows moved behind the glass like human fish in a murky aquarium. A few minutes later, Rob entered the lobby through a cleverly concealed corridor and came toward me.

"Julia. How nice to see you!"

"I hope I didn't arrive at a bad time."

He smiled. "No. Not at all. How are you? I was just finishing up a project and getting ready to head out for lunch. Come on back."

He indicated I should precede him down the hallway. We were treated to a few curious looks from people we passed. Was it because he was so handsome and I was an eligible female? Or did he have a reputation in the office? At the end, the hallway turned right into another section.

"Keep on going to the end. My office is the corner one. Let me take your jacket."

"That's all right, I can't visit for long. I had to come downtown today so I thought I'd stop by for a minute. I have a quick question, if you can answer it."

"Please, have a seat." He ushered me into his office and sat behind his desk, leaning back in a plush ergonomic chair."

"Actually, I wanted to show you something. I'm hoping you recognize this." I unzipped my purse and pulled out the bracelet. I'd rewrapped it in tissue paper. I wanted to show it to Rob without its Rochecault box, to gauge his reaction.

"It's something we ..." A little white lie, but I didn't want to tip anyone off that I'd searched Moira's apartment alone. "Something we found in Moira's apartment, and Geneva thought it might belong to Brooke." I placed it in the middle of his desk and unwrapped the tissue. Rob looked at it for a moment and said nothing.

"Could this by any chance belong to Brooke?"

"I don't think so. At least, I don't recognize it. Where did you find it again?"

"In a drawer in Moira's apartment. It looks like sapphires and small diamonds and something else too."

"Well, you know, it could be a fake, some kind of iolite quartz or something."

I pushed the bracelet closer to him across the desk. "It appears to be the real thing to me. And I'm sure the setting is platinum. Here, have a closer look."

Rob picked up a pair of reading glasses from his desk and slipped them on. He lifted the bracelet in its bed of tissues and held it under the desk lamp for a closer examination.

"I don't know what to say, Julia. I've just never seen this before, so I don't think it's Brooke's. She does have a few nice pieces in a safe at home. I can ask her. But if it's Moira's, I really can't imagine how she would have been able to buy anything expensive."

"I thought it was worth a try to ask. I'm sorry to bother you at work."

He shrugged. "I'm no jeweler. I don't know if I could tell real from fake anyway. Maybe you should have it appraised."

"That's an idea. I just thought I'd ask before I gave it back to the Learys. I left a message for Brooke, but please tell her not to bother."

"Yes." Rob looked down at his hands. "She's ... having a very tough time of it right now. You can understand." Then he glanced up. "Listen, I'm just about finished with this." He waved his arm over several stacks of paper on his desk. "Why don't you join me for lunch?"

I hesitated. I had to admit to a certain amount of curiosity about Rob. Besides, I thought I might be able to pump him for more information about Brooke and Moira's relationship.

"Sure. Why not?" I smiled.

"Great. Tell you what. Let's go to the Palace, the Garden Court Restaurant. I haven't been there for a long time. How does that sound? You can help me celebrate my proven innocence, thank God."

"The Palace? Wow. You know, I haven't been to the restaurant since it was renovated. I'd be happy to."

"We can take my car. It's parked downstairs, it'll save us the walk. I've got to be back here in a couple of hours for a meeting anyway."

The Palace Hotel is old, and some say it's haunted by its builder. It's one of the few remaining structures in San Francisco that survived the great quake of 1906, only to be burned in a later fire. A recent restoration returned the hotel to its turn-of-the-century grandeur, complete with Austrian crystal chandeliers, marble columns, potted palms, and a center courtyard restaurant topped with a stained glass dome. The original builder, William Ralston, had not lived to see his dream realized. When a run on his bank in 1873 left him destitute, he was seen thrashing in the Bay while taking his daily swim. A few days later, his body surfaced. Autopsy results indicated he died of a stroke, but history buffs still claim it was suicide.

The maitre d' seated us quickly even though we had no reservation. I hoped Rob was footing the bill and glad I hadn't worn jeans. I decided to splurge on the glazed duckling. Rob opted for oysters.

Once the waiter moved away, Rob said, "Brooke and I have decided to bring Ashley to the wake whenever it's held, but just for a little while. The hell with Dan and what he thinks. It may sound strange, but children can have a hard time dealing with death and this may make it easier for Ashley."

"So do adults. Have a hard time, I mean. But why does Dan seem... I guess what I'm asking is, what happened to cause Dan's bad feelings toward you? Was he always like that?"

"I believe so. On Dan's part, at any rate. Frankly, I think he's jealous."

"In what way?"

"Of my success. Of the money I make now. I think it's a working class attitude toward someone who's raking in big bucks. But believe me, I didn't always have a large paycheck, especially when I worked for the DA's office. That was a pittance." He laughed. "Look, Julia, just between you and me ..." He hesitated. "I don't think Dan's the nice guy he pretends to be. The family won't admit this, but I wouldn't be surprised if he wasn't somehow involved in drugs with Moira."

Steve the mechanic's remarks about Moira and her brother flashed through my mind. "Do you know something you haven't told the family?" I asked slowly. "Dan seems ..."

"I know. Like a really regular guy who works hard for a living. Runs his own business and all that stuff. But he and Moira used to hang out a lot together and she never had any money, so how did she afford some of her habits?"

"I understand she caused some trouble for Brooke in the past."

Rob grimaced. "You better believe it. One time, she stole Brooke's credit cards and went on a binge. She ran up thousands of dollars before Brooke discovered their loss."

"What did Brooke do?"

"Well, she didn't realize it at first. She reported the cards as stolen, and then later figured out it was Moira. God, I was pissed. Brooke wouldn't press charges and paid off all the cards. That was the kind of crap Moira pulled. You can see why I didn't trust her around Ashley." Rob put down his silverware and took a sip of water. "Frankly ..."

"Yes?"

He hesitated for a moment and then made up his mind to speak. "This might sound terrible, but hear me out."

I waited.

"Both Dan and Moira stand ... stood ... to gain if Brooke were to die."

I paused with my fork halfway to my mouth. "What are you saying?"

"Brooke has the money in our family. Certainly more than I do. She has a trust fund set up for Ashley, and I'm the executor of that, but a good part of her money is in trust for her mother, and Dan's the executor. If something happened to Brooke, God forbid, Dan would get his hands on it. He could go through everything."

"What does this have to do with Moira being shot?"

Rob hesitated. "I know this will sound awful ... but what if ..." He hesitated again. "What if it was Brooke, not Moira, who was the intended victim? Brooke goes down to the garage every night to let the dog out. What if they intended to shoot her, but ended up taking a shot at me?"

"They?"

"Whoever was there in the garage with Moira."

"That's horrible. I can't even conceive of that, Rob."

"I know. I hesitate to even say it. But the thought has crossed my mind. Julia, that night ..." Rob trailed off. "Was Moira able to speak? Did she say anything to you?"

I didn't want the picture of Moira bleeding to death to flash in front of my eyes. I did my best to push it away. In retrospect, though, I was almost sure she was gone before I even reached her. "No. Nothing." I shuddered. "Can you think of any reason she would have had to be in the garage in the middle of the night?"

"Anything's possible. Andy's car was there. They'd been fighting all day. Maybe she was thinking of taking off. Maybe she was meeting someone." He shrugged his shoulders. "I just don't know."

"I spoke with Moira's ex-boyfriend Steve, and Rita, the waitress who worked with her at the Alibi."

"You did? Why?"

"Geneva asked me to help her find out what was going on in Moira's life. I thought maybe people would speak more openly to me than to someone in her family."

"Did you learn anything?"

"Not really. Rita thought Moira was involved with someone besides Andy. She saw someone pick her up one night. And her ex-boyfriend Steve seemed to think she was cheating on him when they were together."

Rob was thoughtful for a moment. "There's another thing that really stumps me. How did Dan get to the house so fast after Moira was shot. I was pretty much in a state of shock, but still, looking back, it seems like he just appeared right away . . . " Rob trailed off.

"Andy called him."

"Even so, the guy lives over by Lake Merced. With no traffic, it would still take him twenty or thirty minutes to get to our house. I wasn't paying attention at the time, but he arrived pretty quick."

I remembered Dan's explanation—that he'd been close by, at a bar—but I didn't want to volunteer anything that might add fuel to the fire between Rob and Dan.

Rob continued. "For all we know, maybe Andy and Moira fought and the gun went off. Maybe it was an accident and he panicked."

I thought about that one. "Possibly. But Andy seemed relatively calm, especially at first, considering what went down. I think he wanted to believe Moira would pull through, or maybe it was shock or denial. I don't know."

"Yeah. And if he did do it, how did he get rid of the gun? I've thought about nothing else the past few days." Rob reached over and put his hand over mine, a curiously intimate gesture that sent a shock up my arm. "It's haunted me, Julia." I could see tears welling up in his eyes. "I'm sorry. I don't mean to get so emotional. It just catches me off guard sometimes."

His cellphone rang. "Excuse me for a sec." He looked quizzically at the caller ID. "Rob Ramer." He listened for a moment, then stared at me and the color seemed to drain from his face. "I'll be right there."

"Is something wrong?" I asked as he slid his cellphone into a pocket.

He looked at me a long moment before he spoke. "My wife's just been arrested."

TWENTY-SEVEN

♈ ♉ ♊ ♋ ♌ ♍ ♎ ♏ ♐ ♑ ♒ ♓

"JULIA, I'M SORRY, I have to go. Will you be all right on your own?"

"Of course. Don't worry."

Rob reached into his wallet and placed a couple of large bills on the table. His hands were shaking. "This should cover it. Are you sure you'll be all right?"

"Yes. Yes, of course. Please don't worry. You need to go."

He stood and stumbled slightly. I saw him signaling to the valet as he neared the front door.

I was just as stunned as Rob. My half-eaten lunch sat in front of me but my appetite was gone. What a waste. I was tempted to ask for a doggie bag, but the idea of dragging leftover duckling around town wasn't very appealing. I signaled to the waiter to bring the bill. He deftly swooped down and left a small leather case on the table. After I added the tip, there wasn't much change from Rob's cash.

I pulled my cell phone out and dialed Mary's house. No answer. The machine picked up. I had no idea who had contacted Rob, but I hesitated to leave any message on the off chance the family wasn't yet aware of Brooke's arrest. I left the restaurant, crossed Market, and trudged up the hill on California to the parking garage. By the time I got there, the muscles around my shoulder blades were in spasm. Undoubtedly from my adventure of the night before. I wondered if Kuan was free this afternoon. I could certainly use his services. I paid the parking fee and picked up Grant Avenue heading into North Beach, grateful I could still drive.

There was no sign on Kuan's door when I arrived. I breathed a sigh of relief. I rang the bell and he opened the door immediately. The strain must have shown on my face. Kuan didn't say a word but pointed to the treatment room, where I changed into a cotton robe. He felt my pulses and touched my shoulder blade and ribs in various spots.

"How did you do this?"

"It's better if I don't tell you."

Kuan shook his head. "You're too reckless, Julia. Your grandmother worries about you all the time, even if she doesn't say much."

"I know she does, but really, I'm fine. Is she upstairs right now?"

"No. She's out. Your secret is safe."

I lay on my stomach on the treatment table, my face peeking through the padded donut hole while Kuan inserted acupuncture needles into my neck, my shoulder, and next to my spine. He was so adept, I didn't feel them at all. The fragrant odor of the mugwort stick filled the room as he heated the needles with the burning herb. I felt the change. Now I could breathe deeply without a twinge. It was heavenly.

When he finished, he said, "Get dressed and come in the kitchen. I have some special tea for you. It will help."

As I sat up, I could still feel the heat in my tender muscles, but everything felt relaxed and back in place. I dressed and headed for

Kuan's immaculate kitchen, where fresh herbs hung from a rack above the counter. He placed two handmade pottery cups on the table and poured from a small teapot.

"This has something to do with the murder after the wedding, doesn't it?" he asked.

"Let's put it this way. I was snooping and had a choice of getting caught or escaping. I managed to escape."

"Hmm." He sipped carefully from the hot mug. "Did you learn anything?"

"I'm not sure." I relented and filled Kuan in on the facts as I knew them so far. I knew that nothing I told him would go any further.

"The most intriguing fact is where this murder took place," he said after I'd finished.

"How do you mean?"

"Why the garage? Was this woman who was killed familiar with that space for any reason?"

"She spent a lot of time at her sister's house. But no one knows why she was in the garage, of all places."

"Yet the only person whose regular habit it was to go down to the garage was the woman of the house, correct?"

"Yes, to let the dog out to her run."

"Very interesting."

"What does that mean?"

"I have no idea." Kuan smiled suddenly. "It was just a thought. A juxtaposition."

"Thank you for the treatment. I'd like to pay you."

"I refuse payment. Go home. Get some rest."

I gave him a kiss on the cheek and a hug and headed out to my car.

TWENTY-EIGHT

♈ ♉ ♊ ♋ ♌ ♍ ♎ ♏ ♐ ♑ ♒ ♓

I TRIED GENEVA TWO more times as I drove toward the Avenues. When I reached the top of the hill on Geary, I remembered the shopping bag in my trunk. As much as I disliked dealing with Celia, there was no time like the present. I decided not to call this time. Why give her a chance to make the errand more difficult?

I cut across Golden Gate Park and picked up Sunset. Celia's house was set back from the wide boulevard on a street that never seemed to be busy with traffic. I pulled up in front and climbed the stairs. Celia hadn't worked in many years. After Michael's father died, she was fortunate in that she could still afford to live in her home. The front lawn was perfect, a postage stamp of lush, brilliant green bordered with hydrangeas. No leaf would dare be out of place in Celia's garden. I lugged the shopping bag up the stairs, forcing myself not to think about the remnants of Michael's life that I'd packed away. After all, the very least she could do would be to open the door and say thank you.

When I reached the top of the stairway, I rang the bell and waited. I waited a few minutes more and then rang the doorbell again. She was home, I was sure of it. She simply refused to have anything to do with me. That old familiar ache rose in my chest. The orphan with her nose pressed against the window looking in on a life she couldn't hope to have. Angry at my automatic reaction, I rang the bell a third time. Finally, I gave up. *Okay, Celia, you win.* I placed the bag at the front door and returned down the steps.

As I was opening my car door, someone called my name. I turned back. It was Maggie, Michael's sister.

"Julia. Wait." She rushed down the stairs, out of breath when she reached me. "I'm sorry, I didn't hear the bell. I was upstairs." She gave me a warm hug.

"Hi Maggie." I smiled. "It's great to see you." I'd always liked Michael's younger sister. I'd never known their father, but they both must have taken after him. There certainly was no spiritual resemblance between them and their mother. "How are you?" I asked.

"I'm fine. I was just visiting at Mom's." Her smile faded. "Julia, I'm sorry she's treating you this way. She's home. She just won't answer the door."

"Maggie, I gave up a year ago, wondering what she held against me."

"It's not just you, I'm afraid. She won't talk to anybody in the family. Doesn't see her old friends. She rattles around that big old house day and night. She's made a shrine of my brother's room. I think she spends most of her time there." Maggie shrugged. "I'm really worried about her, but I just don't know what to do. That's why I try to stop by whenever I can."

"I wish I could help, but I'm likely the last person she wants to see. You don't have to apologize for her."

"I know that. I just don't think you need to be treated like that. We all hurt. It doesn't help to be cruel to you. Michael really loved you. I just hope you always remember that. Don't let my mother's behavior color your feelings about him and what you had together."

Tears sprang to my eyes. I hadn't expected this greeting and hadn't thought it would strike such a chord. "Thanks, Maggie. I do appreciate that." Her eyes were Michael's eyes, the same green flecks in the brown that gave them a hazel tinge.

"You can call me anytime."

I glanced up at the front door. Maggie had left it wide open. I spotted Harry, Michael's dog. When Michael and I had first started seeing each other, we went bicycling in the park whenever we could. One day, I spotted something moving under a bush and halted. We investigated and found a beautiful white poodle, half starved, smelling very bad and suffering from infections. He'd obviously been abandoned and someone had beaten him severely. Michael left me to watch over him and hurried back to retrieve his car. We loaded the bikes on the back and I held Harry on my lap all the way to the emergency vet. Michael paid for all his treatments and then adopted him. His budget as a student was tight, but he didn't hesitate to help a wounded creature. I think that was when I fell in love with him.

"Harry's with you?"

Maggie followed my gaze. "Harry! What are you doing?" Harry had knocked over the shopping bag and was sniffing it. When he heard his name called, he raised his head, one of Michael's gloves in his mouth. He whimpered and looked at us.

"Oh, God." Maggie said. "He knows that's Michael's glove. Poor guy. Come here, Harry," she called. Harry dropped the glove and bounded down the stairs. He came straight at me and leaped toward my face. "He remembers you." Maggie said.

"Of course he does." I bent down and hugged him as Harry left slippery kisses on my face. I looked up at Maggie. "I'm so glad you've kept him."

"I'd never let him go. I just love Harry to death. It's like having a part of my brother to hold on to."

Seeing Harry had brought a rush of memories. I had to get out of there before I turned into a blubbering idiot. I hugged Maggie and thanked her. As I started the engine, she leaned in the window. "Just remember, Julia—it's not you. It's nothing you've done."

I nodded, blinking back more tears, and drove away into the park. When I reached the Botanical Gardens, I pulled over and wiped my eyes in an effort to clear my head. Seeing Harry had stirred a memory. I tried to retrieve it but it eluded me, just out of reach. Whatever it was, it would come back. I checked my watch. A little after two o'clock. Matt wasn't due to arrive for his reading until five. I had some free time and tried to figure out the best use of it. I did need to reach Geneva and bring her up to date on the little bit I'd learned. And I wanted to find out if she was aware of Brooke's arrest. I called the Leary house. Again, no answer. I turned the car around and headed for 35th Avenue.

TWENTY-NINE

♈ ♉ ♊ ♋ ♌ ♍ ♎ ♏ ♐ ♑ ♒ ♓

As I turned the corner, I spotted Geneva's car pulling up to the garage door. I cruised down the street and parked in front of their house. Mary stepped out of Geneva's car and, without a word, climbed the stairs and entered the house. Geneva waited on the sidewalk for me.

"I've been trying to call you," I said.

"We just came from making arrangements. The wake is tomorrow night at seven at Nordenson's on Sloat. Can you be there?"

"Of course. I'll bring Gloria. I know she'd want to come."

Geneva's face looked terribly drawn and gray. Dark circles colored the pale skin around her eyes. "You haven't heard the worst part yet. Brooke's been arrested."

"I know."

"How?"

"I was with Rob when he took the call."

"Rob? Why?"

"The bracelet. I thought on the off chance it belonged to Brooke he might know. But he didn't recognize it."

"Oh. I forgot all about the bracelet." Geneva rubbed her forehead. "Let's go inside."

I followed her up the stairway to the front door and waited while she hung her coat in the closet. She peeked down the hallway to make sure her mother wouldn't overhear our conversation.

"Marjorie's doing what she can to get Brooke released. Ianello told her they discovered emails between Brooke and Moira proving they were planning to kill Rob."

"Are you telling me the police think they *emailed* each other about a murder plot?"

"It's completely crazy. The police confiscated Moira's computer after she died, remember? The emails were deleted but apparently some computer forensics person checked it. They explained it to me but it went right over my head. You can delete emails but they remain on the hard drive somehow, and then there are copies saved on the server for a certain number of days. I didn't really understand it all. Then they got a warrant and took Brooke's computer at home and the one in her office too. Look, even if it were true, which I don't for a minute believe, Brooke would never have dragged Moira into anything. She was always getting her out of scrapes, not into them."

"Did Moira have access to Brooke's computers?"

"Well, she went to Brooke's office sometimes. Oh God, what are you saying? That Moira sent them to herself—something like that?"

"It's possible."

"I can't take all this in."

"Why in heaven's name would they want to kill Rob?" I asked.

"Supposedly the motive was insurance money." Geneva laughed harshly.

"But Brooke really doesn't need the money. How much insurance are we talking about?"

"Five hundred thousand. Frankly, it's really not much of a policy for a man in Rob's position."

The whole concept was astounding given what I knew of Brooke. "Do you believe this?"

"Not for a minute!" Geneva said vehemently. "It's completely ridiculous. I don't know what they found in the emails, but it's not true. I will never believe that. They must be desperate to close this case, that's all I can say. When I saw you pull up, I was actually hoping you had some good news for me. Have you found anything out?"

I filled Geneva in on my conversations with Rita and Steve. "But I think there's more. I think Rita's holding back something. In fact, if I can, I'm going back there this afternoon to try to get it out of her."

"I had no idea there was another man in Moira's life. A black sedan, you say?"

I nodded. "I know that's pretty vague, but the picture I got was of someone far more affluent than the crowd that hangs out at the Alibi. I caught up with Andy the night before last. He was tying one on big time at the Plough."

"What did he have to say for himself?" Geneva's tone was caustic.

"He thought there was someone else in the picture too. He's been suspicious of a guy who's a bartender at Macao. I went there yesterday to try to find him."

"Did you?"

"No. It's a long story but I think the place is a clearing house for heavy drugs."

"Oh, great! I hope to God Moira wasn't involved in anything like that."

"Did Moira ever mention a guy like that?

"Yes. Andy's an idiot—he's talking about Tony. He and Moira were friends, that's all."

I took her statement with a grain of salt. It was quite possible Moira and Tony were something else and Geneva would be the last person to know.

"If they were more than friends, I'll find out," I said.

"How?"

"I don't know yet, but I'll think of a way."

"Oh, Julia, before I forget to tell you ..." I waited. "We got a call today from the Inn. Sally Stark passed away."

A chill ran up my spine. "What? How? I mean ..."

"They had no other information. It was just a courtesy call to let us know. I guess they're running tests or they'll be an autopsy." She looked at me. "What's wrong? You look so upset."

"Uh ... it's nothing. It's just a shock." I didn't want to tell Geneva what Moira said in the car after the wedding. Not that it made a bit of difference in the end, but for right now, it was better left unsaid.

Geneva walked me to the front door, once again checking that her mother was safely in the kitchen. "There's more, Julia. Now that the autopsy finished, we know Moira wasn't pregnant. That's such a relief. Here's the bad part—the bullet that killed her was definitely a .22 caliber."

"Not such good news with David's gun missing, is it?"

"No," she replied. "I'm just panicked about it. So is David. I'd give anything to know who took it from our car. Without that... there's no way to prove one way or the other if it *was* his gun. I just hope they'll release Brooke tomorrow. She should be at the wake. Now I wish we could postpone it, but it might not be possible with all this happening. You'll come tomorrow night?"

"I'll be there. Call me in the meantime if you need anything."

THIRTY

♈ ♉ ♊ ♋ ♌ ♍ ♎ ♏ ♐ ♑ ♒ ♓

THERE WAS STILL TIME to stop by the Alibi. I tried to recall what had been nagging me about my conversation with Rita. When was that, anyway? The days were passing but didn't seem to be in any logical order. The day before yesterday? I cast my mind back. Something I'd asked her and then felt I hit a nerve. I was sure she was holding something back, but then we moved on to another topic. What was it? Suddenly I remembered. I'd asked her if there was anyone else she'd seen Moira with, other than Steve and someone in a black car.

I pulled into the parking lot across the alleyway from the bar and entered from the back door. The place looked dingy even in the bright light of day. Warm afternoon sun filtered through the grime of the front windows. This time two younger men sat at the bar watching a soccer match. Rita leaned against the counter. Her body language was suggestive. One arm rested on the counter, giving the guys a good shot of cleavage. She was doing her best to pull their attention away from the game. Judging by the men's intent expressions, she was wasting her time. The sound from the TV was deafening. She turned and spotted me. Her smile vanished. I'd rained on her parade.

I grabbed a stool and waited for her to approach. She looked disgruntled.

"You haven't told me everything, have you?"

"Whadda ya mean?" Her lips twitched again. This girl should never play poker. "I told you everything I know."

"Come on, Rita. You're holding back. I knew it the other day."

Her jaw tightened. "What do you want from me?"

"I want everything you know. And you haven't told me everything. Maybe you didn't like her. Maybe she was a pain in the ass, but she had a family and they're wonderful people and they're in bad shape. I need your help. I need to know everything you know."

Rita's shoulders slumped. "Oh, Christ." She threw the rag down on the bar and headed for the back door. I followed her. Outside, she pulled a pack of cigarettes out of her apron and lit up, inhaling deeply.

"I asked you if there was anybody else hanging around Moira besides Steve. You didn't answer my question."

"There was somebody else," she admitted grudgingly.

"Who? Was it the guy in the black car?"

"I don't know." She caught my expression. "I don't think so, though." She took another drag from her cigarette and was polite enough to blow it out the side of her mouth away from me.

"Tell me what you don't know then."

"This guy ... he'd sometimes come in and hang out at the bar. Moira used to talk to him, but she didn't seem happy about it."

"Another boyfriend, maybe?"

"Nah. Don't think so. I couldn't figure it out. She'd get real nervous when he came in. Like she was in trouble with him or something." Rita hesitated. "To tell you the truth, I wondered if he wasn't a cop. Dressed casual, but something about him … his body language … I don't know."

"What did he look like? Do you remember?"

Rita shrugged. "Kinda burly, big guy. Reddish hair. Dressed in slacks and a jacket, shiny shoes. A little too clean-cut, I guess." She laughed. "Maybe that's why I got the cop vibe."

There were a lot of men around Moira. This guy at the bar. Steve, and Andy, who took Steve's place. But Andy didn't strike me as the type to drive a black sedan. I couldn't remember his car from the wedding, other than Brooke driving it home because Andy was drinking, but if memory served me, it was a silvery-gray coupe. And if that was the case, then the driver of the black sedan was yet another man, and perhaps the object of Moira's intense attachment.

The Pluto transit had been hitting her natal Venus. Somebody very important was in the picture. Who was Moira's real lover? I knew she had one. I just didn't know who he was.

THIRTY-ONE

♈ ♉ ♊ ♋ ♌ ♍ ♎ ♏ ♐ ♑ ♒ ♓

I PULLED OUT OF the alleyway and headed down Waller. The church where Rita claimed the local drug connection hung out was a block and a half away. I drove as slowly as possible. The only man I spotted was a janitor hosing down the sidewalk in front of the entrance of the church. I was starting to wonder if Zims, the old vet, was a myth. Maybe he conducted business inside the chapel. Frankly, in this neighborhood, nothing would surprise me.

I kept going and headed out on Geary to the Avenues, passing by the Honda shop. Glancing over, I noticed the metal gate was down and the shop was closed. Steve was such an unpleasant character I couldn't imagine what Moira could have seen in him. When I reached my apartment, I parked on the street and ran up the stairs. Wizard padded down the hall to greet me, his bell jingling. I scratched his ears and doled out some food. He circled and rubbed against my legs ecstatically until I dropped the nuggets into his dish.

Something was hovering at the edge of my consciousness, but it still eluded me. Something to do with seeing Michael's dog Harry today. I reached down and rubbed Wiz's tummy. If it hadn't been for Wizard, I might have adopted Harry myself. Although he was better off with Maggie. My schedule is far more erratic and a dog is a lot more work.

I washed up and brushed my hair, adding a little makeup. I checked the apartment and straightened up my desk, making sure I had my tape recorder, water, and tissues at the ready for Matt's session. I slipped into a skirt and fresh sweater, made a small pot of coffee, and then lit a cone of incense, placing it in the belly of the Buddha. Everything was ready.

Matt arrived exactly on time. Once jovial and larger than life, he was now quiet and seemed subdued. The stockbroker façade had dropped away.

"Come on up, Matt. Would you like some coffee or tea?"

"No thanks, Julia. I'm fine." We'd reached the top of the stairway. "By the way, I should 'fess up. I Googled you."

I turned to look at him. "You did what?"

"I hope you don't mind."

I shrugged. "Not at all. I could have offered you some references if you were concerned."

He smiled. "Why didn't you tell me?"

Here it comes. "Tell you what?"

"That you were the astrologer that broke up that preacher's cult last year. I had no idea you were so well-known."

"Oh Matt," I groaned. "Please. I'm not famous, I'm not rich. I'm a pretty good astrologer, but I doubt I'm any better than many others."

"Well I was impressed." He laughed. "Maybe you should see what the world is saying about you."

I led him down the hall to the office. "Frankly, I'd rather not. I'm just grateful I got through it all." I avoided mentioning a former friend who hadn't survived.

"Shall we?" I indicated the client chair. Matt sat and I turned the screen slightly so he could visualize what I was referring to. From my study of his chart, I suspected his problems were romantic.

"Well, Julia, what do you see? I've never done this before, so..." He laughed again. "I guess I'm a little nervous."

"Most people are, the first time, but that'll disappear when you understand more. Now, I see you've just gone through a Saturn transit over your fourth house cusp. That's an important transition. You're concerned with building a more secure foundation in your life. Financially and emotionally, you're ready. However, I also see there's been a recent disappointment. Several months ago. A romantic disappointment. Saturn by transit opposed your Venus and made a hard angle to your Moon. That must have been quite lonely and tough."

Matt nodded. "Amazing. You're absolutely right. You know, I really hustle to make good investments for my clients, and I'm doing all right. But I want to do more."

I ignored his effort to change the subject. "I think that's brilliant and very much in line with Saturn's transit over the fourth house cusp. But let's talk about your emotional life."

Matt cleared his throat, obviously not so comfortable.

I waited. He didn't respond. "There was a breakup, I assume?"

"Yes. I got involved with someone who... wasn't free, and I... I guess I got in over my head. I feel really bad about it. I'm still having trouble with it and I can't seem to get her out of my mind."

"Do you have her birth information? Perhaps we could have a quick look. It might give us some insight."

"Only her birth date, no time or anything. It's October third. She's a Libra."

I started to plug the information into the program and stopped, my fingers hovering above the keyboard. He had given me Brooke's birth date, fresh in my mind from Geneva's notes.

"Matt, I have to stop you. I think I know who this woman is."

"You do?" He looked quite surprised.

"Geneva is my client, and she gave me her family's information."

"Oh. Oh, I'm sorry. I'm so embarrassed." He wiped his forehead. "I just don't know who I can talk to. It's been awful. It started when she and Rob were having trouble, about a year ago. It didn't last very long though. I met her at Geneva and David's. I've thought maybe I couldn't forget about her because I feel guilty, or because I know it's taboo, you know what I mean?"

I nodded. "Forbidden fruit and all that stuff. Look, because Geneva's my client, I really can't talk about Brooke's chart. I can look at the composite between your chart and hers, however."

I clicked on the button that would generate a chart of midpoints to describe the relationship and studied it a moment. I turned the screen toward Matt again so I could point out the placements I was talking about. "There's a twelfth house Sun. That is not positive. Not in a composite or relationship chart. Either a secret relationship or something that can't quite come out into the light of day. And that Sun has an opposition from Uranus near the seventh house cusp."

"What does all that mean?"

"Even if Brooke had been free when you met, there would have been difficulties. It's just the very nature of the relationship. Some other circumstance would have existed that wouldn't have allowed this relationship to 'come out,' and there would always be an instability about it. With Saturn transiting over your fourth house cusp, you're looking for something solid, someone you can build a future with."

Matt was silent.

"I'm sorry. It wasn't her and never will be. Not under any circumstances." Perhaps harsh words, but a reality I'd had to face in different circumstances.

"You're right. I know you're right. I've wracked my brain over this thing. I know I have to forget her."

I couldn't ask the question directly, but I was fairly certain Matt had not heard of Brooke's arrest, and unless I wanted to be the astrological town gossip, I wasn't about to inform him. He would probably be attending Moira's wake. I was sure he'd hear of Brooke's arrest soon enough.

"Do you see anyone coming along in the near future?" he asked.

"Let's have a look." I went back to his chart and used a timer to advance his progressions. "In about a year, you'll be in a committed relationship. That's definite. It's *possible* you'll meet her in about four months' time, when Venus progresses to your natal Sun. Can't guarantee that part, it's an educated guess, but you've got the next year to be single."

"Whoa. That's scary. I'll have to think about that one."

I smiled. "Be careful what you wish for."

Matt left, much more cheerful than when he arrived. I closed up his folder and filed it away. I was sure no one suspected his relationship with Brooke, and I certainly wasn't free to blab about it anyway, even if I were so inclined. I also didn't want to be the one to tell him that the police believed Brooke and Moira had exchanged emails plotting Rob's death. It was simply too ridiculous.

Was Geneva correct in suspecting Andy? He could be guilty, whether he'd pulled the trigger or not. If Moira had found out that her identity was being used for real estate deals, maybe she was getting ready to blow the whistle on Andy or his boss. If so, the possibility of jail time could be a very compelling motive for murder. Dan hated Rob and would blame him for Moira's death no matter whose gun had killed her. Rob, on the other hand, suspected a plot against Brooke on the part of Moira and Dan to get access to the money in Brooke's trust fund. If anything, that was a motive that made monetary sense.

I couldn't think what else I could do. I could try again to locate Tony, the bartender at Macao, although the idea of returning there gave me the shudders. Maybe Zims really did exist, but what information he could offer would be dubious if not downright suspect. The guy was a drug dealer, after all.

I could even call Detective Ianello and tell him what I suspected about Andy and turn over Moira's tax form to the police. Had those papers we found stuck behind the broken drawer been misplaced, or had Moira hidden them there? Had she been aware her identity was being used all along, or had she recently discovered what Andy was doing? If there were records on her computer, the police might already have figured all that out. Maybe Andy was completely innocent of any involvement with Moira's difficulties. Maybe the tax form listing real estate had absolutely nothing to do with him. But Dan's comment about Andy's under-the-table real estate deals was too much of a coincidence. It was time to find out.

THIRTY-TWO

♈ ♉ ♊ ♋ ♌ ♍ ♎ ♏ ♐ ♑ ♒ ♓

ANDY'S BUILDING ON COLE, a two-story, spruced-up Victorian, was painted yellow and divided into four apartments. The front door was an old-fashioned double door with beveled glass panes. I pushed the button that said *A. DeWinter*. A moment later, the door-knob vibrated in my hand. I entered the hallway. A door opened on the left of the small lobby and Andy looked out, surprised to see me.

"Julia!"

"Hi Andy. I just stopped by on the off chance you'd be home. I hope you don't mind?" I was just observing the niceties. At this point, I didn't care if he did mind.

"Not at all, come on in. I'm always here. Most of my work is book-keeping for my clients." He held the door open for me. "Listen, I'm really sorry about the other night. I was a real mess. I'm sure you can understand."

Andy's apartment consisted of a living room that faced the street through tall ceiling-high bowed windows, with more than likely a bedroom, kitchen, and bath at the other end of a long hallway. A large desk faced the front windows, piled with folders, more papers, and a laptop. Andy stepped over to the desk and closed the laptop. I guess he didn't want any snooping on my part.

"Have a seat. What can I do for you?"

"Detective Ianello stopped by my apartment the other day."

Andy groaned. "Yeah, he's been here too. Asking a lot of the same questions over and over, the same ones they asked me downtown."

"He seemed to be particularly interested in what you were wearing that night. I told him you had on jeans and a jacket."

"That's right. I don't know why he thought it was strange. I don't wear pajamas. Moira pulled off my clothes and I passed out. When I came to, I just grabbed the closest thing. It was cold that night. I think he thinks I was lurking around in the backyard or something. He kept asking me if I knew that David kept a gun in the trunk of his car."

"Did you?"

"Nah. I wasn't paying any attention. I may have seen David showing Rob something in the garage the night before the wedding, but it didn't really register. At least I don't think so. I didn't see a gun. Not that I'm conscious of."

"Who's the guy at Macao you said Moira was very friendly with?"

Andy's mouth twitched slightly. "I don't remember his name."

I waited.

"I don't. Really. I just know he bartends there, and I know he goes to Berkeley 'cause Moira never shut up about him. She was always going on about how nice he was and how smart he was and all that crap." Andy sat on his desk chair and crossed his arms over his chest.

"So I guess you do bookkeeping for the owner of Macao. And you're involved in some real estate deals too."

Andy became very still. "Who told you that?"

"Dan mentioned it."

"Dan's got it all wrong." Andy rose from his chair and walked over to the desk. He started rearranging the piles of papers. "Besides I'm not licensed by the state to broker any real estate deals. Dan was mistaken."

"I see." I did see. He was lying through his teeth.

"Maybe you and Moira were investing in real estate?" I said quietly.

"That's ridiculous." He answered too quickly. "I don't own any real estate, and as far as I know, neither did Moira. Is there anything else, Julia? Because I'm real busy right now. Got a lot of work to get done." A small tic had started under his left eye.

I thought of Geneva and the Learys and what they were going through. I had no more patience with anybody's lies. My anger was going to boil to the surface and I wasn't sure I could contain it. Somehow I forced my voice to remain calm. "I think you're a damn liar, Andy. I found a tax form at her apartment. A form that proved she was declaring real estate investments. I checked out those properties."

He glared at me. "I have no idea what the hell you're talking about."

"You were using her identity, weren't you? Did she find out? Is that what you were really arguing about at the wedding?"

"That's crazy." He moved awkwardly and his arm collided with a stack of papers on the desk. They fell to the floor, scattering in all directions. "I think you should leave now." He advanced toward me. Involuntarily, I took two steps back. "Who do you think you are, coming here, accusing me of this shit!"

"Did she threaten to blow your cover?

The blood had drained from Andy's face. His complexion was ashen. "How can you say that? I would never have hurt her. Never!"

"And your pals at Macao? What about them?"

He gritted his teeth. "Get out! Get the hell out of here. Before I do something I'll be sorry about."

I didn't need another invitation. I was out the door in three steps, slamming it behind me. Somehow I reached the sidewalk. Outside on the street, I looked back at his front windows. He stood there staring at me, a phone held against his ear. I felt his gaze boring into me as I headed for my car. My hands were shaking. If Andy had shot Moira, or if his dealings had caused her death, I wanted to tear his throat out myself.

THIRTY-THREE

♈ ♉ ♊ ♋ ♌ ♍ ♎ ♏ ♐ ♑ ♒ ♓

I RAMMED MY KEY into the ignition and drove into the park. I was on auto pilot, not even sure where I was heading. I kept taking deep breaths until my head cleared. My cell phone rang as I passed the Conservatory of Flowers. I pulled over and hit the brakes, making a conscious effort to pull myself back into the here and now. It was Gale.

"Julia, get over here. Right now." I could hear Cheryl in the background giggling.

"What's going on?"

Cheryl grabbed the phone. "We're celebrating. We won. We won." She crowed cheerfully.

Gale came back on the line. "The judge ruled today. Sam just called us. And Frank's so upset he's been leaving nasty voicemails all afternoon on Cheryl's phone. He should've had a lawyer. But I guess he figured dental school qualified him to practice law." Gale shrieked with laughter.

"What's the final outcome?"

"Cheryl gets half the house, so she'll have enough to buy a nice little apartment in the city near us, *and* half of Frank's sizeable pension fund. Pretty cool, huh? Don't know how he's going to support his underage pregnant girlfriend, though." Gale hooted with laughter once again. I could hear glasses clinking in the background. "Anyway, we're celebrating tonight at my place. You *have* to come over right now. I've ordered out for sushi and we're having wine."

"I'll come now." I didn't trust myself to be alone.

———

Gale's condo is a corner unit in a sleek high-rise on Russian Hill. Her years in real estate had served her well. Two sides of the apartment have large windows overlooking the northern part of the city. The view toward the east is anchored by Coit Tower and Telegraph Hill. To the north is the Bay with the Golden Gate Bridge an illuminated marker on the far west. The sun had set and the lights of the city were twinkling below. It was breathtaking, but I had to admit to a teeny bit of vertigo and the fact that I'd be terrified in an earthquake.

"Honey, don't worry," Gale always says. "These buildings are built to *sway* in an earthquake. If anything happens, just hold on to a doorjamb and try not to lose your balance. They're a lot safer than the older buildings."

I pulled into the carriage area and waved to the valet. He came rushing over and opened my door. "Hi, James. How are you?"

"I'm fine. Good to see you again." As the regular valet for guests on weeknights, James was used to my little red Geo and kind enough not to sneer at it, as another valet and a doorman had done. The cars that lived and visited here were priced at least fifty-thousand dollars more. I'm attached to my little car, though, and wouldn't trade it in for anything. It's dependable, always starts, is easy on gas, and has gotten me out of a few tough scrapes.

Gale and Cheryl were laughing hysterically when I reached the front door of the condo. I could hear them as soon as I stepped off the elevator. I rang the bell and Gale opened the door a moment later. She was dressed in a flowy sort of caftan-like outfit she'd picked up in Morocco and was decked out with large pieces of handmade African jewelry.

"Did you have to bribe the whole tribe for that?" I was referring to her necklace made of hunks of stone and copper strung together with leather strips.

"Oh, shut up," she laughed. "Come on in and help Cheryl celebrate. Kick off your shoes. The sushi's already here."

I took her advice and settled into the cushions with a large glass of wine. She passed me a tray of sushi. Not my favorite thing to eat. I always worry it might be dressed with poisonous blowfish, but I was so hungry, I wolfed down several rounds. Spelling each other when one ran out of breath, Cheryl and Gale happily, and somewhat tipsily, gave me a blow-by-blow account of the judge's order. Frank and his girlfriend had been charged with contempt of court. He was released on his own recognizance later in the day, but would now have to find a lawyer and appear in court again.

"Julia, I've been so scared, not knowing how I was going to survive or make a living, and I was so intimidated by Frank, I couldn't think straight."

"Be happy. You're starting a brand new life, and you don't deserve to walk away with nothing."

Cheryl was thrilled with the settlement and, hugging Gale, broke down in grateful tears. Gale was a born mother, and I knew she was secretly thrilled to have engineered Cheryl's successful divorce. "I still can't believe what he did. I actually fell for it. I'm so ashamed," Cheryl went on. Tears came into her eyes. "I guess I just needed to see one more time what a selfish ass he is."

We were silent for a few moments, sad that Cheryl had been so vulnerable to Frank's manipulations. Gale finally said, "So Julia, where were you today? Tell us what's going on. Bring us up to date."

I decided not to mention my confrontation with Andy. I didn't want to hear anyone's advice at that moment, nor did I want to rain on Cheryl's parade. "You've never met Geneva, my friend from school…"

"No, but you've mentioned her often. Cheryl told me part of the story. I can't believe you know these people. I mean, it's really shocking. And you were there."

I grimaced. "I truly wish I hadn't been."

"So what do you think? What do the stars have to say?"

I shook my head. "Can't talk about that at all, you know that."

"Can you talk about the murder?"

"I can tell you what happened. It's no secret." I gave Gale the condensed version of events, editing out my questioning of Rita and Andy. They listened, rapt and wide-eyed.

Cheryl spoke first. "So now the police know the murder weapon was a .22 caliber gun. So it definitely wasn't the husband?"

"Couldn't be. Rob's gun was only fired once, and that bullet was lodged in the opposite wall.

"And the second gun is still missing? That's the one that belonged to your friend's husband?"

"David's gun is missing, but there's no proof it was the gun that killed Moira, although it certainly looks suspicious. The police have torn the house and the entire property apart and can't find any other gun. So, it's likely that someone else was in the garage with Moira that night. Someone who took off with the gun."

"Did everyone come running at once?"

"I was sleeping in the den above the garage, so the shots were probably much louder where I was. Ashley, their little girl, sleeps on the third floor and didn't wake up at all, thankfully."

"So who wasn't where they were supposed to be?" Gale cut straight to the chase.

I explained the layout of the house and the old servants' stairway. "It's possible someone could have returned to an upstairs bedroom from the back stairs. They'd have to be pretty quick, though. It's also possible Moira was planning to take off in Andy's car, or she was meeting someone in the garage who we don't know about. Mary was standing on the stairway when I went through the foyer. Matt came down the stairs a few moments later."

"You didn't see anyone else?"

"Not at first. Matt and I had just decided to go investigate, but the door that leads down into the garage was locked. Then Rob opened that door from the other side to tell us he'd shot someone. We followed him back down to the garage and … I was in a state of shock, I guess. I wasn't watching who was there and who wasn't."

"Think about it now."

"Well, Matt was right by my side, and Rob of course was already there. Mary was at the bottom of the stairs in the garage, but I didn't actually notice Andy until the ambulance took Moira and Brooke away. And then Dan showed up very quickly. Andy had called him."

"So any of the others could have been in the garage and come back into the house through the yard and the back stairway, couldn't they?

"I suppose so. But then how could they have gotten rid of the gun? There wouldn't have been time. The house and neighborhood have all been searched. The police probably quickly realized two different guns were involved."

"And the missing gun? Could it have been hidden somewhere?"

"I don't see how. The search was very thorough. And it still hasn't turned up. The real question is why? Why would anybody want to kill Moira?"

"What does the family think?"

"Geneva suspects Andy because he and Moira fought so much. Dan dislikes Rob intensely and tends to think he's behind this somehow. Rob ... he had a theory I won't bore you with, and I have no idea what Brooke's theory is.

"What do you think of the husband?" Cheryl asked.

"Rob? He's very good-looking and seems to be a concerned guy. He's really torn up about this. It must have been just awful for him to think he shot his wife's sister."

"I'll bet he's a phony. I'll bet he's got a girlfriend on the side." Cheryl was now definitely slurring her words. "But if you're involved in this, you better include me. I'm ready for some adventure in my life now."

I laughed. "Don't get your hopes up. I don't have much more I can do to ferret out dirt on Moira. In fact, Geneva's still trying to find birth information for Rob. I don't know if she can get Andy's information. I certainly can't, since I just had a rather nasty confrontation with him." It wasn't the moment to tell them about

Macao or the drug shipment, not yet, nor my suspicion that Andy was involved in money laundering schemes. Gale would have a fit and would lecture me mercilessly. I wouldn't tell Geneva yet either. I needed time to cool off and think clearly.

"You mean you haven't seen their charts yet?" Cheryl asked, amazed.

"Geneva will call me soon. She's trying to get the info."

"How boring," Cheryl answered, trying her best to land her wine glass safely on the coffee table.

Gale piped up. "Look, you two, I want you to stay here tonight. You both look exhausted and you've both been drinking. Stay over, okay? We can grab some breakfast down the street at the wharf tomorrow."

I was too tired to argue. Gale put Cheryl in the guest bedroom, which, with its own bathroom, was a safer bet. She really had polished off several glasses of wine. I crashed on the sofa in the office, and fortunately the sushi settled well in my stomach. I only hoped the thoughts rattling around in my head didn't result in nightmares.

THIRTY-FOUR

♈ ♉ ♊ ♋ ♌ ♍ ♎ ♏ ♐ ♑ ♒ ♓

THE NEXT MORNING, WE took my car. Parking near the wharf is difficult at best, even on a weekday—we stood a better chance of finding a spot with my Geo. From the crest of Russian Hill, we had a panoramic view of the bay. The sky was cloudless and the deep blue of the Bay sparkled like scattered diamonds as wind currents ruffled the waters. The buildings of Alcatraz were stark white against the bare cliffs of Marin.

I trailed a cable car, full to capacity, and did my best to keep one set of wheels off the metal tracks and not skid down the hill. We descended to Bay Street, past Aquatic Park and the cable car turnaround. The tourist season was in full swing. The park was already crowded with portable stalls selling souvenirs and jewelry, a juggler doing tricks and a guitar player with his case open for donations. We cut down Jefferson to Millie's Crepe House.

We were the first customers of the morning and settled in at an outdoor table, perched on a small pier a few feet above the water line. We were bundled up in sweaters Gale had loaned us. The smell of fresh fish and brine filled the air and seagulls swooped and cried above us, ready to dive for crumbs. Cheryl and Gale ordered omelets and I chose the blueberry crepes. We dug in as soon as our waiter arrived with our orders.

Gale sprinkled salt on her dish. "I've got to go into the shop today and organize some things for the psychic fair next week, but I want you to stay in touch with me."

"Sure. Any special reason?" I asked.

"I have a distinct feeling there's more you're not telling me. I think you're more involved than you should be."

"Gale, I haven't even set up all the charts."

"Yeah, well, I know you. You're like a pit bull once you get an idea in your head, so just be careful. Some of these people may not be as nice as you think they are. One of them is already dead."

"Whatever happens, Julia, you can count me in," Cheryl offered.

Gale turned to her. "And you too. You're a babe in the woods. You'll get yourself in trouble. I just know it. Now that you're a gay divorcée, you have to be careful. There are a lot of sharks out there, not just in the Bay."

"Yes, Mom," Cheryl replied, smiling.

It was then I remembered the precious package I'd been carrying around. "Oh, I completely forgot. I meant to show this to you both last night, but it slipped my mind." I pulled out the sapphire and platinum bracelet, now back in its Rochecault box. I showed it to Gale.

"Did you say this woman was a waitress at a bar?"

"Pretty strange, huh?"

"Well, somebody with some serious bucks bought this for her then."

"That's what I want to find out. I haven't shown it to Brooke yet, but I ran it by Rob, and he didn't recognize it. Geneva's afraid that Moira might have stolen it."

Cheryl leaned back in her chair, sipping coffee. "I know where this came from. I know the shop."

"Rochecault, right?" I said.

"Yup. I have a friend who works there. Very pricey place. It's on Maiden Lane near the Gucci shop. Maybe she can tell us who bought it. I'll go down there with you if you want."

"That'd be great."

Gale turned to Cheryl. "Don't forget about the open house on Sunday. I've spoken to the realtor and she's expecting us."

Cheryl nodded. "I haven't forgotten. I'm just not sure…"

"I'm sure," Gale said. "Julia, I want you to come and see it too. I really want Cheryl to get this apartment. I think it's a great deal. Just right for her. Fabulous location and now she'll have some money to work with."

Cheryl groaned. "Look, I appreciate what you're doing, but I don't think I'm ready for this yet."

"You're ready, honey. Don't doubt that." Gale gave me a penetrating look. "And as for you…" She trailed off without finishing her sentence. I avoided her look and didn't reply.

We settled our bill and clambered back in the car. Traffic was heavier now. We escaped the tourist fray at the wharf and headed back up the hill. I pulled into the circular drive to drop Gale off. James wasn't on duty at this hour and the doorman stared at us as though we'd taken a wrong turn.

"Snobs," I muttered under my breath.

Gale waved at the doorman, who, recognizing her, hotfooted it to the passenger door and quickly opened it.

"I think I'll have a word with him. He better treat you right when you pull up to my house." Gale climbed out and Cheryl moved into the passenger seat. Gale turned and leaned down to the passenger window. "Remember what I said, Julia. I don't want to see either of you in any trouble."

We nodded and smiled.

She shook her head in frustration. "Ciao. Kisses." She waved back at us as she entered her building.

I appreciated her concern, but I was slightly miffed that she considered me such an idiot I wouldn't be able to stay out of trouble. It was a good thing I hadn't mentioned getting locked in the storeroom at Macao with illegal substances.

We exited the semi-circular drive and turned toward town. Cheryl was on her cell, hoping to reach her friend at the jewelry store. She clicked her phone shut. "We're in luck. Shahin's there today. I told her we'd be in to see her."

I followed Bush Street down to Union Square. The square rises above the bordering streets in a mound topped with a concrete plaza and a spire commemorating the Civil War. The regular denizens were in attendance, but a milling crowd was setting up booths for an art fair. An elderly man bundled in sweaters sat on a bench feeding pigeons. At another bench, a teenage couple was locked in a clutch. Cars had lined up to enter the parking garage under the square and I joined the queue. Pedestrians jaywalked around the car as we inched forward. When we finally neared the entrance, I breathed a sigh of relief the lot wasn't full.

Maiden Lane is a narrow street between Grant and Stockton that runs into Union Square and lays claim to some of the priciest shops in the city. We waited at the traffic light and hurried across the street. Rochecault was halfway down the narrow street, next to a restaurant with outdoor tables. Unusual estate pieces and handmade creations were displayed in the window. We stepped into the front vestibule and Cheryl rang the bell. A young woman with short dark hair looked up from the interior of the shop and pressed a buzzer allowing us entry through a second door.

"Cheryl! Hi." The woman waved from behind the counter.

"Shahin, this is my friend Julia."

She smiled widely and shook my hand. Her complexion was smooth and dark. She had a brilliantly white smile and a wide generous mouth with full lips.

"Hi, Julia. Cheryl tells me you have something you think was purchased here?"

"I'm fairly sure. It belongs to a friend who found it in her sister's apartment. We were hoping you might be able to tell us anything you know."

"Let's have a look."

I dug through my purse and opened the box once more, spreading it out for Shahin's perusal. She took a jeweler's loupe from a drawer under the counter.

"Oh. Yes. I've seen this before."

"Do you remember who bought it?"

She thought for a moment. "It does look very familiar. But I can't recall right now. We sell estate jewelry and one-of-a-kind pieces like this, sometimes made on the premises. This design is unusual, and the precious gems and semi-precious—two different tones of blue—

give it a lot of depth. The platinum too. It's beautiful. Let me ask Amir—he's one of the owners. He might remember." She walked through a door into the back of the shop and returned a few moments later.

"Yes. He remembers the piece. He said it was sold a few months ago. I'll check our ledger book." Once again, Shahin walked to the end of the counter and disappeared behind a screened-off area. She returned immediately carrying a large, bound ledger.

"You write everything down?"

Shahin nodded. "We have computer records too, but the guys here are kind of old-fashioned. They like to keep a handwritten record as well."

She opened the book to early March and ran her finger down the columns. After five pages, she spotted it.

"Here it is. See, here's the description. Here's the jeweler's name and the date. April 5th. It was sold for $5,500."

"With a credit card?" I held my breath.

"No. Cash. Not even a personal check. Wow!"

"Is that the buyer's name in the last column?"

"Yes, we do keep a record in case there's a repair needed, and we send out reminder cards when holidays are coming up, that kind of thing. We can't give out customer information though. I'm sorry."

Shahin looked at Cheryl and gave her a wink. She jotted down a name and address on a pad of paper and slid it across the counter toward Cheryl. "Sorry Cheryl, I can't help you with this," she added in a slightly louder voice for the benefit of the man working in the rear of the store.

"That's all right. Thanks anyway. We appreciate your time," I replied.

Shahin buzzed us out of the shop. On the sidewalk, Cheryl pulled the slip of paper out of her pocket.

"Wait. Not here." I spotted outdoor tables next door. "Let's get a cappuccino." We grabbed a table and a waiter immediately swooped down and took our order.

"That was awfully trusting of your friend. How do you know her?"

"We were in a French cooking class together a few years ago and we've stayed in touch since then."

"Now let's see what's on that paper."

Cheryl had stuck the note in her purse. She dug it out and passed it over, peering over my shoulder.

"'L. Barron, 443 Vallejo Street.'"

"Do you think that's a phony name and address?" Cheryl asked.

"Who knows? We don't even know if it's a man or a woman."

"We could go ring the bell and see who answers."

"And if there really is an L. Barron, and he or she calls the police? What if Moira stole it from him or her? I really don't want to bring any more trouble down on the Learys."

Cheryl was thoughtful for a moment. "You said Geneva didn't recognize it. So either Moira stole it somewhere or she had a wealthy benefactor. How do you know this sugar daddy wasn't a sugar mommy?"

"I hadn't thought of that, but anything's possible. If you're going to steal jewelry from someone, you usually wouldn't be able to get the box it came in too, would you?"

"No, I guess not," Cheryl agreed. "And Moira herself could have bought it and used a phony name and address. What about this Andy guy she was dating?"

Our waiter arrived with our cappuccinos. I waited until he moved away before answering. "There are some suspicious things about his financial state. But he doesn't appear to have a lot of money."

"Wealthy people don't necessarily walk around with that kind of cash, either. Of course, it's the best way of not leaving a paper trail." Cheryl sipped carefully at the foam at the top of her cup. "Listen, maybe I'll buzz through the Gucci shop and browse a bit, now that I'm here and have some bucks coming to me. Want to join me?"

"Love to, but I'm going to try to visit Brooke."

"That sounds depressing."

I nodded in response. "No doubt, but she's still in the city jail. Although Geneva said if they were going to hold her, they could move her someplace else. And speaking of depressing, I'll be at the wake tonight, but it won't be late. If you're free, do you feel like a drink after? There's a place I'd like to check out."

"I'm game. Give me a call later."

We finished our drinks and parted on the corner of Maiden Lane. I headed back to the parking garage and retrieved my car. I drove across Market, turning on Howard, and followed it to 7th Street. A dirt parking lot nearby charged only twenty dollars for the day. What a bargain. This was a San Francisco far removed from the glittering heights of Telegraph Hill or Nob Hill and the breathtaking views of the Bay. The closest water was China Basin, once only neglected piers built on sunken ships and filled land. Market Street cuts a diagonal swath through the city and has always been the dividing line between the right and the wrong sides of town. As time passed and the land south of Market, now called SOMA, became more and more valuable, the developers have taken over, building a civic center, a new museum, and condos in an area called "South Beach" in realtorese speak.

Granted, there were fewer vacant lots and industrial storage properties now, and office space once housed on Union Street had slowly moved to upscale new quarters around China Basin, but the heart of the area had not changed. Truly organic neighborhoods take time and aren't thrown up quickly by developers. At night, few residents walk the streets in spite of the occasional restaurant or club opening. In my opinion, the city still psychically resists spreading over that boundary.

The wide stairs of the jail at 425 7th Street were thick with bird droppings. Garbage swirled on the sidewalk and against the curbs. I pushed through the door of the squat gray stone building and stood in line while visitors placed items on the moving mini-tarmac of the security station, much like an airport. I passed through the metal detector. After that, a California Department of Corrections officer held out a large device like a padded microphone and passed it all around me, up and down, to check for weapons.

Once through, I filled out a form with my information and the name of the prisoner I was visiting. I was then allowed to enter a large waiting room, painted in two-tone industrial green with benches along the sides of the walls and parallel rows of benches filling the center of the room. One wall had narrow rectangular windows, covered with metal bars, just below ceiling level and at least twelve feet from the floor. The entire room was illuminated by neon-tubed light fixtures hanging from the ceiling on chains. The overwhelming odor in the room was disinfectant overlaid with fear and sweat.

Perhaps thirty people were waiting for their visit with a prisoner just as I was. Every ten minutes, a guard entered the room through a locked double door and called out a name. Someone would rise, raise their hand, and move quickly toward the guard and through the door.

The time passed excruciatingly slowly. Under the pallid glow of neon lights, we all looked like prisoners of war. Most of the waiting were women—wives, mothers, girlfriends, and sisters of the incarcerated. Two tattooed men in droopy gangbanger pants who sat together looked like they belonged on the other side of the door.

After an hour's wait, a female guard called my name. I followed her down a long hallway and through another set of doors. I was wanded once more, my purse and jacket were taken from me, and I was asked to pass through yet another metal detector. Then I was shown into a small narrow room, one wall fitted with bulletproof glass and a long vinyl counter running under the glass. A telephone receiver hung on either side of the glass. I took the molded plastic chair on my side of the partition and waited. Eventually, the door opened and a female guard escorted Brooke into the room. She looked even thinner but still moved with grace. She stopped short when she saw me and hesitated. Then she sat down slowly on her side of the plastiglas and picked up the telephone.

"Julia..."

"I hope you don't mind that I came to see you," I said.

Brooke's normally pale highlighted hair looked heavy and matted under the neon lighting. She wore no makeup and only a two-piece bright orange shirt and pants, with no belt. Her skin was strained tight over the bones of her face and seemed almost translucent. She looked down at her hands, clenched together on the counter.

"No, I appreciate your coming." She stifled a sob. "It doesn't look good for me."

"Don't say that. If you're not guilty, stick to your guns."

"Oh, Julia. Attorneys and prosecutors and judges play just as many games with your life in this world as in the corporate world. Just insisting on your innocence doesn't cut any ice. There's not one woman in here who's guilty. Didn't you know, we're all innocent?" she said with a bitter laugh.

"What does your husband have to say?"

"Rob's been fantastic. Thank God. He knows I love him and I'd never have done anything so ridiculous."

"What do you know about these emails the police supposedly have?"

Brooke's shoulders slumped. "About a year ago, Rob and I were fighting a lot … we were even talking about a divorce." She twisted her fingers nervously. "Moira, I remember, sent an email that said something like 'Let's bump him off for the life insurance,' but she meant it as a *joke*. I know she did. I don't think I even responded to it. It was just at a time when she knew we were fighting and maybe talking about going our separate ways."

"But weren't there others?"

"Yes. That's what I don't understand. Moira would have had to be the one to send the other emails. But I can't imagine her doing that."

"Geneva said she used to visit you at your office."

"Oh, sure, she'd come by to see me. A few times she brought Ashley in, that sort of thing. I've tried to remember … I know she used my computer sometimes to look things up."

"Did anyone else have access to your office computer?"

"No. No one outside the company, certainly."

"What about your computer at home?"

"Well ... yes. Moira used it occasionally."

"What did the emails say?"

"They were really ... other than the one that was obviously a joke ... they were ambiguous for the most part. The police confronted me with them. They said things like, 'When are you going to wake up, what are you waiting for?' And then supposedly I wrote back stuff like, 'You'll have to help me. I can't do it alone.' And another one from Moira said, 'I know you want to get rid of him. You let me know what you need from me.' But I swear, Julia, I know I didn't write those—at least I don't *remember* writing them. And I can't imagine why Moira would write those things to me. But it had to be Moira. Who else had access to my house and my office? It breaks my heart to think that, but it's the only explanation. Moira loved me, I know she did. But she resented me too. In her mind, I was everything she would never be. This was something she did to herself. It wasn't the way I felt about her. I loved her with all my heart. My baby sister who could never seem to find her way. So no matter what I did or didn't do, I was always wrong." Brooke's voice broke, but she took a deep breath and continued. "Julia, the only person with a motive for killing Moira was Andy. They fought a lot. I know my sister was out of control sometimes, but they had some violent arguments. Believe me, if anyone in our circle is guilty, it's Andy."

I did my best to gauge the depth of her honesty. I have a tendency to take people at face value. I've learned the hard way to reserve judgment. After all, I didn't really know Brooke Ramer. Could she be a manipulative, cold-blooded woman who could set her sister up to commit a murder? Had she planned to make Moira the scapegoat for removing an inconvenient husband? I remembered her Sun-Venus conjunction in Libra in the eleventh house. I just couldn't believe her capable of anything so dreadful, and neither could her family. Moira, on the other hand, had always been in trouble. It made much more sense to imagine Moira preparing a scenario that would cause trouble between Brooke and Rob. Motivated by resentment and anger, she might not imagine the consequences of her actions.

"I'm so glad Rob's been supportive."

Brooke nodded. "We worked all that stuff out last year. But at the time, it was tough. I felt like we were facing a divorce."

"I heard Rob wanted another child. A son."

"He and his first wife weren't able to have any children, so it was important to him, but..." She trailed off. "I just didn't want to have any more children. We have Ashley and she's older now, and she's fine as an only child. I felt if I had another child, it wouldn't be possible for me to keep up my work schedule, and my career is very important to me... was..." She laughed bitterly. "I guess that may be moot right now, huh?"

"Rob was a widower when you married?"

"Sondra's death was terrible for him. He stayed very close to her sister Pamela, though. She thinks the world of Rob. He even gave her half of Sondra's life insurance money. He felt terrible about what happened, especially since the two sisters had no other family."

"That was very generous of him."

"Yes, I know. We've stayed in touch with Pamela. We always invite her to holiday dinners with the family. Rob doesn't want her to feel that she's alone in the world." Brooke's eyes took on a faraway look. "You know, this time last year, we were on a boat trip. Funny how one day, one minute, can change every aspect of your life."

"You have a boat? That's lovely."

"Oh, we don't. It belongs to a friend of Rob's. He keeps it moored in the Marina, but we have the use of it whenever we want. His friend travels a lot for his business and can't really keep an eye on it, so he likes us to use it whenever we can. It's a good-sized sloop with a full cockpit and galley. Rob was saying just yesterday that when this thing's sorted out, he wants to plan a trip." She smiled sadly.

"I can't believe they're denying you bail."

Brooke shook her head. "The police play politics too. Rob worked in the DA's office before he went to a private practice and I'm the editor of a high-profile magazine. The prosecutors want to look like they're doing their job. But we're really not that wealthy, at least not in terms of cash. I'm afraid the legal fees will eat most of it up."

A buzzer sounded and the same female guard opened a door behind Brooke. Her shoulders sagged.

"That's it. Our time's all gone. Thanks for coming, Julia." She attempted a smile without much success as she was led away.

The wind whipped dust and trash up in the gutters as I left the building. I walked along the sidewalk, heading back to the parking lot. It was only mid-afternoon, but the air had turned cold. I wrapped my jacket tightly around me and walked as fast as I could through the lot, trying to remember where I'd parked. The parking guard had collected his fee in advance and now had disappeared. I unlocked the car and climbed in out of the wind, then navigated over the metal teeth set in concrete at the exit and headed home.

The visit to Brooke had been draining. I couldn't begin to imagine what she was feeling, locked up as she was. If she were found guilty, her life would be over—her career, her marriage, and her relationship with her daughter. Even if she was eventually released, how could she rebuild a life? The only blessing she had at this point was the fact that her husband, and her family, believed her innocent.

I maneuvered out of downtown and as I drove west on Geary, I made a quick decision and moved into the left-hand lane. I headed toward Waller and passed by the Alibi bar. I drove a few more blocks, pulled a U-turn, and cruised down the street one more time. A couple came out of a bookstore. A girl with purple hair rearranged a sign in the window of one of the tattoo parlors and some teenagers were hanging out in front of a smoke shop.

I finally spotted him. A man in a wheelchair in front of the church near the corner of Clayton. I parked at Stanyan and walked back. He was corpulent, perhaps early sixties. His legs ended at his knees, but his arm muscles bulged under a sweatshirt. He wore several layers of clothing. His face was round and babyish with a few days growth of orange-and-gray stubble. Aviator glasses covered his eyes. A baseball cap was pulled down over long greasy hair. His wheelchair was a complicated affair with hand controls and several rubber wheels. I hoped he wasn't carrying any weapons anywhere in his gear. On his lap was a stack of pamphlets. As I came closer, I could see they were religious tracts.

"Are you here to talk about Jesus?" he cried out to me as I crossed the street. I stopped and watched him carefully. The curb was so deep we were almost eye to eye.

"No, and I don't want to see him, either."

He laughed, throwing his head back and treating me to the sight of a row of decayed teeth. "Well, lady, if you're not into visiting Jesus, then why come to me?"

"Are you Zims?"

"At your service." He leered at me.

"I'm here about Moira Leary."

His face darkened. "What about her? Are you a cop?"

"Hardly. Her family wants to know."

"Crazy bitch. I heard what happened. Doesn't surprise me."

"What was she using?"

"Mostly coke, but she was movin' over to meth. Nobody woulda needed to kill her. She woulda taken care of that herself. Of course, you understand I just heard about this. On the street, you know. Nothin' to do with me."

"'Course not." I replied dryly.

He watched me for a moment. "What's it to you anyway?"

I remained silent and pulled a twenty dollar bill out of my wallet and folded it up. He snorted in derision. I pulled two more twenties out and folded them up with the first and held the cash up. He snatched it with surprising speed, tucking it into one of the pockets in his many layers.

He looked at me over his aviator glasses. "I wasn't doin' any business with her, you know. Not after she got busted."

That made my ears go up. "When did that happen?"

"'Bout a month ago. I saw the whole thing. They picked her up and took her away. Then they dropped her back a few hours later."

"She wasn't charged?"

247

"Nope." I waited and watched him closely. "Maybe they wanted something from her. Maybe it wasn't about drugs. But after that, I didn't want nothin' to do with her."

I tried not to look at his missing legs. He caught my eye.

"'S okay, lady. I'm used to people staring."

"I heard you're a vet."

"Yeah. A long time ago, 1969. Another life. God bless America." He gripped his controls and suddenly wheeled away, leaving me standing on the street with an empty wallet.

It wasn't my lucky day. A ticket was stuck under my windshield wiper. I pulled it out and shoved it in my purse. I didn't want to think what the fine was. I'd hyperventilate later. If Zims could be believed, Moira was picked up by the police and then released. Or picked up by somebody. Was it a drug bust? Or maybe the cops wanted an informant in the neighborhood. That would line up with what Rita had suspected, that the man who stopped into the bar to see Moira was a cop. Then again, maybe it had nothing to do with drugs. Either way, she not only hadn't been charged with anything, she'd been escorted back.

Andy claimed Moira was cheating on him. Steve thought her brother was supplying her with drugs or the money to buy them. Moira was in possession of a very expensive item of jewelry and was worried she was pregnant. If there was yet another guy, who was he?

THIRTY-FIVE

♈ ♉ ♊ ♋ ♌ ♍ ♎ ♏ ♐ ♑ ♒ ♓

I TRUDGED UP THE front stairs to my apartment. I looked up and gasped involuntarily. Matt was sitting on the top step by my front door.

"Matt! What are you doing here?"

"Julia, sorry. I just wanted to talk to you for a few minutes."

"This is kind of a bad time." I was wondering why he hadn't just picked up a phone. His visit was peculiar to say the least and I had no desire to invite him in.

"I just talked to David. He told me about Brooke's arrest. Do you know what's going on?"

"Not in detail. I just came from seeing her."

"You did?" Matt's face paled. "How is she?"

"Not great, as you can imagine."

"Where is she?"

"She's at the 7th Street jail. But it might not be such a good idea for you to show up there. You'd be giving the cops a lot to think about."

Matt nodded. "You're right. I don't dare go to see her. It could cause a lot of trouble with Rob. No one knows about us and I want to keep it that way."

"Not even David?" I queried.

"Especially David. I wouldn't want him telling Geneva. Not that I don't trust them—I do. They're both good friends. It's just that neither Brooke nor I wanted to involve them. It was just better they not know about us." He sighed heavily. "Look, I'm very nervous. I really hope you won't ever mention what you know about this to anyone. I never thought when I gave you her birth information that you'd recognize it."

"I understand. You don't have to worry. Anything you tell me in a reading is absolutely confidential. I can't tell anyone else. It's completely private and will go no further. Not even to Geneva. Of course, if you tell me you've committed a crime, that might be different." The words slipped out of my mouth before I thought about them.

Matt's face turned pale. "Oh God, you don't think *I* had anything to do with Moira, do you?"

"No, I don't." I realized as I spoke that I really didn't suspect Matt. He was staring at me. "Don't worry. Your secret about Brooke is safe. Unless *you've* told someone else, or Brooke has. But no one will ever hear it from my lips. You're my client."

He took a deep breath and his face relaxed. "Thanks, Julia. It could really screw things up for me. Business-wise, I mean. My firm handles Rob's investments. Not to mention the trouble it would cause for Brooke. You understand?"

"I do."

"I'll let you go then. I appreciate it." He turned and walked down the stairs.

Matt was definitely suffering from a guilty conscience, but if his affair with Brooke came to light now, the fallout could be disastrous for her. She could lose the support of her husband. Not to mention how the police might read it. I couldn't help but wonder if their affair had really ended several months before. Was it stretching it to think a single attractive male would still be so smitten a year after the relationship was over? So smitten, in fact, that he was driven to talk to an astrologer? Perhaps I'd been a little too gullible in believing his version of events.

THIRTY-SIX

♈ ♉ ♊ ♋ ♌ ♍ ♎ ♏ ♐ ♑ ♒ ♓

I HOPED TO HAVE a chance to talk to Geneva before the wake. I knew she was on thin emotional ice, and I was far more worried about her than I was about Brooke. I'd called Mary Leary's house, but the only response was the answering machine. Geneva was probably at the funeral home by now. I left a message on her cell to call me if she was able to. Then I munched on a dinner roll and fed Wizard.

Rummaging in the hallway closet, I found a navy dress and jacket appropriate for the wake. I even had a pair of navy blue heels. My grandmother would be scandalized if I hadn't produced a pair of shoes to match my outfit. I may not have much in my checking account, but thanks to her samples, I have plenty of clothes. I switched purses, gave Wizard a big hug, brushed cat hairs off my jacket, and trotted down the stairs to the car.

I reached my grandmother's house in twenty minutes. As usual, parking was impossible and I pulled up to the garage door. Fog had rolled in with a vengeance and was billowing in from the bay. I rang the bell, then, using my key, opened the front door. I called up the stairs to Gloria's apartment.

"Hello dear. Come on up," she replied. "Kuan's here too. We're just having some tea."

I climbed the stairs and walked down the short hallway to the kitchen. Mahjongg tiles were laid out on the kitchen table. "I'm getting an education in strategy." She looked up at me.

"Julia, how are you?" Kuan stood and gave me a kiss on the cheek. "You look very nice. So sorry it's for a sad occasion."

"Aren't these fascinating, Julia? They're so beautiful! These are Winds and these are Dragons. Would you like some tea?"

"Thanks, no. We have to hit the road if we're going to make it in time."

Kuan said, "You two go ahead. I'll clear up before I go downstairs."

"Are you aiding and abetting my grandmother's gambling?" I asked.

"Yes. Of course. In fact, she's pretty good."

"I want him to teach me *Weigi* and *Chien-tsu* too. I just love those names, don't you?" Gloria turned to me with a smile. "So exotic."

"Sounds like something you do in an opium den. Come on, let's go." I waved to Kuan. "Just make sure she doesn't lose her house, okay?"

He chuckled in response but gave me a hard look, as if he knew that I was the one getting involved in things best left alone.

THIRTY-SEVEN

♈ ♉ ♊ ♋ ♌ ♍ ♎ ♏ ♐ ♑ ♒ ♓

NORDENSON'S WAS A RAMBLING one-story, cinder-block building plastered in white stucco on the outside and painted pale green in the interior rooms. Bland landscapes and floral prints were hung at strategic points along the walls. The air from the vents was perfumed with a slight tinge of formaldehyde. Two large men who looked like members of the Leary clan stood guard at the archway to a room decorated in more soft greens. They watched carefully as guests signed in. I was sure I'd seen both men at Geneva's wedding.

Gloria and I signed our names in the guest book and entered. Mary, Geneva, and Dan Leary sat in chairs placed at an angle to the casket and diagonally facing the seating within the room. The casket was open. I stood back while my grandmother knelt and closed her eyes in a silent prayer. Then she made the sign of the cross and rose to greet the Learys. Mary clutched a tissue in her hand, her eyes swollen. Geneva introduced my grandmother to Mary. Dan nodded, but otherwise sat silent and stone-faced.

I knelt at the bier and said a prayer, not just for Moira but for all the family. Before the wedding, I hadn't seen Moira for at least four years, and although the undertaker's art had done its amazing work, she looked much harder in death than her twenty-eight years. I'm not a big fan of wakes and funerals—I've always thought cremation's a much cleaner way to be disposed of. The whole prospect of being buried in the ground seems gruesome, no matter how watertight the undertaker might claim the casket to be.

I rose and turned. My eye caught Detective Ianello standing against a side wall. He nodded in my direction.

When I reached the Learys, I kissed Mary's cheek and held Geneva's hand. She indicated she wanted to talk. I nodded and said I'd wait till she could get free.

I followed my grandmother to two empty seats in the third row. David was sitting on the side, keeping a close eye on Geneva. The guests whispered quietly among themselves, creating a low hum in the room. We had no sooner settled in than I felt a shift in the atmosphere. I looked up. Rob stood in the archway, holding Ashley's hand. One of the Leary cousins stepped in front of Rob. I was sure they knew he'd been absolved of any guilt in the shooting, but apparently there were still suspicions or resentments, no doubt fueled by Dan.

Geneva shot a look at Dan, who finally nodded to the two men. They stepped away from Rob. Ashley walked slowly into the room. She was wearing a white blouse with a large collar and a long black velvet skirt. Her small patent letter shoes peeked out from under her skirt, and her light brown hair was pulled back with a velvet ribbon. She'd been coached well. She knelt at the bier, held her hands together in prayer, and closed her eyes. I could see her lips moving as she prayed. Rob joined her. He closed his eyes for a few moments in silence and then glanced at his daughter. Ashley was staring at Moira's body in the casket. She whispered something to her father. He nodded and rose. Ashley crossed herself, then turned and ran to her grandmother as Rob returned to the foyer. Mary reached for her granddaughter, hugging her tightly and holding her in her lap for a long minute. Geneva smiled and stroked Ashley's hair.

"I love you, Gramma," Ashley said. "But I have to go. Daddy's waiting for me."

"That's all right, dear. You go ahead. I'll see you soon." Mary kissed her granddaughter's cheek and gave her one last hug as Ashley bolted after her father.

Geneva looked up and caught my eye. I couldn't read her expression, but her face looked strained.

"Pssst," Gloria hissed in my ear. "Is that the sister's husband?" Her dark eyes were fixed on Rob.

"Yes."

We stayed until the room filled with more well-wishers and mourners. Eventually, I saw several people slipping off to a private room across the lobby. I felt duty bound to stay the full three hours, but after one hour, my leg was falling asleep and I was having trouble keeping the rest of me awake as well.

"Dear, let's go across to the other room. I'm sure we can find a good stiff drink there," Gloria said. "I don't know about you, but I could use one. This is ghastly!"

I had to agree. "You go first, and I'll come in a few minutes."

It seemed as though most of the visitors were paying their respects, sitting for an hour with the family, and then leaving, but at all times the room was filled with hushed conversation. An elderly woman entered and spoke to Mary Leary. Mary started to cry and Geneva put an arm around her mother until she regained control. I gave up my seat and, carrying my purse, tiptoed out toward the lobby.

Gloria had a head start. She was standing next to a tall, white-haired elderly gentleman, swigging from a silver flask he'd offered her. I raised an eyebrow at her. She shrugged and smiled. An informal bar had been set up in spite of the funeral director's wishes, loaded with bottles of wine, whiskey, and beer, with a tray or two of hors d'oeuvres.

Gloria waved me over. "Julia, this is…"

"Patrick McGee." He extended a beefy hand. "But call me Pat. I'm Mary's brother. Terrible business, this."

"Yes." I smiled back.

"Can I get you something to drink, darlin'?"

I usually never drink anything stronger than wine, but watching Gloria take another swig from Pat's flask, I was tempted. "No, that's fine. I'm driving tonight."

A tall woman in a dark business suit stood near the impromptu bar. Her hair was pinned back in a tight bun at the nape of her neck, highlighting her strong features. She wore very little makeup but was striking nonetheless. She glanced toward our little group and then seemed to make up her mind. She skirted the imposing figure of Patrick McGee and arrived at my side.

"Excuse me, are you Julia?"

"Yes." As I turned, I saw Geneva standing in the archway between the two rooms. She moved quickly toward us.

"I see you've met each other already," Geneva said. "Marjorie is Brooke and Rob's attorney."

"We haven't actually met," I said. "But I saw you in the lot outside the courthouse with Rob."

Marjorie grimaced. "Oh, yes? That's right—we had a meeting downtown. I've heard a lot about you. It's great to finally meet you."

Geneva turned to my grandmother. "It was very kind of you to come, Gloria."

"Of course I would come. I'm so sorry for your loss. Please come visit me sometime whenever you can."

"I will." Geneva gave my grandmother a kiss on the cheek. "Let me drag Julia away for a bit. I need to talk to her."

Gloria's eyes turned toward the archway. She looked momentarily confused. I followed her gaze, but saw only Detective Ianello lurking behind a column. She regained her focus and turned back to Geneva. "Go right ahead, dear."

Geneva asked, "Can we go outside for a while?"

Marjorie and I followed her. We walked through another room which led to a hallway with a side entrance. We pushed through the heavy door and let it slam shut behind us.

Outside, it was chilly but quiet. Geneva rubbed her arms for warmth and turned to Marjorie. "Have you filled Julia in?"

"I was just about to."

"It's a nightmare, Julia. They've charged Brooke with conspiracy to commit murder." Geneva's face was flushed and her tone angry. "They're saying the emails between Brooke and Moira are hard evidence that the two of them were planning to kill Rob. It's ridiculous. They're not going to release her."

"What exactly did they say, these emails?"

Marjorie shrugged. "They're rather vague. Implying that when Rob's out of the way, they can split the insurance money. Words to that effect."

That confirmed what Brooke had told me. "What about Rob?" I asked. "What does he say about all this?"

"He's completely blown away," Geneva said. "He doesn't believe the charges against Brooke at all. I don't know what to think. We're burying my sister and now my other sister's in jail. Why is this happening to us? I don't for a second believe Brooke would have cooked up a scheme like this. Neither does Rob. I *know* she would never do anything like that ... ever. Brooke was always very protective toward Moira. Even if by some stretch you could imagine Brooke planning anything like that, she loved Moira to death. She would never have let her in for any harm or danger or anything illegal. Brooke is the most loving, honest, ethical person on two feet." Geneva's voice rose in pitch and I worried she was on the verge of hysteria.

Marjorie shot a glance at me and then turned to Geneva. "You've got to stay calm and get through this. The cops can be major screwups. People are arrested all the time on very thin evidence, particularly when the police are under pressure. Hang in there. I'll know more soon."

Geneva nodded mutely. She was shivering in the night air. "I should get back. I just wanted to make sure you two met and had a chance to talk." She turned and pulled open the door to the funeral home and stepped inside. When the door shut behind her, Marjorie turned to me.

"I do think their case against Brooke is thin, unless there's more I don't know about. They're theorizing that Moira was supposed to commit the murder, but maybe she balked and Brooke shot her. Knowing Brooke as I do, I just cannot imagine that."

"That's ridiculous. If so, how could she have disposed of the gun?"

"Exactly! Was everyone checked for blood spatter that night?"

"Well, yes. We were checked. There was blood on my robe. But then, I'd knelt down next to Moira and Rob grabbed a blanket to cover her. But other than my robe and the blanket, they found no other traces."

"Frankly, I think they should take another look at Andy."

I was on the alert, curious why Marjorie too had zeroed in on Andy, but I still wasn't ready to tell anyone what I suspected about his dealings. "Do you have any particular reason for saying that?"

"The family feels Andy was pathologically jealous, maybe even violent, but they could never get Moira to talk about it. They were more than a little worried about their relationship even before all this. Do you remember exactly where Andy was at the time of the shooting?"

"Not really. I was almost hysterical myself. The first time I remember seeing him was in the garage after they took Moira away in the ambulance, but he could have been there the whole time."

"I see," Marjorie responded.

"And with that back stairway..." I trailed off. "Anyone could have left the garage by the door to the yard and come in through the kitchen and the service stairs."

Marjorie was silent but listened carefully.

I hesitated, afraid of the answer. "Marjorie, if by some chance the police are able to build a case against Brooke, and she were convicted, what would happen?"

Marjorie's face looked grim. "To be technical, she's been charged with conspiracy to commit murder. If they can prove that she and Moira were involved in such a plan, and someone died as a result of that … whether or not Brooke fired the shot … I'm sure you know about the felony murder rule in California."

I was at a loss. "No … sorry."

"If someone is killed or inadvertently dies in the commission of a felony, it can mean a life sentence without the option of parole."

I felt my stomach lurch. "Are you saying this could apply to Brooke?"

"Yes. Conspiracy to murder is one thing, but if the felony murder rule applies, well … California is actually rather draconian in that regard. This is very serious for Brooke."

"I see. Then it's your task to prove her innocent."

"I certainly hope I can. Julia, I better get going. It was nice to meet you. I hope we meet again in more pleasant circumstances."

"Good night."

Marjorie headed for the parking lot, her heels clicking on the pavement. I watched until she reached her car. I heard the beep of her alarm just before she climbed in. I wouldn't wish her job on my worst enemy.

When I re-entered the funeral parlor, I spotted Geneva talking to a fair-haired woman in a long dark coat. She turned toward me as I approached.

"Julia, I don't think you've ever met Pamela."

I smiled and shook the woman's hand. Her face was thin, almost gaunt. White orthopedic shoes peeked out from beneath her dark slacks. Geneva looked at me expectantly, as if I should recognize the woman, but I was drawing a blank. Geneva picked up on it and said, "Pamela's sister Sondra was married to Rob."

"Oh." I shook her hand. "Yes, Geneva's mentioned you often."

Pamela smiled sadly and turned to Geneva. "I was so upset when I heard what happened. And so sorry for your family."

Pamela had seen my glance at her white shoes. "Sorry I had to come dressed like this. I just left work and didn't have time to change." She smiled. "I'm a nurse at the VA. Cardiology Unit."

"Rob has left," Geneva said, "but I'll make sure he knows you were here."

"Please do." Pamela turned to me, as if in explanation. "Rob and I have stayed close, and I just love Brooke. If it weren't for Rob's support after my sister died, I don't know where I'd be." She turned back to Geneva. "Is there anything I can do for you or your mother?"

"Thanks. We're really all set. We've arranged everything, but please, I hope you'll stay in touch with my mom after the dust settles."

"I will." Pamela squeezed Geneva's hand and headed for the main room.

Geneva whispered, "Julia, I have to talk to you."

It was obvious she didn't want to be overheard. I led her to a quiet corner of the lobby away from prying ears.

"My mother told me today..."

"Yes?"

"That night... that dreadful night... oh God, please don't tell *anyone* this... not even Dan... my mother told me she went upstairs to get Rob and Brooke after she heard the shots. Rob of course was in the garage, but when she got to their bedroom, Brooke wasn't there."

I thought a moment. Could Brooke have slipped out of her room to see Matt while Rob was downstairs in the library? Geneva didn't know about Brooke's affair, and I couldn't tell her.

"What if they make my mother testify? It will just add weight to their charge against Brooke."

"I'm sure there's a rational explanation for everything. You just have to keep it together for yourself and David and your mother."

She took a deep breath. "You're right. I know you're right." She leaned over and hugged me. She'd lost several pounds and her arms were painfully thin. Her skin felt hot to the touch, as if she were burning with an internal fever.

"I'm falling apart these days. But I'm certain of one thing. I have absolute faith Brooke is innocent. I refuse to believe otherwise. Have you been able to learn anything more?"

I stalled. "Nothing significant so far, but we'll catch up soon." It wasn't the right time to tell Geneva about Andy and his bookkeeping connection to Macao, especially when she was in such a vulnerable state.

"I'll try to give you a call tomorrow," Geneva said. "I have to go give Dan a break." We hugged one more time and she left the room.

I returned to the side room where I'd left my grandmother. Now she was standing next to the long table with a glass of wine in her hand. Patrick McGee was moving in for the kill. Gloria continued to smile, but there was a glassy look to her eyes. I stood close to her and she pressed her pointed toe against the side of my shoe. I took this to mean, *Get me out of here.*

I picked up my cue. "I think we better go. I'm really tired."

"Oh, so soon? What a shame," Patrick replied.

"Pat, it was so nice to meet you," I said. "I hope we see you again at a happier time." I grasped my grandmother's elbow and steered her through the crowd.

When we reached the front door, she said, "Julia. There's something I have to tell you."

"What?"

"You're killing my arm."

I turned to her. "Is that what you wanted to tell me?" I let go of her elbow. "I'm sorry. I figured it was the only way to rescue you from that guy who was trying to pick you up."

"I thought he was rather attractive, you know, big and ruddy and Irish, with that gorgeous white hair," Gloria mumbled as we descended the steps of the funeral parlor. "But he never stopped talking!"

"Would you like to go back? I can set up a date for you."

"I can set up my own dates, thank you very much. I may be an old lady, but I'm still cute and definitely not dead."

"I'm only teasing you." I gave her a kiss on the cheek as I bundled her into the Geo.

When I climbed into the driver's seat, Gloria said, "I saw someone I know in there tonight."

"Really? Who was it?"

"That dark-haired, slick-looking man standing in the archway."

I thought back to where people had been milling about. "I noticed you were looking at someone. Do you mean Detective Ianello?"

"Detective? He's a cop? Does he know the Learys?"

"He does now. That's the detective in charge of the case."

"No! Paolo Ianello is in charge of this case? I don't believe it!"

"How do you know him?"

"Well, I should say I knew the family. From the neighborhood. The father was a miserable man. He was abusive to his wife and probably his kids too. His wife, I mean Paolo's mother, Clara, was the sweetest woman but she just couldn't seem to stand up to her husband."

"That's a little difficult when someone weighs two hundred pounds more."

"Oh, he wasn't very big. Fat, but short. A little Napoleon. Brutal man. Anyway... Clara, his wife, could never have afforded anything from my shop. Her husband had the money, but wouldn't give her any. I used to tell her to stop in when she could and a few times I gave her some dresses that hadn't sold. She didn't want to take them. She felt she was taking charity, but I told her not to worry about it. It was the end of the season and I had to move them along. Her husband was in the food business, so we worked out a swap. She'd bring me olive oil and vegetables, saved me from having to shop and that way she didn't feel like she was just taking."

I had a feeling there was more to this story. "What happened then?"

"One day her husband stormed in my shop. He was a nasty little brute of a man. He was screaming in Italian and cursing me. He had a bag with all the dresses I'd given her and he pulled them out and ripped them to shreds in the middle of my shop. Scared some customers away too. I was furious. I used to keep a baseball bat under the counter and I hauled it out and went after him. I was so mad I chased him halfway down the street. I never caught up with him. He just ran like the weasel he was. Believe me, if your grandfather had been alive, he would have knocked on his door and taught him a lesson or two."

"Did he ever bother you again?"

"Me? No. But I kept that baseball bat handy just in case. If he had the nerve to come back, I was gonna crack his skull with it."

My eyes widened. It was hard to imagine my diminutive grandmother being such a tough cookie.

"He never came back, but neither did Clara. Next time I saw her, she had bruises on her arms and a black eye and she ran away from me. It just broke my heart."

"I wonder if the son recognized you tonight."

"Wouldn't be surprised if he did. All those kids probably got an earful and a beating too. And for all I know, maybe he's followed in his old man's footsteps, beating up women. Like father like son."

"Whatever happened to the family?"

"The kids are all gone in different directions. Both the parents are dead. And now Paolo's a cop. Strange. Hope he turned out better than his father."

We took 19th Avenue, the main thoroughfare that cuts through the Sunset, following it into Golden Gate Park. The wooded area was free of traffic and we wound along the road lined with eucalyptus trees. I cracked my window slightly and cold air poured in. My grandmother was strangely silent. I wondered if she was still thinking of her friend from the neighborhood.

I looked over at her. "A penny..."

"I was thinking about that handsome man—that's the sister's husband, isn't it? The one who shot the girl?"

"Yes. Well, except he didn't."

"Didn't what?"

"Shoot her. The bullet came from a different gun."

"I'm confused."

"Someone shot at him and he shot back. They couldn't be absolutely sure until the autopsy. The bullet that hit Moira didn't come from his gun."

"Still, he has some brass showing up at the wake like that."

"That's one way to put it. I guess he wanted to make sure his daughter paid her respects."

"Hmmph," Gloria responded. "I don't know about the wisdom of that! What's he going to tell her? 'This is your aunt, she's dead because somebody shot her in your house. We thought it was Daddy at first… accidentally.' I can see why the family didn't want him there. But, my! He's certainly handsome!" My grandmother was an aficionado of good-looking men.

"True. He also seems like a very nice guy and very upset about what happened."

"When did you talk to him?"

"I was there that night, and then he showed up at Geneva's sister's apartment when I was helping her clear it out. And I've talked to him a couple of times since."

"Why did he go to the girl's apartment?"

"He said he wanted to talk to them. To Dan and Geneva."

"What's there to say?"

"Atonement. I think he was just desperate to convince everyone that he didn't mean any harm."

"That's all well and good, but this is something that family will never get over, no matter who did it. I feel just terrible for them."

Gloria leaned her head back and stared at the passing houses for the rest of the ride into North Beach. By the time we reached Castle

Alley, it was after ten o'clock. My grandmother climbed out of the car and told me to drive safely. She turned back and said, "Just remember, dear. Never marry a short man."

I smiled and waited with the engine running until she'd climbed the stairs and closed the door behind her. Kuan's living room light was on, so I knew he was keeping an eye and an ear out for her.

THIRTY-EIGHT

♈ ♉ ♊ ♋ ♌ ♍ ♎ ♏ ♐ ♑ ♒ ♓

I DIALED CHERYL'S NUMBER while I waited at the traffic light on Montgomery. She answered on the first ring. I was a little nervous about returning to Macao, but since the place would likely be filled with customers, I pushed my fears aside.

"You still up for that drink?"

"Sure. Pick me up downstairs."

When I pulled up in front of Cheryl's building, she was waiting on the sidewalk wearing a little black cocktail dress, a wrap thrown over her shoulders, and very high heels. She clambered into the car.

"Did you have a place in mind?"

"Yes. A place called Macao. Moira worked there occasionally."

"Ooooh. Nice. I've heard about it! It's down on the Embarcadero? I'm up for it."

"Maybe it's a complete waste of time, but I want to check the place out at night. Besides, it's the only thing I can think of to do right now." I filled Cheryl in on Brooke's arrest and Moira's wake.

"Maybe we'll meet a friendly informative bartender. So, what do you really think? Do you think the police might be right? That Brooke planned to murder her husband?"

I thought for a few moments before answering. "I don't know what to think. Moira wasn't exactly what you'd call well-balanced. It might make sense if it were Moira sending emails to cause trouble between Brooke and Rob. She had access to their house and also her sister's office. She could have used both those computers and her own too."

"How well do you know Brooke?"

"I can't say I know her well. But she's an extremely bright woman and this thing sounds screwy. If you're planning to murder someone, sending emails doesn't make a lot of sense. But I'm worried it might be enough to convince a jury."

I took Broadway straight down to the Embarcadero. We followed the waterfront along the eastern side of the city until we reached Pier 3. I drove past the club and managed to find a metered space. We parked and walked back along the deserted sidewalk. The fog hadn't reached this side of the city yet and the air was still clear and chill. Lights from the East Bay reflected in the black waters lapping against the pilings. I shuddered when I thought of my close call two nights before on the pier.

The entryway under the canopy was brightly lit tonight. The fish still swam in their underground river and I wondered if they were on the menu. A tinkling fountain I hadn't noticed at the door completed the water theme. Inside, my eyes took a moment to adjust to the dim lighting. On a slightly raised stage at the rear of the large room, a pianist sat at a baby grand playing a jazz standard. He finished his piece and another man in formal wear stepped onto the stage next to a stand-up bass. A moment later, a slender blonde woman arrived and pulled the microphone from its stand. The music started and the singer launched into a Billy Holiday tune.

We found a small table in the middle of the room, close enough to enjoy the music but not so close we couldn't talk. I ordered two Macaos for us when the waiter came.

Cheryl looked at me quizzically. "What's a Macao?"

I shrugged. "We'll find out."

"It's so nice to be out on the town." With a toss of her head, Cheryl indicated a man seated midway at the bar. "Hey, check out that guy at the bar, Julia."

I followed her line of sight and stifled a gasp. "Cheryl..."

"What?"

"I know him."

"You do?"

"It's Matt," I whispered. "From the wedding. He was there the night Moira was shot. He's also my client now."

"No kidding. Did you know he'd be here?"

"No. No idea. Surprise to me." I realized I was staring. As if he could feel my gaze, Matt turned, and, after his initial surprise, a look of recognition spread across his face. He raised a hand in greeting and, carrying his drink, navigated through the maze of tables toward us.

"Julia! Fancy meeting you here."

"Hi, Matt. Join us. Please." I indicated the chair between me and Cheryl.

"Thanks." He sat down in the empty chair.

"What brings you here?" I asked.

"My office is right across the street at One Embarcadero. I stop in sometimes for a drink before heading home."

"This is my friend Cheryl."

Cheryl smiled at Matt. "Nice to meet you."

The waiter returned and placed two tall frosted drinks before us with thin green shoots of lemongrass peeking out of each glass.

Matt took a sip of his own drink. "Actually, I was kind of half hoping I'd run into Rob tonight. There are some good investments I'd like to talk to him about."

"Rob comes here?"

Matt nodded. "Sometimes. Under the circumstances, I didn't want to bother him with a phone call."

"He was at the wake earlier tonight. He brought Ashley."

Matt grimaced. "Oh. Yeah. Well, to tell you the truth, I suppose I should have gone too. I just couldn't handle it. I made my excuses to David. I hope they're not upset with me about it, but you know … this whole thing has been too much." He hesitated. "Julia, there's something I meant to ask you. Have you ever done any astrological work with stocks or companies? You know, like predicting if a certain company's stock will rise?"

"I haven't, although there are people whose specialty that is—business consultations and so on."

"Really!" His interest was definitely piqued.

"It's not my area of focus, but some of the same rules apply."

"Maybe you could put me in touch with someone like that? Could astrology be used to predict a company's growth?"

"Oh, I'm sure it could. It would be very important to cast the chart of the business correctly. For example, you'd have to know when the partnership papers were signed, or exactly when a corporation was formed, but it's definitely possible. I know a few astrologers who do that kind of work almost exclusively. There's one in particular I know personally. I'll send you an email and pass on some names."

Matt turned in his chair and stared at the front entryway. "Hey."

"What is it?"

"Oh, nothing, I guess." He twisted back in his chair. "It's strange. I could have sworn I saw Rob."

I turned and saw a man with dark hair moving away from the glass entrance toward the sidewalk, but he was so far way I couldn't be sure. I looked at Matt. "Was it him?"

"Nah, I guess not." Matt shifted his attention back to us. "Can I order another for both of you?"

"I'm fine."

"Cheryl?"

"Okay. Thanks." She smiled brilliantly in Matt's direction.

Matt signaled to the waitress, who nodded and moved away to fill his order. He turned his chair slightly toward Cheryl. "Have we met before?"

Cheryl continued to smile. "I don't think so."

"Weren't you at Geneva and David's wedding?"

"No. I've never met them. They're friends of Julia's." She nodded in my direction.

"Well, that's too bad. Wish we'd met there."

Matt was definitely interested, and Cheryl was enjoying the male attention. And I was the invisible girl. I continued to sip my cocktail while Matt downed his freshly ordered drink. On stage, the singer worked her way through a few more torch songs. By the time the set finished, my glass was empty. I glanced toward the bar and spotted a bartender I hadn't seen when we first arrived. He was in his early thirties, Asian. Tall and slender and his head was shaved. This had to be Tony, the Berkeley grad student and friend of Moira's. I wasn't sure there was a way I'd be able to talk to him alone, particularly with Matt and Cheryl at the table. I sipped the melted ice from my drink while the two of them chatted, oblivious to my presence. It was time to go.

I nudged Cheryl under the table and, picking up my cue, she gave me a quizzical look but gathered her purse and jacket.

"Leaving so soon?" This was addressed to Cheryl.

"Well, yes, we both have to be up early tomorrow."

"Maybe I'll see you here again, I hope."

Cheryl simpered. "I'm sure you will."

They continued to smile at each other. I left some bills on the table and slipped my jacket on as I stood up.

"Good night, Matt."

He stood and held Cheryl's chair. "Night. Drive safe." He smiled at Cheryl again and handed her a business card.

We made our exit to the street.

"He's very cute, Julia."

"Ya think?"

"Yes, I do. And nice too."

"Mmm. Seems so."

"You don't sound very excited. But I know what you need."

"What?"

"You need to start dating again." I didn't respond. "Maybe we should come back here again?"

"I'd have to take out a loan to drink here on a regular basis."

"Do you think I should have stayed tonight?"

"Nooooo."

"What if he thinks I don't like him?"

I laughed. "I think he got the message ... loud and clear."

"Do you blame me? I mean, I have to start somewhere. Dating, I mean," Cheryl replied defensively as she settled into her seat.

I looked over at her and smiled. "You've made a good start."

She sniffed and didn't respond.

I dropped Cheryl at her apartment and, without mentioning my plan, returned to Macao. I parked the car half a block away once again and walked back. A good three-quarters of an hour had elapsed. Matt was nowhere to be seen. The band was playing another set, and several of the tables were still filled, but the seating at the bar was open. I climbed onto a stool. The same bartender approached and placed a napkin in front of me.

"What'll it be?"

"Are you Tony?"

He smiled. "Yes."

"I'd like to talk to you if I could."

"About?"

"Moira Leary. I'm a friend of her sister's."

His face underwent a shift. "Not here."

"Where?"

"I'm off in an hour. Meet me at Wong's. On Jackson. Please order a drink." He seemed nervous.

"Can you bring me a Coke?"

He nodded.

When he returned, I paid the tab and added a tip. "I'll be there."

———

I finished my Coke and left the bar. I didn't hang around but drove straight back to Chinatown. Wong's is an all-night hole-in-the-wall on Jackson, with dusty windows and plastic flowers on the tables. They serve coffee, tea, and pastries, both Chinese and American, and not much else. I parked in a red zone near the doorway to the diner and waited. I hoped Tony would show.

Forty minutes later, I spotted him walking up the hill. He entered Wong's and took a seat in the rear, far away from the front windows. I left my car in the red zone and joined him at his table. He was sipping a coffee.

"Can I get you one?"

"No thanks, too late for me."

"I've got some studying to do tonight, gotta stay awake. Look, I didn't want to be seen talking to anyone there, especially about Moira."

"Why?"

"We're watched all the time. I work there to pay for school. It's real good money but I have to be careful."

"You were seeing Moira?"

"No, no. Just friends. I liked her. She was great, but she was real messed up. She was in a lot of trouble. I heard about what happened."

"What kind of trouble?"

Tony was silent.

"Drugs?"

"Well, maybe that too. But the cops were pressing her for information about her boyfriend."

"Andy?"

"Yeah, that's the guy. He keeps the books for Luong Cheng, the owner of Macao. At least that's the official story."

"What's the unofficial?"

"Take a guess. I suspect the feds are sniffing around Cheng for a lot of reasons. That's why I don't want to be seen talking to anyone, particularly a non-Asian."

"Where's the money coming from?"

He looked at me over his cup of coffee. "I'm Chinese, and Cheng and his crew are Vietnamese, but I pick things up even if I don't speak their language." He took a sip of his coffee. "Could be coming from any number of things, but let's put it this way. I don't think you'll find a lot of green cards among the kitchen staff. One night, Moira was in a real state. I kept pressing her to tell me what was wrong. She finally broke down and told me some stuff." Tony sighed. "Apparently she got busted. They picked her up and then let her go. She was under pressure to get information about what her boyfriend did for Cheng. She was between a rock and a hard place, if you know what I mean. Frankly, I don't think she knew that much about what was going on. But listen—whatever happens, that didn't come from me."

Tony's information tied in with what Zims had told me. The cops, either city or federal, had picked Moira up and then let her go for some purpose of their own. If Andy thought Moira would turn on him, he'd have a damn good motive to get rid of her.

"I hope they catch whoever did this. I really do. She was kinda nuts, but she had a good heart. Listen, I'm gonna take off now. Can you wait a while before you leave, if you don't mind?"

"Okay." I wondered if he wasn't being overly paranoid, but maybe he was just afraid of losing his job.

Tony left and I ordered a cup of tea and a pastry and consumed it slowly. After another forty-five minutes, I left Wong's and returned to my car. I drove over the hill on Sacramento and then cut down to California. Traffic out of town was light. I didn't notice anything unusual until I crossed Polk. That's when I saw the dark sedan following me.

THIRTY-NINE

♈ ♉ ♊ ♋ ♌ ♍ ♎ ♏ ♐ ♑ ♒ ♓

THE SAME HEADLIGHTS STAYED behind me for several blocks, remaining about two car-lengths behind. I'm very careful about locking my car doors, especially at night, and I look over my shoulder when getting into my car too. I clicked the door locks again for good measure. Two cars passed me in the next lane, but the car behind remained at the same distance.

When the next light turned green, I accelerated quickly and kept my speed up for the next few blocks, hoping a police cruiser wasn't waiting in an alleyway speed trap to ticket me. The car following matched my speed. Why would anyone be trailing me? And if they were, how long had I been followed?

I cast my mind back, trying to remember if I'd noticed anything outside Macao or earlier. No one had been around. I hadn't seen any cars pulling out behind me. But then, it had been the last thing on my mind. I was only intent on meeting Tony.

After the next light, I slowed to a crawl, watching to see if the driver would become impatient and pass me. Again, the car matched my speed. A chill ran down my spine. Someone was definitely following me and they didn't care if I knew.

I quickly reviewed my options. I had no intention of leading a stranger to my apartment. Of course, I'd found my wallet open—exposing my driver's license—that night in Moira's apartment, so if my follower was the same person who'd attacked me, he would already know where I lived. I nixed the idea of heading for my grandmother's house. I didn't want to bring any trouble to her doorstep, nor to Gale's. Plus, that would involve driving back toward Russian Hill. I could return to Cheryl's, but I didn't like the thought of being unprotected on a deserted downtown street when I got out of my car. Whoever he, or she, was, I had to lose them.

When I reached Divisadero, I turned left and headed for a neighborhood that I knew was a warren of intertwining streets. I made a fast turn heading west on Turk and an even faster right on Baker, leading me up Terra Vista. By now I was too frightened to even look in the rear-view mirror. I raced up Terra Vista and took the corner on two wheels. I didn't see car lights behind me as I turned the corner, only the ambient glow of headlights down the hill. I drove halfway down the block and spotted a long driveway leading to a garage at the rear of a house. I pulled down the driveway and parked behind the house. I doused my headlights and turned off the engine. My hands were sweating and my heart was pounding.

I hadn't imagined the black sedan following me. I had no idea what kind of car it was—only black, late model, and could have been a Mercedes or a Cadillac; I honestly wouldn't know the difference unless I saw an insignia. My engine made small metallic pinging sounds as it cooled. I waited but heard nothing. I carefully rolled down my window and listened. A glow from headlights highlighted the tall tree branches in the next yard. I heard a car moving slowly down the street. The motor was almost silent, but I could hear the crunching of dry leaves under tires. He was searching. I'd temporarily lost him, but now I was trapped in a driveway behind a private home. I prayed no one in the house would turn on outside lights or do anything to signal my presence. How long would he cruise the street?

Ten minutes elapsed but it felt like an hour. I twisted in my seat and once again saw the same glow of headlights. Again I heard the crunching of leaves and small branches under tires. The car came to a stop directly in front of the driveway. Its headlights were fixed against the wall of the house next door.

My mouth was dry and I could barely swallow. If the driver found me, what would he do? What could I do? I could lean on the horn and hope to wake the occupants of the house. The arrogance of following me in such an overt manner was more frightening than an attempt to track me covertly. Was someone trying to discover where I lived, or did they already know? Did someone wish me harm or were they only trying to frighten me? If so, they were doing a damn good job of it.

My heart was racing. I closed my eyes and deliberately slowed my breathing and prayed. Then I heard an engine rev and tires squeal. The sedan barreled down the street as if angry to have lost me. But I was too afraid to turn my car around and pull out. It could be a trick. He could be waiting at the foot of the hill.

I was cold now and shivering, and I wanted to be home in my own bed more than anything in the world. I had to take a chance. I turned on my parking lights and saw that the driveway continued on past the garages. A narrow space next to the last garage led to an alley behind the homes. I started the engine but left my headlights off. I followed the concrete path along the side of the garage and through the opening to the alleyway. It led to an intersecting street. At the corner of the alley, I hit the brakes and looked around carefully. Nothing moved. I glanced up at the street sign. *Fortuna Street.* I almost laughed with gratitude at the name. I wiped tears from my eyes and took a deep breath. Following Fortuna, I reached Turk again. No other cars were on the street. I turned west toward the Avenues, keeping a lookout, but I didn't spot the black sedan again.

When I reached home, I pulled the car into the garage, made sure the heavy door was properly locked, and climbed the back stairs to my kitchen. Wizard padded out to greet me. He tried to make a dash for the yard, but, struggling to hold on to my purse and keys, I grabbed him at the last moment. I didn't want him out this late at night, and I was too tired to have to call him in later. I reached down and closed the hatch on his kitty door before he could get free. He looked at me and uttered a low growl in his throat.

"No. Sorry. It's been a rough day and a rougher night. You're in." I doled out a couple of kitty treats and dropped them in his plate. He attacked them at once. I turned off the kitchen light and in the dark, peeked out the living room windows to the street below. I saw no cars that seemed out of place. Then I walked down the stairway and shoved the bolt across the front door. Wizard eyed me strangely, sensing something was out of kilter.

Upstairs, I shed my jacket and poured a glass of wine. The light on the answering machine was blinking. Gale had left a message reminding me of the open house on Sunday. Cheryl hadn't spoken of it earlier, and I suspected she might bail on the whole idea. Then I kicked off my shoes and shed my clothes. I slipped into my flannel pajamas, propped some extra pillows on the bed, and settled in.

I thought about the couples I knew. Cheryl dealing with a divorce, Brooke in jail and accused of planning her husband's death, Moira dead and forced to turn over information on her boyfriend to the police. David and Geneva seemed the only happy people in the world, in spite of their family difficulties. Only Gale was completely content as a single woman. Maybe I was better off in my alone state than I knew.

Wizard climbed onto my lap and started kneading the comforter furiously. Was Cheryl right? Was it time to consider dating? The thought of it brought no joy. If someone told me to climb Mount Everest with no equipment, it would seem an easier prospect. But if I didn't take a chance, I'd be a woman alone with her cat forever. I finished the wine, turned off the bedroom lamp, and snuggled down under the comforter. I heard the foghorns in the distance as my eyes closed involuntarily.

FORTY

♈ ♉ ♊ ♋ ♌ ♍ ♎ ♏ ♐ ♑ ♒ ♓

THE NEXT MORNING I stumbled into the shower. I'd slept way past the time I usually wake. I downed some coffee, fed Wizard his morning meal, and threw on jeans and a sweater. Once the coffee kicked in, I spent the next couple of hours catching up on emails, client appointments, and the Zodia column. By then I was famished. I made some toast and sat down to review the notes I'd made of my conversations with everyone who knew Moira.

Again, there was something niggling at the back of my mind and I couldn't quite get hold of it. Rita had seen Moira getting into a large dark car in the parking lot of the Alibi. She was sure Moira had been picked up by a man. Was it the same black sedan that had followed me last night? Did Rita know more about cars than I? Maybe she'd noticed the make and just hadn't mentioned it.

It was past noon, so Rita might be at work. I slipped on my jacket and headed back to the Haight. When I reached Waller, I drove around the block and pulled into the Alibi's rear lot. A few cars were parked on the cracked asphalt behind the bar. At the far end was an older, dark blue two-door. I drove closer. It was Rita—I could see her curly dark hair through the window. She was turned sideways, gathering her things. I climbed out and walked over to the driver's window.

I tapped on the glass but Rita didn't move. Her face was turned away from me and her head lay against the headrest. I stood still for a moment and then slowly circled the car, moving around to the passenger side. Something was very wrong. My heart was skipping beats. Against my will, I forced myself to look inside. Rita was propped up, facing the passenger window. Her swollen tongue extended from her mouth and raw bruises marked her neck. Her eyes were open and sightless.

I backed away and bumped into a chain-link fence at the side of the parking lot. Nausea threatened to overwhelm me. I hung on to the fence for support and bent over to catch my breath. Shuddering, I took deep breaths until my stomach was under control. I staggered back to my car, found a bottle of water in the trunk, and downed a large mouthful. I had to walk slowly. My legs were stiff and the world was spinning. Inside the Alibi, the bartender, a partially bald older man in a white T-shirt, was wiping down the bar. He looked up as I approached.

"Please call the police," I croaked.

"What's that, lady?"

"The police. Call the police, right away," I managed to say. "Rita's in her car in the back. She'd dead."

He stood staring at me for a moment, trying to take in my words. Then he ran to the end of the bar and out to the parking lot. I followed him, watching him run to Rita's car. He stopped a few feet away and then slowly backed up. He turned to look at me.

"Did you see what happened?"

I couldn't speak. I opened my mouth but no words came out. I shook my head. "I just pulled up and found her."

"Stay here. I'm calling the cops. Don't touch anything."

He returned a moment later and waited with me. Ten minutes later we heard sirens. A cruiser pulled down the alley and a man and woman emerged from the car.

They too walked slowly around Rita's car, and then the female officer returned to the cruiser and radioed it in. I gave the other officer my name and information. Told them I'd only met Rita once or twice at the bar, didn't see anything, and had no information. My speculation that Rita had known something important about Moira would seem too far-fetched. They would never understand and it would take too long to explain. When another patrol car and a police van pulled into the parking lot, I slipped away and climbed into my car. No one was paying the slightest attention to me.

I started the engine and drove off, careful not to look in Rita's direction. I'd contact the police later, but I didn't want to stand there waiting to explain things to local cops on the beat. I drove home, pushing the thought of Rita's face out of my mind. She had known something. She knew the car or she could identify it, or she'd seen the man who'd picked up Moira that night. And that's why she was dead.

FORTY-ONE

♈ ♉ ♊ ♋ ♌ ♍ ♎ ♏ ♐ ♑ ♒ ♓

GENEVA SAT QUIETLY AND listened. She picked obsessively at a thread dangling from a small pillow on her lap. When I finished, she said nothing. She stared at the floor. I'd told her everything I had learned and everything I suspected, but I still had no idea who'd shot Moira, much less why.

"If Moira was being used by Andy to cover up money laundering, why didn't she come to us?" Geneva asked. "Why didn't she tell us?"

"Maybe she was afraid you wouldn't believe her. It strikes me that no one lent her much credence on any subject."

Geneva's face paled. "Fair enough." She put her hands over her face and burst into tears, long, wracking sobs. I jumped up and sat on the arm of her chair. *Damn.* I'd done it again. Open mouth, insert foot. I put my arms around her and held her while she cried. After a few minutes, her chest stopped heaving and she took a deep breath, wiping her eyes.

"I'm sorry, Julia. I didn't mean to lose it like that."

"No, I'm sorry. What I said was … I didn't mean it as a criticism. I wouldn't say anything hurtful to you for the world."

"But you're right. You're right. We were so tired, tired of her screw-ups and escapades. Tired of excuses and so tired of always bailing her out."

"Please, please don't beat yourself up. Don't torture yourself with guilt."

Geneva nodded, wiping her eyes. "Easier said than done. But what makes you think there was another man in her life? Explain it to me.

"Well, call it an educated … no, call it I'm 99.9% sure. In her chart, Pluto by transit has been hitting her natal Venus off and on for the past year. She's been involved in an affair, most likely a secret one, and this has been very intense and powerful. Now, you could argue that Andy is the person she was involved with, but frankly I don't think so. Whatever their relationship, it hardly struck me as anything more than contentious. So that's why I believe there's someone else."

Geneva sighed. "And you think this man killed her?"

"I don't know. I really don't. And I don't even know if it was a man."

"What do you mean?"

"We don't know she wasn't involved with a woman."

Geneva gasped. "I never even thought of that. Are you saying my sister might have been gay?"

"Not at all. I'm just trying to remain logical. It isn't possible to predict gender from a chart, assuming we even had one for another person. Moira was involved in an affair. It was intense. It was consuming her. It may have even been secret, but there's no guarantee it was with a man."

Geneva was quiet for a long time. She finally took a deep breath. "You were right the other day."

"Right about what?"

"Studying Moira's chart. You warned me. You said I might not like what I found out."

"Are you sorry I'm doing this? Do you want me to back off?"

Geneva shook her head vehemently. "No. I have to know. I have to know the truth about what happened that night. What on earth led to my sister's murder."

By the time I left Mary Leary's house, Geneva was calm, but she was still sitting in the same position, picking at threads from the pillow. Her eyes had a far-off look.

———

When I reached my apartment, I dropped my purse on the floor in the hallway, hung my jacket on a chair, and stumbled into the bedroom. I couldn't think about Moira any more. I couldn't think about Rita. Both of them young, murdered, and dead. I fell onto the bed, clothes and all, and pulled the comforter over me. I sank into a sleep so deep I'm certain I left my body behind on the planet and ventured somewhere else.

When I finally woke, it was dark outside. I dragged myself off the bed and walked around the apartment turning on lights. I fixed a cup of chamomile tea. I needed a respite from the turmoil and my own thoughts. I needed to stay in my cocoon. I needed to be domestic. And I was starving. I dug one of my grandmother's care packages out of the freezer and thawed it in the microwave. This one was slices of steak with mushrooms, onions, and carrots.

I cleared away the dishes and washed everything. Then I fed Wizard his dinner. The phone rang but I decided not to answer. I didn't want to hear from anyone. Not the Learys, not my clients, not the police, no one. But then curiosity got the better of me. I saw Cheryl's number on the caller ID and picked up.

"What are you doing tonight?"

"I'm hiding out. I just warmed up some food and I plan to watch a movie. How 'bout you?"

"It's Saturday night! I was hoping I could talk you into going back to that bar on the Embarcadero."

Cheryl's spirits had improved a great deal since the court hearing. I really didn't want to tell her about discovering Rita's body. At least not yet. "Hate to disappoint you, but no way."

"What a pooper you are."

"Why don't you come over? We can watch a movie and drink some wine. Stay over if you like."

"Oh gee, whaddya got? *Brain Eating Mummies Devour LA?*" Cheryl was referring to my undying love of grade-B sci-fi's of the 1950s. I also love old mummy flicks. Whether it's an Egyptian priest cooking up tanna leaves or a giant octopus destroying the Golden Gate Bridge, no matter what, everything always turns out just fine.

"My DVDs are American classics!"

"American cult dreck."

"I won't take offense. Most people just don't get it."

"Right. You and Wizard are connoisseurs."

"See if I invite you again."

Cheryl laughed. "I'm just teasing you. Don't really feel like a domestic night tonight, but thanks."

"I'll see you tomorrow?"

"Tomorrow?"

"The open house."

"Oh, yeah … I guess."

"Gale has her heart set on your getting that condo."

"I know. Don't get me wrong, I'm curious, just don't know if I'm ready. Oh, that reminds me—I've got to call her back anyway. She left me a message. Wanted to know how we made out at Rochecault. I'll see you tomorrow."

"'Night."

Part of me regretted turning Cheryl's invitation down, but I was glad to be battening down the hatches. I popped a bag of popcorn in the microwave and a DVD in the player. Wizard followed me into the living room and settled on my lap while I munched out. By the time the popcorn was gone, Wiz was snoring and the atomically mutated giant ants were dead in the desert. I knew all would be well and I could sleep.

FORTY-TWO

♈ ♉ ♊ ♋ ♌ ♍ ♎ ♏ ♐ ♑ ♒ ♓

WHEN I WOKE THE next morning, I had a burst of energy prompted by a large cup of coffee and the dust bunnies I could see under the sofa in the living room. I dressed in jeans and a T-shirt, dumped Wizard's cat box and filled it with fresh litter, vacuumed the apartment, closets and all, washed the kitchen floor, changed the sheets, did two loads of laundry, and even watered the potted plants at the front door.

By then I was starving. I downed some toast slathered with jelly and a poached egg. The open house was scheduled to start at one o'clock and I knew Gale would be the first one there. I showered and dressed in a skirt and sweater, slapped on some makeup and grabbed my purse.

That's when I saw the light blinking on the machine. The phone must have rung while I was in the shower. I hit the message button. It was Geneva, calling with the birth information she'd finally discovered. I'd have to listen later. It was close to noon and I didn't want to be late meeting Gale.

The condo that Gale had found was on Northpoint close to Fisherman's Wharf, in an older building renovated into four separate apartments. I found the address and after several turns around the block managed to snag a parking space. The building itself was tall and impressive, with a narrow lane at the side leading to garages in the rear. The front apartments on each of the two floors boasted curved glass windows. I knew the unit for sale was in the rear, which often meant no view of the street and no fireplace, but I'd reserve judgment until I could see it. Best of all, there was no elevator, and this would keep the homeowners' fees low. A curving stairway with a polished mahogany handrail led me upward.

The door to the apartment was open. I heard Gale's voice and entered a living room with windows on the side of the building only, but it did have a fireplace.

"Julia, there you are. This is Joyce."

The realtor smiled and I shook her hand. "So glad you could make it. You're considering a purchase?"

"Oh, no. Our friend Cheryl is. She should be here soon."

"Well, please have a look around. It's a very unusual apartment."

"Julia, come and see the rest. I think she'll love it."

Gale took me by the arm and led me down the hall. "It's laid out kind of oddly 'cause each floor was split up, but I think it works. You saw the living room. And it has a fireplace! I guess the house originally had two on each floor, so each apartment has one. Isn't that wonderful?" Gale was excited. "And it's just come on the market. Believe me, at this price, it's gonna be snapped up."

The second room off the hallway was the bedroom. "It's a little dark cause the windows are on the side here too, but wait." Gale led me to the end of the hall and I entered a kitchen that was huge.

"Ohmigod." The back wall of the kitchen was a series of windows overlooking the houses below and the bay. "I can't believe this view."

"I know. It's fantastic. A clear view of Alcatraz and everything, and it's so light and bright in here. You can see the sailboats on the Bay. And look, there's another room off the kitchen. Could be an office or a second bedroom.

"You could serve dinner to thirty people in this kitchen. It's amazing."

"I can't wait for her to see it. I swear, she better like it. I'll knock her silly if she doesn't."

"Where is she?"

"I don't know. She was supposed to meet me here half an hour ago. I'm a little irked. She better not get cold feet."

We sat on the chairs in the kitchen and enjoyed the view for a few minutes until we heard more voices at the front door. Gale jumped up and went down the hall to see if Cheryl had arrived. She returned to the kitchen shaking her head.

"It wasn't her. Where the hell is she?"

"Have you tried her cell?"

"Yes. No answer. I don't think she would have forgotten."

"No. But maybe you're pushing too hard. Maybe she's not ready yet."

"Nonsense," Gale replied. I raised my eyebrows at her but didn't say anything.

"Call her again." I waited while Gale dialed the number.

"No answer. I'll try the shop." I waited patiently while Gale let the phone ring several times until the answering machine picked up.

"She could be there and just not answering."

"True. Well, I can't see the point in waiting. I've got to get going, but I'll stop by the Eye and see if her car's there."

I didn't know if Cheryl was avoiding the open house and Gale's pressure or if we should be worried about her. "You know what, I'll go by her apartment and see if she's home."

"Okay. That sounds good. Call me later." Gale breezed out of the kitchen and I heard her thanking the realtor. I made my escape while Joyce was busy with a new prospect.

When I got to Cheryl's building, I rang the bell several times, but there was no response. Through the glass, I saw a man heading down the stairs and toward the front door. I waited as he came out and then grabbed the door and let myself into the entry hall. I didn't want to wait for the ancient elevator. I climbed two flights up the curving stairway to Cheryl's floor. At the door of 2C I knocked. If she was here, she'd come to the door. I called her name and knocked again. No answer. I waited a moment and finally gave up and called it a day. It wasn't like her to hide out and just not show. Where was she?

FORTY-THREE

♈ ♉ ♊ ♋ ♌ ♍ ♎ ♏ ♐ ♑ ♒ ♓

I MANEUVERED OUT OF downtown and was almost home when I thought of Pamela, Rob's former sister-in-law. She'd mentioned she worked in the Cardiology Unit of the VA Hospital. The hospital is at Clement and 38th, just a few blocks from my apartment. This fell into the category of no stone unturned. Instead of heading down the hill, I kept going and followed the signs for visitor parking. I pulled into a lot just east of the hospital building itself.

Several people sat in the lobby, waiting on hard plastic chairs that lined the walls. An information kiosk stood in the middle of the floor but it was unattended. Our tax dollars at work. The sign told me the Cardiology Unit was on the second floor in the west wing. Yellow arrows on the floor pointed toward an elevator bank. I took the elevator and continued in the same direction until I reached a set of double doors labeled *Cardiology* in large block letters.

A square work area enclosed the nurses' station. I had no idea if Pamela would be on duty today. It was a long shot, but I hoped for the best. I didn't think there was much she could tell me, but at least I could swear to Geneva that I'd covered all the bases I could think of.

A young woman in a turquoise smock and black slacks sat behind the counter shuffling sheets of paper. When she was satisfied they were in order, she quickly slipped each into patient charts lined up on the desk. I approached her and asked for Pamela, suddenly realizing I had no idea of her last name.

The woman looked up and smiled. "She's with a patient right now, but she'll be right back."

"Thanks." I leaned against the counter and looked around. The station had a direct view of six rooms, some of them wards. Another set of double doors at the end of the corridor were designated Cardiac Care Unit. The padded door opened and Pamela appeared, heading in my direction toward the nurses station. She was wearing green cotton pants, as if dressed for the operating room, and a long white smock decorated with a busy pattern of bumblebees. Her pockets bulged with various instruments and a stethoscope hung from her neck. Her hair, straight and blonde and lined with gray, was pinned back behind her ears. She was shorter and heavier than I remembered, or perhaps it was her gaunt face that had made her seem thin that night at the funeral home. She walked briskly toward the nurses' station.

I followed her with my eyes. "Pamela?"

"Yes. Can I help you?" She barely glanced at me as she rounded the corner by the desk.

"Sorry to bother you at work. I just thought this might be a good chance to talk to you."

She looked up at me and tilted her head in a quizzical gesture. "Oh. Oh, I'm sorry. I didn't realize. We met the other night, didn't we? You're Geneva's friend."

"Yes."

"Are they all right? Has anything happened?" Her expression was alarmed.

"No. Sorry. Didn't mean to alarm you. Nothing new, just the same old bad news."

"Oh, you scared me. Listen, I pulled a double. I'm on this evening too but I'm about to take my dinner break. You're welcome to join me if you like. It's just the cafeteria, nothing exciting."

"That's fine."

We took the elevator down to a level below the lobby. Pamela walked quickly, as though one of her patients might be on the verge of cardiac arrest. I had to hurry to stay abreast of her. We stood in line and Pamela waved to a woman behind the counter. The woman promptly filled a plate with a serving of meat loaf and gravy, mashed potatoes, and peas. I followed Pamela through the line and filled a cup with coffee as we approached the cashier.

"So, what can I do for you?" Pamela asked as she plunked her tray down across from me. "You'll have to excuse me while I shovel food in. I only have a half an hour and I could be paged at any time."

"I understand. I hope you don't mind my coming here?"

"Not at all. Fire away."

"Well, Geneva, as you can imagine, is desperate. First the police questioned her husband, and now her sister's been arrested. She's asked me to talk to anyone who might have some knowledge about Moira. I thought of you because you're in touch with Rob, and I know he and Moira didn't get along."

Pamela looked up from a forkful of peas buried in mashed potatoes. "I hope you're not suggesting that Rob . . . I mean, I know at first he thought he'd accidentally shot her, but he had no idea . . ."

"Oh, no. I'm not saying that at all. I'm just curious if you have any thoughts. You're still connected to Rob and the Learys."

"I really hope you're not hinting what I think you're hinting at. If you're suggesting that there's anything underhanded about my relationship with Rob, you're just plain crazy." Her reaction made me take two mental steps back. "Rob to this day makes sure I'm doing okay. When my sister died, it was Rob who shared her insurance money with me, and that was when he wasn't making much money. He's been nothing but kind and considerate, and I won't hear you or any other nosy son of a bitch say anything against him." She was pointing her fork at me, accentuating every statement with another jab.

"Pamela, slow down. You've got it all wrong. I'm not accusing anyone. I'm doing this for Geneva." I wasn't sure she even heard me.

"And don't forget, I actually like Brooke. She's been extremely considerate of my feelings ever since she and Rob first met. I think she's a great gal! So, no, I don't believe she could be involved in anything that would hurt Rob." Pamela wiped the gravy off her plate with a last piece of meatloaf. So if there's nothing else . . ."

"Actually, there is." I hesitated. "Can you tell me how your sister died?"

Pamela's face hardened and she wiped her lips with a thin paper napkin. "If you must know, my sister took a header down a flight of stairs and broke her neck. She was diagnosed as bipolar, but frankly, I think she was just a selfish, high-maintenance pain in the ass. And, who knows, maybe if she'd lived, they would have divorced anyway.

Am I sorry she's dead? Yes and no. Yes, I'm sorry when anybody dies, but did I have a high opinion of my sister? The answer's no."

I was speechless in the face of her outburst. She'd made so many wrong assumptions, I couldn't begin to reply.

"And now I've got to get back to my floor unless you have any further questions."

"Uh, no."

"Oh … by the way … in case you're harboring any suspicions, I was working a double shift when Sondra died and Rob was out of town on a case."

Pamela picked up her tray, dumped the contents in a large waste container, and pushed through the door to the hallway without another word.

I was frozen in my chair after Pamela's diatribe. Her reaction was the last thing I'd expected, and I needed a minute or two to collect myself. I finished my coffee, threw the paper cup in the trash, and headed back to the lobby and the door to the parking lot. I was home within ten minutes and very glad to bolt the door behind me.

FORTY-FOUR

♈ ♉ ♊ ♋ ♌ ♍ ♎ ♏ ♐ ♑ ♒ ♓

IT WAS LATE AFTERNOON and I knew Wizard would be hungry. I
filled his dish with some fresh food and checked the answering machine. No new calls. I played Geneva's message again and noted all
the birth information. My head felt as if it was ready to burst, but I
clicked on the astro program and forced myself to set up the charts.

I sat staring at the computer screen for a long time. His birthday
was October 6th. He would be thirty-nine this year. He was born in
Los Angeles at 9:31 p.m. His Sun was conjunct Pluto and his Venus,
Mars, and Uranus formed a stellium in Scorpio. A deep need for
power and control. His Moon and Neptune were in Sagittarius very
close to his seventh house cusp, connecting with Moira's Sun and
Moon. He had had a tremendous hold over her. He would appear
sensitive and compassionate, but at a deeper level, he had the ability
to manipulate others ruthlessly. He was a Svengali, able to display
whatever characteristics suited his own immediate needs. How
could I have been so blind? The Uranus connection would make

him unpredictable and explosive. And all of this fell in his fifth house. He would use sexual energy to gain his ends.

And where was Cheryl? Had she returned to Macao by herself? Had she stumbled into danger? A low-level feeling of dread had been dogging me since the open house. Now I felt a full-blown rush of anxiety. I had to find her. I'd start with her apartment. I'd find someone to open it up if necessary.

I threw my jacket on and rushed down to the car. As soon as I started the engine, my cell rang. It was Gale.

"Where are you?"

"In the car. I'm going back to Cheryl's. I'm really worried about her."

"Me too, but I just picked up the new *Eccola!* Have you seen it?"

"I actually have it, in the car, I think. I got one from Brooke's office when I was there. Hang on." I pulled the car over to the side of the street and left the engine idling.

"Look inside, where they list the editor and the staff."

"Okay. What am I looking for?"

"The Assistant Editor."

My eye scanned the page and I found it. "Lana Barron."

"Oh ... oh ... L. Barron, the person who bought the bracelet at Rochecault?"

"Cheryl told me all about that. Interesting coincidence, isn't it?"

"Very. Not exactly sure how it fits in yet, but I want to tell you my theory. I'll call you when I get to Cheryl's."

"Stay in touch and stay out of trouble."

"I intend to, now that I know who did it. I'm just not certain how or why."

I reached Cheryl's building in record time and, ignoring the *no parking* signs, pulled up in front. The sky was dark with a threatening storm. The building lights had not yet come on. Had it only been a few hours since I was last there? I stood on the sidewalk and looked up at Cheryl's windows but didn't see a light. I ran up the front steps of the building and hit the buzzer.

He stepped out of the shadow of the columns. I took a step back, my heart thudding wildly.

"Hello, Julia." Rob smiled. "I knew you'd turn up sooner or later."

I began to tremble but didn't want him to see that. "What do you want?"

"I want you to come with me." He smiled again.

"And I would do that... why?" I did my best to muster some courage.

"Because I have something you want—or should I say, someone."

I felt my heart sink. He had Cheryl. "Why her?"

"Simple. I had to get to you before you did any more damage. Get in." He pointed to the driver's door of my car and walked around to the passenger side. "Just drive nice and slow down to the Marina."

A cold sweat broke out on my forehead. My hands were shaking, but I managed to start the car and drove straight up the hill to the top of Powell. Rob indicated a turn that took us down to Van Ness. I drove, occasionally glancing in his direction. He seemed completely relaxed, a folded jacket over his right hand covering a gun. I wracked my brain for some way to attract police attention, but without spotting a cruiser on the street, I couldn't imagine how I could do that.

"Drive nice and slow and don't think about doing anything funny. If you do, you'll never see your friend again."

We cut down Lombard and turned onto Marina Drive.

"Take this turnoff coming up."

I pulled into the drive leading to the yacht club, following it to the edge closest to the docks, and turned off the engine. "Now what?"

"Get out slowly. Don't try any tricks." I climbed out and Rob followed me. We approached a gate in the chain-link fence separating the parking area from the docks. Rob pulled a key ring out of his pocket and tossed it to me.

"Unlock the gate."

I considered what he might do if I tossed the keys over the fence into the water. But after Gale's call, I knew he wasn't working alone. Now I understood how he and Lana, the Assistant Editor, had managed to set Brooke up. I unlocked the gate and we stepped onto the wooden pier. I pulled it shut behind us and Rob indicated we should head down the dock.

The boats were bobbing slightly in the current, their masts upright, their sails down. The sky was darker now, with heavy, water-laden clouds. The wind had picked up, blowing in short intense gusts. Water slapped against the hulls of the boats and the pilings of the pier. The smell of ocean brine filled the air. The pier was deserted. There was no one in sight to call to for help. Unlike some of the other Bay Area marinas, this one allowed no residents.

Rob smiled and hummed softly to himself as he followed me. Near the end of the pier, he said. "Stop right there." We were next to a long sloop with an aft cabin.

"Climb aboard and watch your step, Julia. I wouldn't want you to fall," he chuckled. His amusement chilled me to the bone.

Once on deck, he pushed me toward an opening that revealed a small inner light. I ducked my head and descended the few steps to a small under-cabin. Cheryl was seated on one of the cushions, in the same black cocktail dress and heels that she'd worn the night we had gone to Macao. She was bound and gagged with strips of white cloth that looked like ripped sheets. Lana Barron sat opposite her, her long legs crossed, with a gun aimed at Cheryl's chest. Cheryl's eyes grew large when she saw me, streaks of mascara marring her cheeks.

"See? I wouldn't hurt your friend. I was very gentle. I wouldn't want there to be any marks on her wrists and ankles later. Although I doubt either of you will ever be found if I've judged the tide and currents correctly."

I shuddered involuntarily. He meant to throw us overboard. An ebb tide must be approaching. Ebb tides in the bay are far more powerful than incoming flood tides. Even ocean liners and military ships will choose to enter the bay on a flood tide, but not when water is moving out of the gate. The Coast Guard is forced to haul in stranded windsurfers on a daily basis, but if anyone has passed the "line of demarcation," an imaginary line extending from Mile Rock off Land's End to Point Bonita in Marin County, it's too late. They are invariably swept out to sea. Even if we could survive the cold water, we'd have no chance.

"Let her go."

"Sorry. No can do. I saw her with you the other night. At Macao."

"So that *was* you!"

"And then I saw her there again last night. I don't believe in coincidences. Picking her up was actually amazingly easy." Rob reached over and stroked Cheryl's cheek. She would have bitten his hand if she hadn't been gagged.

I felt a hot rush of anger well up. Lana smiled but remained silent. "And then of course I knew you'd try to rescue her, like the little do-gooder you are."

"And Rita?"

"Poor Rita. I'm afraid it's all your fault," Rob said lightly. "That day at the Palace restaurant, you told me you'd questioned her. I couldn't take the chance. She might have seen me picking Moira up outside that disgusting bar."

"I see." I was doing my best to breathe normally. "And Moira?"

"That was unfortunate. That wasn't my plan, you see. Poor deluded Moira. I had her convinced only Brooke stood in our way. She was supposed to shoot Brooke in the garage when Brooke went down to let Cassie out. That was the plan. She was so in love with me. It was really too bad she couldn't stay the course. It would have been the perfect murder. She would have been caught, of course, and then it would have been my word against hers."

"You wanted Brooke dead?"

Blood rushed into his face. "She thought she could divorce me!" he shouted suddenly, spittle forming on his lips. "My perfect blonde wife thought she was too good for me." He took a deep breath and gained control once more. "I couldn't have that, you see."

I hoped that if I could keep him talking long enough, I might think of some way for Cheryl and me to escape. "What screwed up your plan?"

"At the wedding, Moira told me she had a change of heart. She was pregnant and she wanted to come clean and tell Brooke everything. She wanted to do things right, she said. She wanted me to leave Brooke for her, if you can believe that."

"But that would have shown up on the autopsy."

"Exactly. Turns out the bitch lied." Rob laughed bitterly. "But I couldn't take that chance, that something could tie me to her. I had to move quickly."

"You poisoned her drink."

"Twice actually, but not poison. Barbiturates. No one would have believed she didn't take them herself, given her history."

"And Sally Stark?"

"An unforeseen glitch."

"And you shot Moira with David's gun."

"Of course."

I gasped. It was clear in a blinding flash. I saw Harry, Michael's poodle, the day I'd stopped at Michael's family's house, with Michael's glove in his mouth. It was the vision hovering at the back of my mind. It all clicked into place. "You trained Cassie." I remembered the muddy prints she'd left on the carpet when she'd rested her head on Rob's knee after the shooting.

Rob smiled slowly. "Isn't Cassie amazing? She's actually a very clever dog, well-trained. All I had to do was let her out the back door of the garage and off she went, over the fence. The gun and the glove I used are somewhere at the bottom of a pond in the Presidio."

"And you and Lana wrote those emails?"

"Oh, yes. Months ago." He nodded in Lana's direction. "If Moira screwed up and Brooke survived, the plan would still have worked. The emails were proof of *their* conspiracy to murder *me*. The police would assume Moira mistook Brooke for me in the darkened garage. I, of course, would play the dutiful husband, believing in my wife's good heart while she and Moira went quietly off to jail. Unfortunately, none of that came to pass, so I had to improvise. Oh, before I forget. Let's have that bracelet you've been showing around town." He grabbed my purse and dumped the contents on to a tiny fold-down table. He grabbed the Rochecault box with the bracelet inside.

"Here you go, dear." He smiled and tossed the bracelet to Lana, who slipped it into a small purse. She stood and walked toward Rob. As she passed him, she laid her gun on a shelf. He slipped an arm around her waist, pulled her body close, and kissed her passionately. She responded to his kiss, glanced over at me one last time, and smiled. She hadn't said a word. She climbed the narrow stairway and clambered off the boat.

"Lana will be happy to provide an alibi for me just in case either of your bodies ever wash ashore, which I doubt, but it pays to be careful."

"So Lana gets the prize, huh? Brooke's career and her husband?"

"Lana and I are so much more compatible. Twin flames, you might say. But enough chatter, ladies. Julia, turn around."

"No!" I spit in his face in a desperate burst of anger.

I never saw it coming. He backhanded me across the face. I went flying into a corner of the cabin hitting my head on a cabinet. Everything went black.

FORTY-FIVE

♈ ♉ ♊ ♋ ♌ ♍ ♎ ♏ ♐ ♑ ♒ ♓

THE FIRST SENSATION I had was the vibration of the motor. I came to slowly, not sure where I was. My cheek and head were throbbing. I didn't know how long I'd been unconscious but I struggled to regain clarity. Then I felt the pitch of the boat. We had left the slip and moved out into the bay. Droplets of rain streaked the portholes. The storm had arrived.

"Mmmm." Cheryl was pushing me with her bound feet. I opened my eyes. At least Rob hadn't gagged my mouth.

"Cheryl," I whispered. "I'm sorry."

Cheryl nodded her head and started to sob. I looked around. We were tied to hand railings screwed into paneling on either side of the cabin. I craned my neck to peer out the tiny porthole next to me. Rob had piloted the boat toward the center of the bay, away from the reefs and shoals. The small sloop heaved and pitched in the rough currents. We were approaching Fort Point, which marked the city side of the base of the Golden Gate Bridge. I figured Rob's plan must be to pass under the bridge and then, after disposing of us, make a

U-turn around its pylons to head back to the Marina. He wouldn't risk going past the line of demarcation in a small boat if the tide was turning. He'd have to throw us overboard past the Bridge and hope the sea currents did the rest.

I had to find a way out of this. I had to do something quick. Across from me were built-in narrow drawers. If I could reach them, I might find a tool or a knife and be able to cut through the cloth restraints that bound me. But there was no way to reach that far, with my hands and my arms bound to the railing. I slipped my shoes off and managed to pull the lowest drawer open. Inside were charts and navigational maps. I tried to reach the second drawer but it was just out of reach. Cheryl saw my struggle and murmured something. Then, shifting as far as she could, she pulled the draw open with her foot.

Something brightly colored caught my eye. It was a utility knife sheathed in red plastic. If I could only move it out of the drawer. I balanced on the edge of the seat and, stretching as far as I could, slipped one foot into the drawer and tried to lift the knife out. It was impossible. Then Cheryl shoved the drawer with her foot. It fell out of the cabinet, its contents spilling onto the floor. The boat lurched and the knife slid away. Silently, I cursed.

I stretched as far as the bindings would allow, but the utility knife was too far out of reach. In spite of the cold, beads of sweat covered my face. The boat lurched again and the knife began sliding in the other direction. As it went past, I stepped on it. I slipped one foot under it and, holding it tenuously between my feet, I leaned sideways. Twisting my body, I managed to drop the knife on the seat cushion next to me. I reached back with my bound hands and grabbed it.

Cheryl watched this procedure wide-eyed. I straightened up and slid the blade open behind my back to start sawing through the strip binding my hands. My arms were still tied to the handrail with another piece of cloth, but as soon as my hands were free, I could easily cut through that.

I was slicing blind with one hand, but I was making progress. The knife was sharp, and after a few false starts, I felt the cloth start to give. I felt a sharp pain on the side of my hand and wasn't sure if I'd cut myself. It didn't matter—I had to keep going. If I could free myself and then Cheryl, perhaps we had a chance.

The cloth finally split just as the door to the upper deck opened. Rob had cut the motor and I hadn't noticed. Quickly I shoved the knife between the seat cushions and grasped the cloth ends, wrapping them loosely around my wrists and holding the binding tight.

Rob glanced at the drawer on the floor and its spilled contents. "Didn't I tell you no tricks?" He reached into the jacket of his windbreaker and pulled out a sharp, serrated knife. Reaching down, he cut through Cheryl's ankle bindings and the cloth lashing her to the handrail. Her hands were still bound. Her mouth was gagged. He lifted her up by one arm and half dragged her up the stairs. She looked terrified.

He returned and cut through the strip holding my feet and attaching me to the handrail. "Don't worry. I have your friend secured to the deck. She's not going anywhere yet."

He pulled me up roughly and shoved me through the door. I grasped the cloth around my wrists, hoping he wouldn't notice it was no longer secure. Cheryl was barefoot, tied to the railing by the cabin doing her best to maintain her balance. We were just under the bridge now and starting to drift out. I heard a blast of the fog-horns above us and the slapping of the water against the pylons. The thrum of traffic on the bridge reached our ears between gusts of wind. Slowly, the tide was carrying us out into the blackness of the nighttime Pacific. We had to escape. The sea offered only a cold and watery death.

Rob shoved me against the cabin and wrapped a cloth strip around one of my arms, tying me loosely to the handrail next to Cheryl. Then he untied her and pulled the gag from her mouth.

"You first, my dear."

"You bastard!" She desperately kicked out at him. He pushed her away, and she slid and fell to the deck. Rob quietly cursed. He reached down to pick her up and heave her into the sea. Cheryl was screaming, one hand clutching the railing in a last ditch effort. In desperation, I looked for something to stop him. I spotted a small blue-and-white buoy attached to a coiled rope two feet away. Dropping my wrist restraints, I grabbed the buoy and its rope with my free arm, and, as Rob straightened up, swung a loop over his head—around his neck—and pulled. Cheryl fell to the deck, still clinging to the railing.

He gagged and reached up for the rope, trying to tear it away from his neck. I pulled harder, barely maintaining my balance. Suddenly, Rob lunged away from me and the rope slid through my hands, breaking my grip. Then he turned and rushed at me. As he came near, Cheryl, in a sitting position, her knees up to her chin, thrust her feet out and tripped him. Rob fell forward, sliding across the deck of the pitching boat. He recovered in an instant and stood up.

At that moment, the sky broke and a deluge descended. A wind swell hit the boat and we lurched sickeningly to one side. Rob held out both arms to regain his balance on the slippery deck. He stood for a long moment, his face registering surprise, realization dawning that he might not regain his balance. Cheryl and I clung to the railing, watching in terror as Rob opened his mouth to scream, his body listing backward into the sea.

I grasped Cheryl's arm with my free hand and hung onto her. The black violent water closed above Rob's head. I saw a hand rise from the inky darkness. He bobbed once. He was flailing wildly, a silent scream on his lips as the current swept him away.

FORTY-SIX

♈ ♉ ♊ ♋ ♌ ♍ ♎ ♏ ♐ ♑ ♒ ♓

THE BOAT CONTINUED TO pitch and yaw. We stood there for precious minutes, unable to speak or to move. I looked to the east and saw the lights of the Bridge receding from us. I felt the swell of the ocean under my feet, moving us inexorably out to sea.

Some instinct clicked in and I was finally able to move. I untied the restraint holding my arm and untied Cheryl's hands. We climbed into the cockpit and, sheltered from the wind, turned the engine over. It caught—we felt rather than heard the vibrations as the motor kicked in. Slowly we turned the wheel until the boat was facing Alcatraz and the City. Then we opened the engine to full throttle, praying it wasn't too late. We had to be able to conquer the tide and not be driven onto the rocky reefs at the mouth of the Bay.

Cheryl ducked below and called 911 on my cell phone to alert the police and Coast Guard. It felt as if hours passed as our engine chugged, moving us incrementally closer to the Marina docks. It was an eternity of fighting the tide before we reached the pylons of the bridge. I felt as if we were moving forward by inches, struggling against a force that wanted to sweep us toward the sea.

A police boat was waiting as we reached the protected reef. Searchlights cut through the dark and the rain. We shut the engine down as we approached the nearest slip, but the impact with the dock sent us reeling. Something metallic caught on the edge of the deck and I realized we were being secured to the pier. A man in a Coast Guard uniform jumped onto the deck. Cheryl and I clung to each other, shivering and soaking wet from sea spray and rain. Two other men climbed aboard and, wrapping blankets around us, helped us disembark.

An ambulance was waiting by the Marina Green, silent, its lights flashing in the darkness. Police officers led us into the yacht club building just yards from the entrance to the boat docks. Inside, we were given hot drinks and fresh dry blankets. We sat on metal folding chairs while the police and Coast Guard officers conferred.

A female officer who looked so young I would have mistaken her for a high school student approached us and pulled up a folding chair. "Is there someone we can call for you?"

Cheryl looked at me and I replied, "Yes. Detective Ianello—SFPD."

The officer raised her eyebrows in surprise.

"Please call him. What happened tonight—it's related to a murder case he's already investigating."

She nodded and started to move away.

"Wait," I said. She stopped and turned back to me. "Are they going to search for . . . for the man who was on the boat with us?"

"That's what they're discussing now. But I don't think it's possible. The Coast Guard will start at first light."

Cheryl and I exchanged looks. Her eyes betrayed the satisfaction of dark justice. No one held out much hope of finding Rob Ramer.

FORTY-SEVEN

♈ ♉ ♊ ♋ ♌ ♍ ♎ ♏ ♐ ♑ ♒ ♓

IT WAS A BASIC beige-on-beige conference room lit with overhead neon lights, one of which buzzed occasionally. Just enough to keep me from nodding off. I sat at the end of a long table, in a cushy upholstered chair, surveying my surroundings at the FBI field office on Golden Gate Avenue. A neglected potted plant took up a corner of the room. Two Customs officials sat to my right, and a man from the Department of the Treasury on my left. A government reporter sat slightly behind me, her fingers poised over her tiny keyboard, ready to take my statement. She stared at the far wall. I wondered if she appreciated the buzzes and pops of the neon lights as much as I did.

One of the Customs agents nodded to the reporter. "We're on the record. The date is August 5th. The time is 1:30 p.m. This is the testimony of Julia Bonatti. Ms. Bonatti, as we explained to you, this will be your official statement regarding what you saw on June 23rd at an establishment called Macao on the Embarcadero. You have sworn that you give this statement willingly. It will be used in evidence in any criminal actions brought against Luong Cheng and possibly others unknown to us at this time. This statement will stand in court and we may possibly call upon you to give testimony in person. Do you understand?"

"Yes."

"Fine. Let's begin."

My statement took no more than half an hour. When I finished, I found Paolo Ianello waiting for me outside the conference room. Macao had been raided a week after our close call in the bay. Whether Don had made good on his promise to alert his contact I didn't know, but obviously this was an investigation that had started long before Moira's murder. Enough hard evidence had been found at the scene to put Luong Cheng and his cronies away for a long time. My statement was nothing more than backup. I'd been told off the record that I would not be called as a witness at any future trial. I hoped they were telling the truth. Andy's involvement in Cheng's money laundering schemes had come to light and he was in custody, also facing charges. In fact, the Customs agents had confided that the information I'd gleaned from Tony, the bartender, was accurate— Andy had already been under investigation.

Ianello stood as I entered the waiting room. He smiled. For once, his face didn't seem wolflike. More like a happy raccoon.

"What are you doing here?" I asked.

"Came to escort you home. Can you use a ride?" Ianello was wearing leather wingtips today.

"Sure can. Thanks." I'd arrived in a government car that had been sent for me.

"Were you scared? About giving evidence?" he asked.

"I guess a little."

"It should be fine. They're just crossing their *T*'s and dotting their *I*'s. I doubt they'll need to call upon you to tie this case up."

"I'm just so glad it's over. Can you tell me what's been happening?"

To date, all charges had been dropped against Brooke and she'd been released. I'd been able to tell Ianello where he could search for the weapon that had killed Moira. He was grateful, but otherwise had been very tight-lipped and unwilling to share any other information about the case.

"I can tell you now," he replied as he swung through downtown traffic. "We picked up Lana Barron the next morning at the *Eccola!* offices." He glanced over at me. "You and your friend, of course, *will* have to give evidence at her trial."

"I know." I heaved a sigh.

"I'm sorry, but you two are the only witnesses we have that she was involved with Rob Ramer. She swears she had nothing to do with Moira Leary's death or Rob's plan to murder Brooke. She went completely blank. Said she never heard of the waitress at the Alibi."

"You believe her?"

"We could see the wheels turning. She was trying to figure it out. Personally, I'm sure Ramer was tying up a loose end with that murder. But unless we find some forensic evidence, we may never be able to prove it," Ianello continued. "We know it was Lana who sent the incriminating emails from Brooke's computer, and Ramer who replied from their home and from Moira's apartment, but proving it in court could be difficult. She's admitted to the affair only and claims Rob promised to divorce his wife." He snorted. "She says she's completely innocent."

He was silent for a few moments. "There's no way I can prove it—and now of course there's no one to prosecute—but I'd bet my last dollar that Ramer murdered his first wife."

I shuddered, remembering how vehemently Rob's former sister-in-law, Pamela, had defended him. "At this point, nothing would surprise me."

"What tipped you off?"

"His chart. Geneva was finally able to get his birth information. When I saw how his planets lined up, it scared me. But when I realized the connections between his chart and Moira's ... well, I knew it had to be him. Moira was just a pawn in the game. His real plan was to get rid of his wife and have Moira take the fall for it."

"He must have had tremendous control over her."

"He did. But she was also in a terribly confused and vulnerable condition, all by herself."

"What clued you in to the dog? How did you figure out he'd trained the dog to get rid of the gun?"

"It was Harry."

Ianello shot me a look. "Okay, I give up. Who's Harry?"

I smiled. "Harry was my fiancé Michael's dog. I ... well, ever since Michael died, I try to stay in touch with his sister. I saw her that week. She had Harry with her, and Harry pulled one of Michael's gloves out of a shopping bag. It was the sight of Harry holding the glove in his mouth. I remembered Rob's dog, Cassie, in the living room that night with muddy paws. It wasn't raining, so where had she been that her paws got muddy enough to leave tracks? It was hovering at the edge of my consciousness, but I'm sorry to say I was terribly slow putting it together. I should have seen it sooner."

"Most people wouldn't even have noticed."

We'd pulled up in front of my apartment building. "Thanks for the lift."

Ianello turned to look at me. "I'm not my father."

"Excuse me?" For a moment I had no idea what he meant, and then I remembered my grandmother's story.

"I know how the Italian grapevine works in North Beach."

"Ah."

"So … just so you know. The apple didn't fall anywhere near that tree."

I studied his face. "It's really not my business. And I wouldn't assume that anyway." I hesitated, but I knew this would be my last chance. "I have to ask you something."

"Shoot."

"The night Moira died. The first time I met you."

"Yes?"

"It's really bugged me."

"What? Spit it out."

"You were wearing the most delicate patent leather shoes."

Ianello stiffened. "Yes." He gave me a hard look. "Why do you ask?"

"I don't know. It just struck me as curious."

"I could tell you, but then I'd have to kill you." A hint of a smile curved the corner of his mouth.

I smiled. "Now I'm intrigued."

"I'm a ballroom dancer. I was at the studio when I got the call." He stared at me intently. "And if you ever mention this to anyone, I *will* have to kill you."

FORTY-EIGHT

♈ ♉ ♊ ♋ ♌ ♍ ♎ ♏ ♐ ♑ ♒ ♓

"Sunflower yellow? What a fantastic color! I approve," Gale sang out as she dumped a box of steaming pizza on the kitchen table. She was referring to the paint that Cheryl and I were rolling on the walls of Cheryl's new kitchen.

"You're a goddess," Cheryl cried. "We're starving. We've been at it for hours. We were just trying to figure out where we could call to order in."

"Well, now you can eat and keep working." Gale wiped off the table and spread out napkins and paper plates. "Don't worry about dieting today, girls."

I kicked off my rubber thongs in case any paint had clung to the bottom and padded across to the table. Gale dished pizza slices onto the plates for us, careful not to dribble melted cheese.

"How much is left to do?" she asked.

I folded an oily piece of pizza in the middle and lunged at the end. "The pantry's done and the ceiling and three walls. Now we just have that last wall."

"Good. Cheryl needs to get out of that hole she's been living in." Gale reached over and squeezed Cheryl's hand.

When Cheryl was waffling about buying the apartment, Gale bought it herself. She was so anxious for Cheryl to get it, and so terrified someone else would grab it first, she decided not to wait. She'd never said a word about it, but one night at the Eye as we were closing up shop, she handed the grant deed and a notarized quitclaim to Cheryl. Cheryl couldn't grasp what it meant at first, and when she did, she burst into tears. And when the sale of her house in Berkeley finally went through, she repaid Gale for the down payment and took possession. I'd never seen her as happy as she was the day we started moving her in. There was still a lot to do—furniture to purchase and dishes to unpack—but slowly it was coming together.

"Julia, I was checking the MLS the other day. I noticed there's a house for sale on Clay Street," Gale continued.

"Yes, I heard. Geneva told me. Brooke couldn't possibly go back to her house to live. Not after what happened."

"What's she going to do?"

"For starters, she's on leave from the magazine and she's taking a long sabbatical with Ashley. They're going to France. Geneva and Mary will miss them a lot, but they'll be able to fly over to visit. I'm sure Brooke will be back eventually. She needs time."

Gale shook her head. "Can't say I blame her."

I fell silent, thinking of the Learys and how their lives had been torn up. They were blessed, though. Moira's shade would be with them always, but the Learys still had each other.

"What about …?" Gale left the question hanging.

Cheryl and I exchanged a look. We shook our heads and left it unsaid. Rob's body had never been found.

FORTY-NINE

♈ ♉ ♊ ♋ ♌ ♍ ♎ ♏ ♐ ♑ ♒ ♓

MIDNIGHT. THE ANTIQUE CLOCK in the living room chimed the hours. My apartment was dark, the only light a bedside lamp in the next room where Wizard snored softly on the comforter. That and the glow from the computer screen. I moved each of the Leary family charts into a separate file. Maybe someday I'd want to look at them again. Someday when it would be easier to remember the events that transpired in those days after the wedding, especially the moments at sea when I thought it might all be over. I wrapped my bathrobe tighter around me and clicked on the next *AskZodia* email.

Dear Zodia:

I've recently lost my wife after a long illness and I can't seem to find a way to cope with everything. I wish I had been a better husband, paid more attention to her. I feel terrible now when I think how much I took for granted. I don't know what to do with all these feelings. My birthday is January 15th, 1956, at 11:10 p.m., Cincinnati, Ohio.

—Man at Sea

Dear Man at Sea:

I am so sorry for your loss ...

My fingers hovered over the keys. There was nothing I could think of to say; no words of comfort or advice seemed adequate.

Outside the darkened windows of my office, the lights of the city sparkled in the distance. I clicked on Michael's natal chart and viewed the transiting planets on that fateful day. Why hadn't I seen deadly elements lining up? Hard transits. Anything. There'd been no warning. Why did he have to die? And why on that day? Why hadn't I sensed the danger?

Michael's face took shape in the glow of the computer screen. My eyes were playing tricks on me. I sighed and rubbed my temples, then closed the program and headed for bed. Tomorrow would be another day, and maybe then I could think of something to say to the Man at Sea.

I slipped under the covers and drifted off, listening to the music of the foghorns.

© www.kazphoto.com

ABOUT THE AUTHOR

Connie di Marco (Los Angeles, CA) is the bestselling author of the
Soup Lover's Mysteries (Penguin), which she published under the
name Connie Archer. She is a member of Mystery Writers of
America, International Thriller Writers, and Sisters in Crime. She
has always been fascinated by astrology and is excited to combine
her love of the stars with her love of writing mysteries. Visit her at
conniedimarco.com, on Facebook at Connie di Marco (Author), or
on Twitter: @askzodia.